NORTH SIDE
HELLION

Ben Broeren

First Print Benjamin D. Broeren Edition 2016
Copyright © 2016

Cover design by Nuria Marquez

Benjamin D. Broeren ISBN-13: 978-0-9967763-4-9

Chicago, Illinois, U.S.A.

Bendbroeren.com

NORTH SIDE

HELLION

Ben Broeren

Part I

Chicago 1920

1

An Insignificant Insurgent

Snow and ice covered the crossing of LaSalle and Division, where the Brass Kerry contained a cacophony of whiskey-infused euphoria despite the first February of Federal Prohibition. Inside the first floor of the red brick high-rise, a roulette wheel spun on a table as patrons gathered for an evening of hijinks. Dozens of thugs, some dressed in pinstriped suits and others fingering silver pocket watches, clustered around two craps tables. As servers poured watered-down beer and distilled spirits for thirsty lips, a haze of smoke from cheap cigars mixed with laughter and unabated breaths to taunt anyone left in the cold.

The cutting chill to the air outside didn't discriminate between those dealing in commerce or crime. Business was booming for almost anyone looking for dough, with no deal missed in this speakeasy, or any other in the Windy City. Who held the purse and pulled the strings made all the difference between laborers, politicians, criminals, and kingpins. It was a world of vice or opportunity, depending on how a young man looked at it.

Sixteen-year-old Aiden McCarthy saw opportunity as

he huddled several hundred paces to the West in an alley near Division and Wells. Snowflakes drifted onto the newsboy cap covering his auburn hair, reflecting moonlight like sparks from a lit fuse. The fog from his breath showed the heat dwelling in his head. With a torn, charcoal paletot overcoat covering his compact, sinewy frame, he flexed his fingers, trying to channel any warmth to tips left uncovered by his mitts.

Aiden wiggled his boot-clad toes while he counted the minutes until he'd have to get the drop on some patsy. The job was to rob a fella, and he drew fuel from an immediate concern to impress his North Side Gang boss. Action, intimidation, and surprise mattered more that any momentary musings on morality. He suppressed any lingering Catholic compassion to keep on task.

From around the corner, he could see the target exit from the Brass Kerry, heading toward the alley. The patsy's six-foot-two height and wide girth showed he was well-fed. The man was likely a bully, coming from a dive well-known for quenching the thirst of Union Stockyard slave drivers. The cauliflower nose on his face blended with a pug's mug, barely outlined from the sputtering street lamps above. There was no room for a halo.

Aiden rationalized his right to take the blockhead's money. From the alley, he shifted from foot to foot and watched his North Side Gang accomplice approach the patsy with the ease of showman to a lion's den. The bells from the nearby Church of the Ascension signaled that it was ten o'clock.

On the face of it, the setup for the robbery seemed to be going according to plan.

Aiden's accomplice was supposed to have drugged their target's whiskey with a dose of chloral hydrate back inside the Brass Kerry. Wooziness and confusion were apparent in the man's slowing westward steps toward Aiden's hiding spot. His tree-trunk legs came to a sudden stop and his shoulders shuddered. A grimace showed suspicion.

"What is happening here?" he asked Aiden's accomplice. "I've never been this drunk after just three drinks. You trying to double-cross me, pal?"

Aiden would have laughed at the two ruffians had he not the intention to rob one them. His accomplice, Danny Keagan, appeared in a pickle, so he shook off his shivers and darted out of the alley to help. A Schrade, push-button knife lay at the ready in his right hand.

The patsy slammed his fist into Keagan's jaw, sending him against a brick wall used to slow his fall to the ground.

Keagan's head swayed before he could regain his composure. He was six-foot tall, but as spindly as a pauper. A kick aimed at his head had yet to connect, being stopped by Aiden's counter kick in the nick of time.

"Back off and hand over your billfold," Aiden hissed from behind their patsy as he pressed the blade of his knife parallel to a robust waist. "I don't want to have to cut anyone."

"What in the devil's name," the man wheezed through a forced chuckle as if socked in the stomach. His shaking knees showed his fading ability to stand upright.

Aiden pulled the knife away and jumped back a step to avoid being crushed by a man almost twice his weight. A flash of shame from his boss and his parents lit his mind before the patsy's thud on the icy ground smacked his own thoughts back to the present. He told himself to rob the patsy and run. No time to dilly dally.

"Slice open the bloody bastard," Keagan said, shaking the matted mop of hair on his head. "The big blockhead about beat the piss out of me."

"Let's just get his dough and get the devil out of here," Aiden said. "There's no need to cut off his bullocks when he's down.

Keagan only gave a nod before being helped off the ground. Aiden then fished the cash from the patsy's billfold, pocketed the money, and swiped a silver pocket watch.

Before the duo could run south of Division on Wells, making their way back to the boss, they saw a witness in front of the Brass Kerry whistling for a cop. Aiden grabbed Keagan and yanked him back toward the alley to lie low and see if there would be trouble.

"Those Paddy jokers should just go back to where Catholics are wanted!" shouted the witness, whose steps tangled in a slight stumble. "Lazy mongrels are almost as bad as the darkies..."

What Aiden thought would be a tattling citizen turned out to be as much of a spectacle as Keagan, him, and the drugged man prostrate in the snow. The ravings were good for more than entertainment.

"What are you doin' there laddie?" asked the officer with a thick Irish brogue. "Yer out startin' such a large fuss you might wake a neighbor or two."

"Hey, you're one of them! Why don't you join them two and go back to Ireland" said the witness. He threw a chunk of ice at the officer as he stumbled forward.

The police officer tripped the drunk with ease and smiled while applying handcuffs. Between the arrest, the prostrate patsy, and the soft drop of snowflakes, the air was quiet again.

Aiden led Keagan to evade more of a ruckus, heading back out of the alleyway toward Wells. The lawman noticed them, prompting Keagan to give a nod and Aiden to give a sheepish wave, not knowing what else to do.

The cop waved back.

"Officer O'Neill gets a cut from the boss," Keagan said before their jog south. "Don't piss on his shoes, though, or he'll grow a public servant attitude. Best to just let him work the law as he likes."

"I'll keep that in mind," Aiden muttered as they headed south to meet the boss.

- - - - -

Dean O'Banion first met Aiden months before the holdup outside the Brass Kerry saloon, over a mile south in the Chicago Loop. O'Banion's lasting impression was that the kid was a pain in the arse. He let Aiden know this on a regular basis despite more respectful rapport ever since.

Aiden had been working as a newspaper peddler for the *Chicago Daily Tribune* when he chanced upon the

North Side Gang boss. O'Banion limped over to him south on Market Street just as a nearby train spewed coal-burning smoke on the 7:43 p.m. Lake Street Elevated Railroad route. As the soot and thunder from above drifted to its constant, hazy buzz, the racketeer boss demanded Aiden carry Hearst's *Chicago American*. It was before Prohibition, and the gang's bread and butter was more in newspapers, gambling and robbery than bootleg.

In spite of O'Banion's gimpy left leg and slight stature, the treacherous tranquility in his eyes and the bulk of muscle in his arms insinuated that he wasn't just a tramp taunting with empty threats. He also flashed a knife.

Giving into O'Banion's demand wasn't an option for Aiden. The threats weren't enough to instill obedience when he saw no benefit to himself or his family. Also, he preferred reading the *Daily Tribune*.

Aiden leaned in and gave a kick to O'Banion's left shin before dodging away. The limp seemed worse as O'Banion staggered with a healthy degree of pain, slashing the air with a Schrade knife.

The young hellion just dodged and smiled before pulling out a small, but effective, club from underneath a roll of newspaper. He let his bag drop to the street before he said,

"You'll never again dance a jig in a pub if you carry on like that."

O'Banion, who had sung and danced while himself an apprentice at a local racketeer's saloon, laughed in spite of himself. He stepped back, raising his hands in mock submission. The North Side Gang boss decided to put words over fists.

"Agh, I'm not in the mood to filet a cocky bastard," he said. "Since I've no lads with me to knock you on your arse, you can go about your business today. You oughta stop by and see me at Schofield's Flower Shop. I might find use for a wise arse like you."

Aiden didn't then realize his luck that O'Banion had no backup and was in a decent mood. After the gang boss threw the Schrade knife into the lad's bat, Aiden stepped back and tilted his newsboy cap with humbled, yet condescending, conciliation. He was told to keep the knife.

A week after their first meeting, Aiden visited Dean O'Banion at Schofield's Flower Shop on State Street. The firmness of a handshake and the almost paternal charm of the thug lured Aiden. The potential for profit and adventure sealed the deal.

Aiden learned much more than the finer points of flower arrangement in the months since. O'Banion's North Side Gang controlled an area dominated by Swedish and Irish immigrants in the Kilgubbin neighborhood around Goose Island. The boss directed gambling, protection, cigars, and bootleg booze from there south to Chicago Avenue

Any of Aiden's qualms about breaking the law dwindled as the money flowed in. The elements of danger fed the intrigue he envisioned for himself. His parents moral disapproval faded to the background over time.

About twenty minutes after the stickup outside the

Brass Kerry, Aiden and Danny Keagan jogged east on Chicago Avenue and made a right on State. They had to report to their boss inside the building where O'Banion ran his legitimate business at Schofield's. The hub of Roman Catholic Chicago, Holy Name Cathedral, was across the street.

Aiden had to suppress a smile while listening to his boss, the Catholic florist and gangster. The flower shop's temperature bordered on tropical, thanks to the orange embers burning in a stove. Lilies, carnations, and chrysanthemums bloomed in pots surrounding several simple, pine work tables, one of which had a mechanical cash register from the turn of the century. Insulated brick walls shielded everything from the icy climate outdoors.

The beads of sweat on Aiden's head weren't only from nerves.

"You see Aiden, keeping on the other side of the law has its advantages," O'Banion droned on while Keagan and Aiden stood before him. "Breaking laws don't matter as much with tribute to law enforcement and officials we help elect."

Aiden nodded and enjoyed the soapbox. His boss asked why they were a bit late and he reported at once about the complications of a drunken witness, Officer O'Neill, and their patsy's fisticuffs with Keagan. Aiden emphasized that he stepped in before Keagan could receive a finishing blow.

O'Banion took an exaggerated step back and gave his associates a sly glance, from one to the other. He whistled before looking at Keagan to address him.

"If you had slipped a proper Mickey Finn to our patsy, the job would have been as easy as ripping off a newsboy," he said. "I mean no offense, Aiden."

After putting out his hand, O'Banion received the looted cash and the pocket watch. He counted upwards of $150 before getting an interruption he likely found rude based on the flush of rouge to his cheeks.

"Actually, it was Officer O'Neill who let us pass," Keagan said. "Without your giving him his weekly bribes, he might have brought down the law."

"Sounds like the bum wanted to kick your arse," O'Banion said."If you would've doped him proper, O'Neill wouldn't have had to take care of a witness. But for Aiden's quick thinking with the knife, you'd be in the emergency ward or in jail."

The cheekbones on Keagan's face drew tight. Aiden figured the North Side accomplice wanted to defend himself, but knew better than to disagree with the boss. He just shifted his anger from his left to right foot.

"Here's twenty clams to bring to you and yours," O'Banion said as he handed Aiden his share. "And you better get your house in order, Danny, or you won't be seeing your share."

Keagan stared at O'Banion like a pit bull shorted out of a meal. Aiden just nodded to the man in charge, said thanks, and rushed out to get home. He wanted to avoid any hot-headed retaliation from his coworker or questioning from his parents.

"If I can keep the local gangster boss in my corner, I might keep things ducky with Ma and Pa," Aiden muttered to himself while in the arctic cold while the jog west kept his blood pumping. "But Christ, Ma is harder to fool."

- - - - -

Aiden ran as fast as he could on Chicago Avenue past Halsted Street to his home, the first story flat of a simple brick row house. After slipping on ice several times, he had enough bruises that he thought it wouldn't have mattered much if he had taken a few blows from the patsy. Chicago winter weather turned out to be a harsh nemesis.

While biting his bottom lip and steadying his right hand with his left, Aiden stuck his key in the lock to his front door. He hoped that his mother, Margaret, would've forgotten about him and gone to sleep. At least his father, Evan, would be asleep, having to get to his barber shop early most mornings. The door swung open like a cork from a bottle before Aiden could sneak inside.

"Oh, where the devil have you been, Aiden," Margaret said, her arms crossed against the outside chill. "It's approaching quarter past eleven and you have school tomorrow. Get your duff inside before you and I both catch consumption."

Inside the relative warmth of his home, Aiden tried to hem together a story before blood could fully circulate to his brain. He said that after he had helped clear the snow in the neighborhood, he tried to get gravel to put down over the remaining ice. But after slipping and falling unconscious, the neighboring Russell couple took him in and made sure he was well enough to return to his mother.

Margaret's glare gave off enough chill to lower the temperature in the room even though a fire had been roaring in the fireplace earlier.

"Well that's a bunch a blarney," she said. "You don't talk smooth enough. The Russells would have just delivered you to our door rather than waste time on you. They're decent enough people, but they're still Protestant. Cut out the bull, won't you?"

Aiden stifled a chuckle as he realized the absurdity of the situation. A little over an hour ago he had been holding a knife to a gorilla's stomach, relieving him of his wallet. He had then charmed the North Side Gang boss for a generous cut. Now, he worried about his mom's wrath. Margaret smacked him on the behind and told him to get off to bed at once.

"I don't wanna hear no more fibs from you," she said. "Your pa will hear about this chicanery and tell you not to be such a wise-arse. At least you don't come back with shiners like you used to have when you hawked the *Tribune*. Get your duff into bed. You'll answer to your father in the morning."

"Yes, Ma," Aiden said with a deferential nod before he went to his room.

While he got into his underclothes, he pondered whether he should be more modest, put his cash under his bed, and and simply study at Holy Name School for Boys instead of running with gangsters. Margaret thought he would have good influences at the school, even though he preferred to be among so-called criminals.

Margaret's ability to detect baloney tempered any

guilt Aiden felt about lying. After getting comfortable and stowing the closed Schrade under his pillow, he pulled his sheets to his chin, and then practiced a self-deprecating grimace to respond to the expected reprimand the next morning. A smirk returned to his face as he drifted off to dreamworld.

As she joined her husband in bed, Margaret harbored no illusions that Aiden would join the priesthood or even be a deacon for one of the largest Roman Catholic Dioceses in the United States. But she hoped that he would at least get a good education and gain friends who weren't all hooligans and hangers-on at pool halls, newsstands, and saloons.

In due time, the McCarthy household fell into a peaceful quiet while the ruckus permeating pockets of Chicago's ever unsleeping streets and speakeasies danced on.

2

The Feminine Mystique

The air was crisp in Washington Square Park Monday morning as the sun peeked from behind fluffy clouds. Soft white light shined on a bohemian community of migrants, charlatans, and evangelists who stood among the trees. Overwhelming voices, sometimes projected atop soapboxes, echoed between Dearborn and Clark Streets. The cacophonous preaching about issues, both real and imagined, earned the park its moniker, Bughouse Square.

On any ordinary day of skipping school, Sophia Golino enjoyed the liberty of the park, where people could rant against patriarchy, greed, and robber barons until their voices grew hoarse. However, today she had slipped out of her studies at Resurrection Academy to spy on her father, Silvio, an up-and-coming lieutenant in John Torrio's Outfit gang. Her father's involvement in the underworld kept her from enjoying the usual show.

At seventeen, Sophia didn't let her father or her mother, Celia, assume that their daughter would join the convent or marry a well-connected *scapolo*. Her boldness, or *impudenza*, as her father called it, set her apart from much of her family, even more than for other *signorine*.

Perhaps most tiresome was her younger brother, Vincent. Almost daily, he threatened to beat up any man with whom she kept company, ensuring that she remained as pure as her *padre* and he wanted so they could marry her off to the highest bidder. Sophia's spirit and smarts had kept her a step ahead of Vincent, with a view into Silvio's illicit gangster affairs. Her restlessness had led Sophia to spy on Silvio's clandestine life with a curious revulsion.

The evening before, she had eavesdropped on a telephone conversation where he made plans with John Torrio to meet in the morning. She deduced from the back and forth that her father would meet with the Outfit boss just south of where her favorite riff raff raised hell in Washington Square Park.

After she had faked illness, she ditched school to spy on her father. She put on a pair of homemade denim pants and a gray pea coat, tucking her chin-length black bob under a cap to avoid the social trappings of being a girl. A streetcar ride north brought her from her house to Bughouse Square.

Sophia could count on her friend, Harriet Rosenstein, for help. The twenty-one-year-old was one of her favorite soapbox preachers, and was more like an older sister than a friend. She listened to Harriet at the park, ravished with the embers of rebellion.

"Why should I be weighed down by one man?" Harriet shouted, towering over a crowd in the park and wearing a torn, gray wool skirt and black coat offset by a red rose above her right ear. "I went to a university. I am smarter, better looking, and more efficient, But men still earn more than me, expect me to clean the house, and not explore the relations of other, more skilled, sensuous suitors."

Sophia wanted to join several other so-called women of ill-repute in the rapture of applause, but she hadn't the time today. She averted her eyes, kept her voice in her chest, and weaved her way toward the base of Harriet's soap box. She beckoned her friend with a nod of the head, wasting no time once the brouhaha simmered down.

"Excuse me, fellow Bughouse dwellers," Harriet emphasized in a mock-hush tone. "One of my lovelies needs me. Charles, take over!"

As Charles Piaf, one of Harriet's handsome paramours, took over a growing, swooning crowd, she stepped down and hugged Sophia. They exchanged friendly pecks, alternating from cheek to cheek like immigrants from the old country.

"As one lovely to another, you're the cat's meow as always," Sophia whispered to her friend. From under the cover of her coat, she returned one of Harriet's flasks she had filled with a bit of Silvio's brandy. "I don't have time to explain, but will you switch coats with me and take my cap?"

The two ladies rushed behind a maple tree as Charles ranted to everyone who was paying attention. They exchanged coats as Sophia smudged dirt on her face and told Harriet that she was looking in on her father.

Harriet nodded and winked as she went back to work the crowds and grab their attention.

"Alas, if I have to look more like a man to be more respected and better paid, I'll play the game," cried Harriet. "Any donation to the liberation of women from patriarchy can be left in this donated cap."

Sophia giggled under her breath before turning her attention from the show.

After messing up her hair to look more like a tramp and to blend in better among the dwellers of the square, Sophia joined another crowd on the south end that was advocating for Marxism and a national proletarian revolution. She obscured her face from her father, blending in with wanna-be revolutionaries as she listened to Silvio's criminal conversation.

Two well-dressed Italian men walked south on Clark, paying little attention to the ruckus in the park. They were only twenty feet away but in a separate world.

- - - - -

Silvio Golino walked south of Washington Park with Outfit leader John Torrio, both donned in pinstripe suits. He straightened his fedora, stopped walking, and then turned to address his boss.

"I tell you Colosimo's bad news," he said to Torrio. "The pinhead doesn't want to move on the moonshine opportunities when it could be most profitable to our business."

Silvio made a valid, yet well-known, case against Chicago Mafia bigwig, pimp and racketeer James Colosimo. "Big Jim," while taking profits from local gambling and his collection of brothels, neglected the opportunity the 18th Amendment to the U.S. Constitution delivered. To the chagrin of his peers in the Chicago Italian rackets, Colosimo was failing to tap into the demand of a thirsty public.

Fellow countrymen with interests in moonshine failed to change Colosimo's mind. He was too comfortable with his ladies of the night and his club's star performer, Minka Summer. He also had powerful friends in the First Ward, with whom he exchanged votes in the red light district for amnesty as a pimp.

"Remember, boss," Silvio said, "Colosimo only wants to sell whoopee and host roulette wheels. That's all fine and good. But he oughta be taken out if he doesn't doesn't wanna sell spirits. Violence don't mix with business, but rules have exceptions."

With fine, combed gray hair and a smooth-shaven face Torrio's face remained pensive rather than hostile. He knew Silvio was right, but still had to play the cooler head. Spilling blood against the overt wishes of their friends in Little Italy, the Gennas, would not only be bad politics, but bad business.

"We still gotta wait until the Genna Brothers get on board," said Torrio. "If we want to have future connections with our Sicilian brethren, we can't show no disrespect. The Gennas not only control most moonshine in Little Italy to the southwest, but they garner a lot of national support with the *Unione Siciliana*."

The veins in Silvio's face stood out as much as his own impatience. Sophia could see the flush of fury from the park. Still, she knew her father would know better than

17

to disrespect his boss.

"The guy's too reckless, Johnny," Silvio said. "I say if I could fail to help him when he trips up in some horrible hit by an outsider, you and me could pay Schofield's for the biggest bouquet ever seen in Chicago. With your guidance, we'd be doin' the Gennas and all the racketeers a favor."

Torrio massaged his hairless chin and watched his lieutenant before giving a brief look to the park and nodding.

"I got a buddy in New York, Frankie Yale, that could help us out, make a hit that couldn't be pinned on us," he said with a calm rationality. "If the Sicilians try to mess with you or anyone in our families, you let Papa Torrio know and we'll make sure certain people happen to vanish."

The Outfit boss looked more like a gentle uncle than a thug as he nodded and clapped Silvio on the shoulder, sneaking a wink.

"You stick to your duties, Silvio," he continued. "I got a fella from the East Coast who's looking to move here to make this city work. Like you and I, Alphonse Capone knows that there's a better racket when the legality of your business depends on who's receiving a cut."

"I'm sure he won't have trouble picking a side after he knows who's in charge, Mr. Torrio," Silvio said.

Back in Washington Square Park, Sophia wandered back to where Harriet's seduced a crowd with the so-called dangers of women's equality. She mulled over her disapproval of Silvio's business ethics. Her mind turned toward her mother per usual when disillusionment gripped her.

"What will happen to me, Vincent, and Mama if Papa gets bumped off in this whole game?" she mumbled to herself.

When Sophia returned her friend's coat and retrieved her cap, she knew she needed something to numb her thoughts. Something stronger than wine or beer.

"I might need a swig of brandy to continue with such charades," Sophia said. "I stole it from an up-and-coming gangster, so I should expect some of the share. What do you say, dove?"

"Now you're learning to act like a revolutionary," said Harriet in a mock motherly voice before passing her flask.

3

Good Company

Aiden awoke that Monday morning with the dull thump of a hand smacking his chest. Even though he was still groggy at half past six, Margaret took pleasure in making Aiden get out of bed to get ready for school at Holy Name. Due to the chipper lilt in her voice, Aiden surmised that she had had a talk with his father. He tried to prepare for Evan's browbeating as he put on some fresh gray trousers and a navy blue sweater.

Over oatmeal Margaret had prepared with a pinch of petulance, Evan lectured Aiden that he ought to be better and keep his nose to his studies to get his high school diploma. His father's arguments were as familiar and conventional as his brown slacks and white button-down, accented only with a navy blue polka dot bow tie.

"If a young, intelligent lad has a degree from a good high school, he can make the world his oyster," Evan lectured. "And you oughtn't make your mother worry so much. You don't want to end up like our neighbor, Seamus, do you, The poor fella gambled and hung around drunks so long he's still in the red."

Evan smacked his *Daily Tribune* for emphasis on the

simple table where they sat in their cozy kitchen and dining room.

Aiden was mock-mouthing his father's words in his head, figuring that Evan worried more than he should. Like most older sons, he didn't think his father gave him enough credit.

He knew in theory that overconfidence could ruin any person looking to make dough off lawbreaking. But that would happen only if he was sloppy or got caught. When his father suggested getting a job in the canning business or as his apprentice, Aiden dismissed any interest in so-called sensibility.

"That's the way to make it in America," Evan said. "You gotta keep your hands on the level and as busy as your mind. Do anything else, and you're liable to find trouble."

"I agree, father," Aiden said with mock-sincerity. "It's my duty as a citizen to follow the laws of the United States government in pursuance of great progress for our family. I've learned my lesson and will, as my headmaster instructs, 'keep my nose to the grindstone.'"

Aiden stared into his father's eyes before Evan shook his head at the boy's cheek.

"You watch yourself with lawbreakers like Dean O'Banion, lad," Evan said. "I can't say how important it is to fold your cards before your bluff gets called out as pure blarney."

Aiden realized his father might be more streetwise than the younger, cocky McCarthy gave him credit. Evan correctly guessed his employer and knew the Irish florist wasn't all on the level. He decided to keep his mouth shut for everyone's benefit.

"And one more thing," Evan continued. "If you keep passing fibs to your mother and smartin' off to us, you won't have to worry about any gangsters. You'd best mind the missus and get ready for school."

Aiden finished his breakfast in silence and wasted no time while rinsing his dishes in the sink, grabbing his books, and donning his cap and jacket. He gave his parents a nod of respect to their stoic faces as he headed toward the door. Margaret stopped him and pecked him on the cheek before he gave a grin and was off.

- - - - --

Aiden sat up straight in the cool room at Holy Name School for Boys, his breath visible. His backside would grow numb against the solid wood chair if he didn't shift from time to time. The move was subtle enough to not distinguish himself from the other boys on either side of him. He stifled a yawn, clenching his jaw to evade further attention from the teacher.

The greatest joy Aiden got from his schooling was the arguments he had with the clergy tasked with teaching him. He was bright in math, science, and English, but his instructors in Catechism and history couldn't decide whether the boy was insane, willful, or both. From his interruptions, they had no evidence to assume he was an idiot.

"Can we be sure that Christ wasn't just a man with good ideas?" Aiden said today. "That says quite a little of mankind to believe that one has to be part deity to atone for our sins. In Luke, Chapter 3, verses 21-22, God

23

proclaims Jesus to be his son. But in the first book of Timothy, Chapter 2, verses 5-7, there is only one God and Jesus is God's mediator to humans. Why does it say two different things in the Bible?

For today's outburst, the headmaster smacked Aiden straight away with a ruler and told him to never repeat such heresy.

Aiden would have liked to respond about the self-righteousness of any man trying to interpret God and life's meaning, but he let it go. He was all for rocking the boat, but didn't wish to get smacked more for trying to pass the time.

He decided he would duck out after his second class and play hooky to keep out of trouble. His absence relieved the teachers enough to look the other way.

Before he would meet with his fellows in the North Side Gang, he headed over to Bughouse Square just before noon to catch his favorite sideshow acts of deviance and political rebellion. There, he saw one of his favorite soap-box hell-raisers, Harriet Rosenstein, carrying on about the "hypocrisy of the status quo." But more interesting than Harriet was an olive-skinned girl around his age. She looked familiar but only noticed her now.

He gulped as he took in her soft, grinning lips, bright hazel eyes, and the stray lock of ebony hair running down her cheek. Her dress at first appeared plain, boyish, and unflattering. However, he was thankful that it didn't hide her feminine curves.

The girl had a rapport with Harriet, apparent as the two swapped coats and hugged. Aiden followed the girl as she skulked around the square. He found her hiding among a group of Marxists professing about how communal ownership would protect the United States from certain doom by robber barons.

The girl grew very serious as she listened to two Italians talking outside the periphery of the crowds. Aiden overheard that they were plotting against James Colosimo and realized he was listening in on the competition. His boss had foretold the scenario behind closed doors, so he listened for names and places that might prove useful.

What Aiden couldn't figure out after listening in on the two Italians was how the beautiful olive-skinned girl connected to them. Was she listening in on the men out of relation to one of them? Or was she interested in the goings-on of Chicago's growing entrepreneurship in illicit goods and services?

That she got sauced after her attention returned to the park made him think that she wanted to escape. She was a fine thing, and he would like to aide her in that escape. He wanted to go up to her and goad her into laughing, to ask her if she had a fella, ruffle her feathers, make her wave her ebony bob back and forth, or to ask her about dancing a foxtrot sometime.

Aiden deduced that this was neither the time nor the place. She appeared to need a good moody, and he didn't want to get involved. He also needed to get a move on if he wanted to listen in on an afternoon meeting between O'Banion and his helping hands.

"Maybe I'll get a chance to chat with the dove another time," he muttered to himself. "It's time for business now."

- - - - -

The North Side Gang members convened inside a
hidden room in Dean O'Banion's favorite saloon on the
corner of Augusta and Milwaukee. In the front room of
Carrie's Ax, customers came to drink liquor and beer
and listen to dark-skinned performers play trumpets
and drums. Nothing illegal had happened at this spot
until the last several months. Ever since, friendly Feds
and police took bribes of cash or liquor to let business
flourish.

O'Banion, his two lieutenants, Earl Weiss and George
Moran, and a few associates, including Aiden and
Danny Keagan, were in the back room. A door hidden
by a moving bookcase allowed them to enter from the
main saloon. The air inside the 144-foot-square room
was hazy as O'Banion smoked cigars with his
lieutenants. The three sat at a small hickory card table
as the associates listened in.

"I don't care what the dagos and their kind do, we're
not bums who make a dime off a dame," O'Banion said.
"They got fourteen-year-old children of God selling
their bodies to hairy goombahs for a dollar a pop. We'll
make enough dough off of our better whiskey. Christ
never had a problem with spirits."

Anyone in the room remained quiet despite a palpable
need for a sliver of levity, at least until Earl Weiss
attempted to rock O'Banion's soapbox. The trim,
twentysomething lieutenant saw how Torrio and
Colosimo made thousands per day, not even having to
work to lure police officers, businessmen, and fellow

power brokers into patronizing their brothels.

"Christ didn't have too much a problem with prostitutes," he interrupted. "He hung out with one before his fellow Jews killed him."

"We don't have problems with the poor prostitutes," O'Banion replied. "It's those bloody johns who take advantage of the gals. Also, lay off the Jews and shut your trap until I'm done talking, Earl. I thought you was a Jew and I hired you."

Weiss said he meant no disrespect, but still didn't understand how it was immoral to capitalize off brothels and permissible to shake down drunks and run hijackings on shipment routes of beer, whiskey, rum, and gin. A look from the boss made him swallow his argument, flex his jaw, and keep his trap shut.

O'Banion explained North Side business was not just about "roughing up dames and drunks." To get an advantage on the Chicago bootleg racket, he had been busy contacting Canadian distillers and breweries through Detroit from well before the federal clampdown of Prohibition. If North Side Gang members were to get rough, it wasn't with anyone who couldn't defend himself.

"Also, if cops want in on our business, I've given them a cut," O'Banion said. "Chances are that the local heat will not cooperate with the Feds, anyway. Dagos to the South are our biggest problem."

He knew Torrio's Outfit and the Mafioso in Little Italy were looking to move into bootlegging to add to their grasp in all other rackets. The problem for the Italians was that "Big Jim" Colosimo was too hopped up on commercial love and selling white slaves to see the opportunity Uncle Sam presented with Prohibition. He acknowledged that "the Colosimo problem might soon be eliminated."

"If the Italians and their friends reach out to us,and find a way to get around Colosimo," O'Banion said, "we'll stand up together against the Huns and Blockheads in Washington."

The North Siders around O'Banion toasted him as leader of the band of thugs in control of alcohol and political clout north of Chicago Avenue.

Weiss sipped his whiskey and hoped that his boss's territorial gamesmanship was realistic enough. Even if the North Siders had a longer history in Chicago, many of the Italian networks could find their roots centuries earlier in the post-feudal remnants of the Roman Empire.

- - - - -

Aiden tried to stifle his coughs as he breathed in some of the cigar smoke in the glorified closet hidden in Carrie's Ax. Between the disagreements with his parents, the overheard conversation outside Bughouse Square and in the back of the saloon, he was growing uneasy.

He had told O'Banion a few days ago that he would threaten with a knife or a baseball bat, but he kept to himself that he wasn't a killer. That his boss would commit a crime of omission by not stopping a murder didn't shake Aiden. He knew the boss couldn't ave the same qualms about killing.

Aiden knew his role was likely to become bloodier the

longer he stayed in the North Side Gang. He would either bloody someone else or be bloodied himself. But the sixteen-year-old in him wanted only to defy caution and so-called good sense, be it from church, school, or his parents.

"At least the Italians and us might rest easy until their king takes a bow," Aiden whispered to Keagan, who stood to his left.

Keagan responded by stomping on Aiden's toe, keeping any verbal response to himself.

Aiden blinked back tears, wanting to punch the bastard, but let it go rather than stoop to being petty..

After O'Banion dismissed the meeting, Aiden figured any information he had about a hit on Colosimo wouldn't be news. He headed back home, not bothering to join the others for a drink. He headed toward safety and kept his thoughts to something he rationalized would make his parents happy. There was no reason to upset them if he'd confine any mischief to the lower levels of the North Side Gang.

"I'll only help harass drunks who might deserve a good drubbing." he said to himself as he approached his house. "At the least, I won't trouble Ma and Pa'll with more scoldings from the headmaster. It's not much worth the effort, anyway."

4

In the Works

John Torrio sat at the edge of the crowd at the Outfit's headquarters at the Four Deuces Club. Several dozen recurring customers swarmed the salon of the establishment at 2222 S. Wabash.

Business was picking up on the first Friday of spring. Torrio recognized bankers, aldermen, and police among his most consistent clientele. He figured more were either on the gambling tables or on the whores working the levels above.

At his oak table, Torrio flicked ash from a poorly-made cigar on the ground. His face remained calm with the drifting smoke and the pleasant burning of the air, but it scrunched in discomfort when a busty, blonde doped-up hooker lost her footing and fell bosom-first into his lap.

He raised her shoulders with a firm grasp on each, avoiding contact with her breasts. They jostled into a standing position, where she wavered to and fro. He shrugged and gave her a forced, patriarchal grin, thinking it would be better for business to dismiss the prostitute's clumsiness without starting an incident.

The lady-for-hire lacked the same sense. She put her right hand on his waist, giving him a direct gaze with her feline eyes as she slowly slid her left hand lower. The glossiness of those eyes turned him off to her callous charms.

"Hey, Johnny," she said with a slur, "I'll let you be my daddy if you want to follow me to the fourth floor. We can chase the dragon or I can show you moves your steady will never let you try. Just let me show you a new world."

In two seconds, Torrio smashed a glass tumbler and held a jagged edge to the blonde. He struck her hand away from his groin as if his wife, Anne, was present. Even though no one around him seemed conscious of events, he had already decided that he wouldn't kill anyone. It wasn't worth the trouble.

"You cheap harlot," he said, bending her hand unnaturally "You'll get out of here with your life tonight. No dirty hooker could amount to a quarter my Anne, but if you ever come back here, you won't be worth an eighth. And that'll be greater than any pervert or pimp would offer."

Torrio broke her pinkie and ring finger with an iron grip before handing her to a doorman. He told the man to keep her alive, but not well. Hired muscle dragged her to 22nd Street and put a few new bruises to her face.

Torrio, meanwhile, lit another cigar before returning his seat at the table. He puffed away and motioned for a kimono-clad brunette server gal to fetch Silvio Golino.

Silvio gave the brunette a quarter after she summoned him from across the room . His blank face hid the unease he felt after he witnessed his boss's reaction to the pushy prostitute. The thoughts running under Silvio's hardened face wove themselves into a tumultuous tapestry. His wish to be Torrio's lead lieutenant would need more finesse than he first figured.

- - - - -

Silvio shuddered when Torrio gestured for them to step outside. Torrio had ordered a doorman to hold an umbrella over him as raindrops fell out of the chilly sky. Hastened by his boss, Silvio didn't enjoy the same comforts. The Outfit boss gave a fish-eating grin and blew warm air in his hands after they exited.

"I called a pal from Brooklyn today," Torrio said after wandering a block from the club without a hint of haste. "Seems that he's copacetic with calculated hits against Colosimo. The Sicilians in Little Italy aren't showing any beef. The Genna brothers should have no problem if someone lacking a sense for business gets bumped off."

"That's great news, Mr. Torrio," Silvio said between the chattering of his teeth. "With my suggestion and your management, we'll keep Italian interests going strong."

Torrio nodded and gestured for them to head back to the warmth of the Four Deuces, showing no remorse for his lieutenant's discomfort when he slapped his cold hands with jovial pretension. He concealed a snicker while Silvio shook his damp, whitening fingers.

"Our man said that the earliest time he can make it to Chicago is a month or so," Torrio said, stopping them both before getting back in the warm, dry club. "I hope I can count on you to keep an eye on things when he shows up. If you do, there's no telling where you can go."

Silvio nodded his head in supposed gratitude. In his mind, he was choking Torrio with strong, still shaking fists, but his demeanor showed only appreciation. He figured he already had a lead on his competition, Alphonse Capone, who had been on his mind since first hearing the name several months ago.

Back in the club, Silvio got two pourings of tea for both of them before settling with Torrio at his table. They sipped and let blood course through their veins as customers around them stumbled and cackled before either heading upstairs for gambling or paid whoopee. When the feeling returned to Silvio's fingers, Torrio teased his subordinate with new information and a request.

"There's also this Capone fella I've been telling you about," Torrio said. "The schmuck won't be here until the Colosimo situation is taken care of, but I hope I can count on you to help him get in touch with the way we do business here. Our biggest challenge is gonna be the Irish."

"You got it, boss," Silvio responded, concealing whatever guile he felt.

Torrio gulped down the rest of his tea and ordered a Cadillac to take him home to his wife, Anne. After a doorman fetched his coat and umbrella, he clipped Silvio on the cheek with comportment far too callous to be cordial. The charming smile on Torrio's face was not warm, but not quite a sneer.

Silvio just nodded with the deference he could stomach as he thought about wiping off the smugness of Torrio's face with a brick. Instead of brooding on his quest for power, he resolved to cave in to his more base needs. He didn't want to head home to be a husband or father. He went up to the brunette server and grabbed her around the waist.

For five dollars, she distracted him on the third floor of the Four Deuces with her smooth, alabaster skin and the curve of her behind and her bust. The hours of ecstasy for him concluded with opium-laced cigarettes. He was asleep and sedated enough to be at peace when his paid company went downstairs for another customer.

5

Opportunity

Dozens of Easter lilies lay on a table at Schofield's Flower Shop, picked free of insects and webbing, and combed over for wilted blooms and chewed leaves, all of which were cut off. Aiden returned the blade to the handle of the Schrade knife after trimming the flowers, at once furrowing his brow and pleased he hadn't yet had to use it to draw blood. When not threatening tramps or soliciting saps, he reckoned that work with the North Side Gang was like any job.

Aiden liked that work was across the street from church and classes. It wasn't hard to keep an eye on Chicago's purveyors of power.

"Please give his grace, Archbishop Mundelein, our utmost appreciation," Dean O'Banion said, escorting a deacon toward the exit. "We are more than happy to help Holy Name Cathedral prepare for our Lord's Resurrection."

The deacon offered his hand once outside, which O'Banion took in both of his. They bid adieu with nods of the head as the cleric said thank you in return.

O'Banion returned to the shop with a smile on his

face, congratulating himself before calling George Moran and Earl Weiss over to deal with other matters.

"Helping those holding the keys to heaven is worth so much more than lost revenue," he said aside to Aiden. "How are those free lilies coming along, lad?"

"Just lovely," Aiden deadpanned.

A cough helped Aiden choke down any backtalk as he returned a smile and got back to work on a few more dozen blooms for the Church. While keeping his hands busy, he propped an ear toward his boss and lieutenants, Weiss and Moran. Although their voices were hushed in a corner of the room, he could make out the words if he strained.

"What's the word, boss?" Moran asked. "You got your finger on the pulse."

"Diamond Jim, as I've said before, is on the way out," O'Banion said. "I know a guy who knows a guy. Papa Torrio's enlisting a strong arm from Brooklyn who doesn't play for the Dodgers."

Aiden tried to remember the name he'd overheard a while back in Bughouse Square as he listened. Suddenly, a pebble hit him on a hand that was holding a lily. O'Banion had noticed his eavesdropping and apparent lack of attention to flowers.

"Hey, lad," the boss said. "Something I can help you with?"

"Frankie Yale," Aiden muttered mostly to himself, but audible enough for inquisitive ears.

Despite the limp, O'Banion crossed the room with the surprising speed of a well-tuned Tin Lizzie. He put his south paw down on the table with a thud, just missing a precious lily bulb. With his other arm, he brought Aiden to a standing position and led him to the corner with his lieutenants.

"Say it again, lad," he commanded, "but keep it on the down low."

Aiden had left his Schrade by the table, not that it mattered much with the North Side Gang boss and top brass in front of him. He decided the truth would set him free. Making up lies was harder under threat of life and limb.

"A while back I heard two Italians talking about Big Jim," he said. "I wasn't lookin for the info, I happened to hear Frankie Yale's name come up. Don't know of the sap, but they seemed to think he could lend a hand."

Teeth flashed on O'Banion's face. The look wasn't unfriendly, if it returned he expected.

"You tend to pick up on things, don't you, you little piss head?" he asked. "That and a thoughtless temper will get you killed if not reigned in. Weiss. Moran. What do you fellas think of our little snoop here?"

Moran, the slightly older and chubbier of the two, gave a wink and nodded his head before noting the lad could be useful. Weiss had a different opinion.

"He's a little young, ain't he?" he asked. "Let him rob drunks and bust heads for a couple of years."

O'Banion swatted his hand and made his point. Aiden's audacity reminded him of himself, and he already had enough thugs. He said as much while giving a not-so-subtle nod to Weiss. The boss still had a calm look as if he were hiding a thought or two.

"You go ahead and keep your eyes and ears open, lad.

But first you oughta get those lilies done. There's no need to save your delicate fingers."

Aiden just smiled with a hint of self-deprecation and returned to his table to trim the lilies' trumpets. When dozens more were complete, he retrieved his newsboy cap and took his leave. He reminded O'Banion he had to be home for supper to keep his ma and pa on an even keel.

O'Banion waved him off, ignoring the possibility that his associate was hiding notions of his own.

6

A Sunny Day in May

Minka Summer stretched her legs as she moved her lithe form, which was lying next to the much larger frame of James Colosimo. Their honeymoon bed was large enough for eight of her and three of him. She liked the big, tall crime boss, even though she didn't find him particularly attractive. She giggled while watching him saw off a muffled snore. The bedside clock ticked as its hands revealed that it was just past eight o'clock in the morning.

A few days ago, Colosimo married the twenty-five-year-old, redheaded chanteuse in northwestern Indiana. The wedding came only one week after the divorce from his last wife, Chicago madam Victoria Moresco. Newspaper coverage of his break from Moresco was second only to the White Sox's first home game loss to the Cleveland Indians.

Minka reminded herself that she wasn't interested in such pedestrian preoccupations as she wrapped her naked body in a silk robe. The new Mrs. Colosimo kissed her husband on his bulldog-like jowls before she padded to the bathroom adjoining their suite at the sprawling Metropole Hotel on South Michigan Avenue. That the space was twice the size of her last bedroom only charmed her more into the prospect of being a Mafia boss's new wife.

Visions of acting and singing beyond the scope of nightclubs and cabarets danced through Minka's head as her eyes flitted back and forth in the mirror. With such dreams, preparation and good looks were as important as talent.

Minka took more time than usual to get dolled up to spend money on little objects with her daddy's money. She ran a gold-plated comb through her crimson-colored, finger-waved, chin-length locks. After applying foundation, eyeliner, and a touch of rouge, she sheathed herself in a trim, knee-length, black dress and donned a red cloche hat only a shade darker than her hair.

"'Good night sweet prince,'" Minka whispered Shakespeare into Colosimo's unconscious ear. "And 'flights of angels sing thee to thy rest.'"

After wrapping herself in a silk scarf, she left a note she was shopping on Maxwell Street to the Northwest, accompanied by one of Colosimo's hired muscle. As she left under protection, she didn't yet know the prescience of her last words to her soon-to-be late husband.

- - - - -

The morning sun illuminated the eastern edge of Maxwell Street before the shops opened at nine o'clock. Few pedestrians would be around until more vendors opened for the early rush. Evan McCarthy found the lack of commotion pleasant

Evan didn't shop much. He preferred to save funds for
when difficult times came. But Aiden's recent behavior
put him in the mood to reward his son. The lad
appeared to stay away from racketeers and pay due
attention to his studies as the school year drew to a
close. At least he showed up for supper on time.

When thinking about Aiden having turned seventeen
a day after the spring opening at Comiskey Park, he also
realized that gift-giving was coming to an end. So he
hiked south along Maxwell Street to make a rare
purchase. He'd pick up some new loafers as a gift before
visiting a friend on 22nd Street.

At Roosevelt, just north of the shoe seller, what Evan
saw made him shake his head and flush with anger as
he blew a flustered breath into the warm air. He was
much more than disappointed and knew how to best
show it.

Aiden was striding north on Ohio Street alongside
Dean O'Banion and other ruffians. None of them
seemed to have any burdens of the world until met with
the five-foot-eight height of an angry father armed with
Irish-Catholic guilt

About a week prior, Evan had visited O'Banion at
Schofield's while purchasing chrysanthemums for
Margaret. He had asked the flower-arranging gangster
in good faith to continue leaving Aiden out of the
rackets, to no avail.

"What are you doing there, lad," Evan said with a
measured calm that froze Aiden in his place. "And you
Dean, I asked ya to keep away from my son."

To Evan's contentment and Aiden's objection, O'Banion shooed away the rest of his gang to keep on walking, nodding to them that there wasn't a problem. The North Side Gang boss stopped in place to respond with more than a bit of deference.

"Your boy was just helping me with some honest work," O'Banion said to a skeptical Evan. "Please don't worry about it now, Mr. McCarthy. Aiden here also wanted to earn you some word-of-mouth for your barbershop. I apologize if there is any confusion. I'm a businessman and the kid's got potential."

Evan shook his head and called Aiden to come home with him. The son brooded, silent as he walked over to his father. In spite of his lack of height, the fury in Evan's face made O'Banion step back.

"You keep away from my son, Dean," Evan said. "If not, I'll make sure your right leg doesn't work as well either."

"Ta, Evan," O'Banion said, a flustered expression on his face. "There's no need for that as I'm well on my way. I won't make you fight for your son, nor is it my place to get in between two Irishmen bonded by blood."

Evan nodded before he continued south with his son, taking him by the left arm. O'Banion and his goons seemed to go in the other direction.

Aiden looked at his pa with curiosity, mixed with apprehension and respect as they continued toward a shoemaker on Maxwell Street. After Evan greeted the merchant craftsman in Yiddish, saying *shalom,* he told Aiden to hurry up and pick out a "decent-priced" pair of leather loafers from the over two dozen for sale.

"Hurry on now," Evan said. "It'll be the last gift I buy you that you haven't damn well earned."

Aiden chose a simple pair of black leather dress shoes. He tried them on without expression before moseying to where his father stood with the merchant.

"I'm sorry, pop," he sniffed, "I should think more instead of disobeying you. I get the increasing feeling I've been a downright dunce."

Evan watched his son give a nervous look as if asking for clemency. It wasn't yet granted.

"Just because I make an honest living, I'm not naive," Evan said. "I got to be more frank with you and treat you less like a child. After this, you'll have to stand on your own two feet. If you keep on like O'Banion, you may, like him, lose the full use of your left leg or more."

Evan declined his son's offer to pay part of the cost of the shoes, Both he and the merchant exchanged a round of Germanic-sounding, spirit-filled Yiddish.

Aiden thought he heard his father call him a *schlemiel.*

"The man here says you look like a putz," Evan said. "I'm inclined to agree with him, but at least if you get tossed in jail you'll have something to keep your feet warm. I hope gangsters taught you how to fight to keep hold of your shoes. Don't expect pointers from me. I'm not in the mood to give them."

Aiden sighed and looked down as cash changed hands. Evan tilted his cap toward the shoemaker, who returned the courtesy before the McCarthys wandered southeast.

"I'm sorry I let you down, Pa," he said.

"Aye, lad," Evan said. "Me, too."

The two McCarthys marched south in silence. Neither noticed the man tailing them.

- - - - -

Silvio Golino drove to a place on 22nd Street between the Metropole Hotel and Colosimo's Cabaret. He waited in the car under Torrio's orders. He had to make sure Frankie Yale made Colosimo disappear, and the Colt revolver resting in a shoulder holster would be his best tool if anything should go south. .

Images of Silvio's wife, son, and daughter interrupted his thoughts of lust, money, and power. He shuddered them off with slight discomfort, pushing aside any moral misgivings of the dangers he could face. His family members, were an inconvenient prop of respectability while he expanded the reach of the Chicago Outfit.

Silvio wanted to make himself number one in Torrio's eyes for no other reason than to become boss himself. He spit out of the window as he kept his eyes toward the cabaret.

"Who's gonna ever remember a name like Capone, anyway?" he mumbled to himself outside the Cadillac sedan. "Keep your eye on the today's prize, Silvio. Take care of "Big Jim" and you'll never have to brown nose a boss or chase tail again."

- - - - -

Drips of sweat ran underneath Jim Colosimo's undershirt when he arrived a few blocks north at his joint, Colosimo's Cabaret. After his coat and hat were taken, he waddled to a dining room in the back and sat in one of the carved wooden chairs as a waiter brought him a coffee to accompany the steak and eggs already waiting atop a white tablecloth. He sat under a hanging fern by the first window of the empty room and finished a Lucky Strike before delving into his meal.

He ate in silence in the back room. The rays of mid-morning sun soaked the carpet as lazily as nicotine seeped into the wallpaper. After a sip of his third cup of coffee, he pulled out another cigarette and lit it before one of his three remaining bodyguards brought him a copy of the *Chicago American*.

On the first page of the third section of the paper, far beneath the fold, Colosimo saw a photograph of his former wife, Victoria Moresco. She was rumored to be "getting rid any dames that went astray of her brothel." The image made him shudder.

His thoughts shifted to Minka and the note she had left from earlier about going shopping. He knew Moresco had the wealth, the means, and the gall to both knock off his young wife and make it look like an accident. He threw down his paper at once and snapped his fingers for his guards.

"Go fetch Minka," he shouted to one. "That old brothel-dwelling witch wants to take away the gal who makes me happy. Charley, you stay here and watch the door until she's safe by my side."

The remaining guard, Charley, went to the door of the dining room, put a hand on his Colt, and blocked the entrance. Colosimo had no concern for his own safety until he heard a silenced round and a thump as if two hundred-fifty pounds had just hit the ground.

"Be still, Colosimo," snickered a menacing voice from behind him. "Here's a little present from Brooklyn."

Frankie Yale put a silenced shot from his Beretta into Colosimo's stomach and adjusted a purple paisley neck tie with his left hand. A loud shot from a Colt hit him in the right arm before he could make an otherwise, well-aimed, fatal shot to Diamond Jim's head.

Charley had squeezed off a final round before dying.

- - - - -

The McCarthy men heard the shot of the Colt while walking south on on Wabash. Outside Colosimo's Cabaret, Aiden spotted one of the Italians who he had seen in Bughouse Square a few months earlier. He remembered talk of assassination as the man ran from a Cadillac into the club.

Curiosity won over good sense when Aiden rationalized a need to keep an eye on competition. He ran after the Italian despite his father's protests. A man with a bleeding right arm and a fancy purple tie rushed out to the street and almost bowled him over. He could hear Evan swearing in the background, but it didn't dissuade him.

From the foyer, Aiden heard another shot amid some yelling in Italian from a back room about fifteen paces away. The man from the Cadillac came from the room with a smoking revolver, stepping with delicate steps over a huge, but without a doubt, dead man lying in a doorway. He pointed the revolver at Aiden.

"You didn't see anything, did you kid?" asked the man before Evan came up behind Aiden. "You weren't even here."

"I told all you gangster bastards to stay away," Evan scolded. "You touch my son, and you'll be picking a fight to the death."

"That's not a bad idea," Silvio said with a toothy grin before he sauntered up to Aiden, resting the gun against his head. "It's your move, pops."

Aiden wanted his father to back away. Evan would only let harm come to family over his own dead body. This humbled and scared Aiden the most.

"I'll be sure to take out the last of yours," Silvio hissed a moment before his attention shifted elsewhere.

In the background, Aiden, Evan, and Silvio all heard the same thing. A host from behind a cash register was ringing the police. No matter who the Outfit or any gangsters had paid off, gunshots from Colosimo's Cabaret couldn't be ignored. As Silvio leveled his gun at the clerk, Aiden saw his moment.

Aiden put his full weight and force into a punch to Silvio's gut before the Italian bowled over in pain. In one of the turning points of his life, he wasn't able to stop Silvio from taking a shot at his father. Evan had been stepping up right behind his son.

"We Irish are hard to kill; you remember that," the elder McCarthy barked through gritted teeth after Silvio's bullet hit him in the knee.

Aiden's world stopped as his father hit the ground. He took a second to look back and hoped his curiosity wouldn't get his father killed. He was speechless, filling with rage as his father's breaths grew faster.

"You think you're miffed," Evan growled to his son. "If you don't get your arse out of here and get safe,

Margaret will kill us both."

After Silvio caught his breath, he pointed his pistol at Aiden. Almost no one in the room noticed as Dean O'Banion then rushed from the entryway, unloading two rounds of his Colt pistol into Silvio's chest.

"Call for a bloody ambulance!" O'Banion shouted to the host. He grabbed Aiden by the arm so they could give attention to Evan. They elevated the bleeding knee with the legs of a chair. O'Banion wrapped his necktie as tight as a boa constrictor around Evan's wound and put fifteen dollars in Aiden's hand.

"You have no idea what went on here," he said. "Officer O'Neill will be the only cop who talks to you. Just take care of your pa."

The host received a ten dollar bill and the same message.

With that, the leader of the North Side Gang fled the scene.

No one noticed the young boy, a year shy of Aiden, with wavy black hair and olive-skin fleeing the scene in tears and rage. The fleeing boy's father lay dead with chest wounds within the foyer to Colosimo's Cabaret.

- - - - -

About a half hour before Dean O'Banion shot her father, Sophia Golino was with her mother, Celia, for morning Mass at St. Therese. At the church, located two blocks east of Archer Avenue and just north of 23rd Street, the Golinos met a thriving number of other Italian-American families at the church for worship.

The high arches and stained glass windows surrounding the rows of pews gave the church a sense of majesty that captured Sophia's imagination. She wasn't as moved by the sermon, but not wanting to offend her mother, she followed the Latin words in her head while moving her lips in unison with those around her.

The two Golino women whispered the *Pater Noster* to themselves as Father Lorenzioni led the entire congregation. Sophia glanced at Sisters of Notre Dame missionaries who had brought several of the Chinese immigrants settling just south of the church.

Sophia found the Chinese fascinating with their dragon-decorated buildings and expressive language. It sounded harsher than the Latin dominant in the church, but the banter reflected such emotional fire. She would like to learn more about the culture but wasn't sure how to penetrate the language barrier. The Orientals nodded their heads while not moving their lips. Their almond-shaped eyes were glued to the priest.

Celia was swift to swat Sophia's knuckles when she noticed her daughter's diverted attentions. She nodded toward the head of the church, signaling her daughter to continue mouthing the prayer.

Celia often cursed the "poppy-headed," Chinese *infideli* and tried to ignore them with polite, dignified disdain while on sacred ground.

"Pay no attention to those hypocrites," she whispered to Sophia after the prayer ended. "They're just trying to pose as Christians to get out of their doomed date with the devil."

Sophia disregarded her mother's distrust of the Chinese, but continued with her automated Latin responses. She thought about her father's involvement in killing while joining her mother to receive Communion. Waves of cognitive dissonance further struck her when Lorenzioni told everyone to go in peace."

Sophia's thoughts also shifted to her brother, Vincent, who was missing with no accusations or condemnation from her mother. She assumed that her brother had clemency if only because he was shadowing his father, no doubt "sowing the seeds of peace."

As the Golino women were leaving St. Therese after Mass, a deacon came up to them to deliver word of Silvio's death. News traveled fastest among clergy and gangsters.

Sophia couldn't control Celia's cries as the deacon helped them to a Cadillac to take them home. As they rode northwest, Sophia held in her emotions and reasoned through any sorrow to let her mother grieve. That killing would beget more killing didn't surprise her. She respected that bit of wisdom she'd found in the Gospel of Matthew.

Back at the Golino household, neighbors were already out greeting them and helping with offerings of food and attentive ears. Above the din of consolations, Sophia wondered were in *inferno* her brother was as she conjured a stoic face for her mother and her neighbors.

7

A Chicago Circus for Colosimo

Before tuxedo-clad coachmen had closed the casket, a penniless immigrant could see James Colosimo's week-old corpse wearing a brown Lucciano Carreli suit with pink pinstripes. The diamond pin on the dead man's lapel was worth more than most people's life savings. The sight of the guards was more for show than the necessity to halt any looting, as no one was stupid enough to make an attempt.

Gorilla-sized goombahs loaded James Colosimo's casket into a Lorraine hearse parked at South Wabash in front of Colosimo's Cabaret a week after the shooting. Two gunmen followed to protect a cargo worth three times the automobile that carried it. The crowd followed the casket-laden hearse west to Clark, where mourners and spectators would join the procession to Chicago's North Side.

The death and gangland brouhaha were unprecedented.

Rays beating down from the sun were warmer than usual, even for May, but the thousands in the crowd remained festive for a funeral. Those who became tired returned to their houses, if they were lucky enough to have them. *Chicago Daily Tribune* and *Chicago American* reporters followed on motorcycles as the crowd came to a halt at St. Boniface Cemetery, north of W. Lawrence Avenue.

Dean O'Banion, George Moran and Earl Weiss, had joined the onlookers during the slow-moving funeral procession in a Packard. The three leading members of the North Side Gang watched as politicians and police officers joined Chicago gangsters and racketeers to pay homage to Colosimo within the cemetery's chapel.

Among those to pay respects were three judges, Mayor "Big Bill" Thompson, the Genna brothers, John Torrio, and a half dozen aldermen, including first ward aldermen Michael "Hinky Dink" Kenna and John "Bathhouse" Coughlin, Colosimo's one time pimp competitor.

Moran, the only devout Catholic of the three North Siders, bowed his head as Coughlin gave a solemn rendition of *In Paradisum*. O'Banion and Weiss mouthed the words of the hymn, showing respect to anyone saying prayers or pretending to do so. They reasoned it wasn't their place to deny a man his blessings.

Minka Summer and Victoria Moresco seemed placid, but spilled occasional tears to honor their late husband and ex-husband. The two seemed to put aside their rivalry to pose for reporters, police, and others who sought to document or sensationalize the murder of the late kingpin of the Chicago Red-light District.

To O'Banion, Minka seemed to be the only one of the two wives who was genuinely sad. He decided to send her a set of chrysanthemums left over from supplying the funeral.

Schofield's Flower Shop staff had arranged and donated a ten-foot, rose-accented cross for the occasion. It stood along with several bundles of carnations arranged for Torrio's Outfit and about six dozen red roses set up for the Genna brothers. Funerals were good for business in some respects.

"It seems that everyone is innocent," O'Banion whispered in Weiss' ear. "Politicians, police, and other pillars of the community are coming to pay respects for this great gentleman pimp."

The lieutenant nodded and gave the slightest hint of a grin.

O'Banion had to snicker to himself when Torrio stepped up to memorialize the departed. Torrio's new alleged protege, Alphonse Capone, stood with studied stoicism in the background as the Outfit leader wiped away tears meant to imply an iota of tenderness to the crowd.

"James Colosimo and I were like brothers," proclaimed Torrio. "We built up the Italian community in Chicago from just a handful of small businessmen and church missions. He will be missed, but never forgotten. Though he is with *il Padre Celeste*, the progress we've started will continue."

The biggest thing that O'Banion regretted about the Colosimo's death was that the Italians would be a greater threat to his bootleg business. Diamond Jim wasn't much of a competitor, not nearly as calculating as Torrio or as hotheaded as the Gennas.

Silvio Golino's death didn't displease O'Banion at all. Keeping Aiden and Evan McCarthy alive lifted any potential burden on his conscience until his attentions were diverted.

Something that seemed out of place to O'Banion was the sight of a young man with a face like Silvio's. A tear ran down the boyish face as he stood with a woman and a young lady who shared a resemblance. He didn't embrace them, but glared at them as if they were a burden. He seemed lost.

O'Banion's thoughts stewed as he took in the spectacle. He figured that the two ladies were Silvio's widow and daughter. The lad was likely Silvio's son.

The North Side Gang boss didn't like to see innocents suffer, hoping the ladies would come to understand that Silvio was a bastard who got what was coming to him. He guessed the son would follow in his father's footsteps. The three were escorted to a much smaller service in a shady plot as Torrio spouted platitudes for the public.

"Can't save everyone, Deanie," he mumbled to himself.

He stayed until the end of Colosimo's service to be courteous. He wasted no time at the end to gather his lieutenants and return to Schofield's for business. Demand had reached new heights since the latest gangland shooting.

8

Healing

It was not a harmonious time at the McCarthy household. Two weeks after the the confrontation at Colosimo's Cabaret, Aiden's mother and father were yelling for different reasons and he was getting tough lessons from both. Neither parent had much to say to him since Margaret and he had retrieved Evan from Cook County Hospital the week before. He had told Margaret about the shooting, O'Banion's intervention, and was otherwise quieter than usual. Aiden waited to be called upon.

"Get your duff over here and bring the laudanum so your pa will stop his bellyaching," Margaret said to Aiden as she washed Evan's knee in the main bedroom of their house.

Evan McCarthy was still in the early stages of recovery, but Margaret staved off infection and inflammation. She cleaned the wound several time a day with iodine and positioned it with pillows, just as the doctor advised. She was also liberal with the laudanum so she could have some quiet, if not peace.

Aiden rushed over to give his father some needed numbness and rest, helping Margaret set up a clean bandage. His furrowed brow and tense lips showed a newfound humility. He more than questioned his future in the profitable lawlessness of Chicago, having distanced himself from dealings with O'Banion and his men since the shooting

Margaret chastised him only once on his involvement with the North Side Gang. She seemed to have an innate sense of the guilt Aiden already felt and devoted most of her time to keeping Evan clean and numb. Her son followed orders to keep the household running as best as they could manage.

"It seems we'll never be rid of the bootleggers and racketeers running this town," Margaret said after finishing with Evan and leaving him to rest. She and Aiden went into the kitchen to boil potatoes and peel carrots for supper. "Prohibition will only help well-connected charlatans and hypocrites who should know better."

Aiden listened to his ma and continued to feel his parents were more savvy than he gave them credit. Evan's words to O'Banion the day of Colosimo's shooting hinted that he shared a history with the gang boss. Margaret wouldn't stand down to guff from anyone, in particular, Chicago ward bosses and others who were "high on themselves."

"Ma, can you tell me more about Pa's story with O'Banion?" Aiden asked. "It's obvious I've been a hellion to have as a son, but I'm keen to know why Mr. O'Banion respects Pa, helped us get out of the hotel, and paid most of the medical bills."

"Oh, so you're saying now that we might be able to teach you something, lad," she said with a mock humility. "Well, then. I'll give you more of a story, so you don't have to take our word for it on how a man who's just seventeen should act."

Aiden grinned at his mother's chutzpah. Her reputation for being a pistol kept him from returning any cheek. He only nodded and muttered an apology. He kept mouth shut and his hands busy with potatoes..

"About a year before you were born, I met your father through my uncle, Karl Reiser," she said. "Uncle Reiser was a skilled safe-cracker keeping his eye out for a young apprentice, which is where your pa comes in. He was nineteen. I had just turned eighteen, and he was the handsomest and most charming fella I'd ever met."

"Pa was a safe-cracker?" Aiden asked.

"Maybe I should'a told you about these things sooner. You might not have acted like such a cocky rube," she said.

"I'm itchin' to learn, Ma."

"Then shut yer trap when I'm talking, won't you?

Margaret explained that her Uncle Reiser took her in after her father had died in the Braidwood mines southwest of Chicago and her mother had died of consumption. Despite taking her in and letting her stay with him in his house in the city, they didn't see eye to eye on ways to make money.

"He was a right bastard," she said. "He wouldn't think twice of beatin' up a poor sort and stealin' from him to earn a dollar. I'd no interest in hurting people for myself to make money. Still, he let me stay at his house as a child while I took lessons at a convent until I got on with your father. Evan was a quick learner, so Uncle Reiser didn't mind when his apprentice started courting me."

Aiden gulped at Margaret calling her uncle a thieving bastard, recalling the times in the past year in which she'd say the same of him.

"So what made Pa take up cutting hair?" Aiden asked and stopped at a glance from Margaret that would petrify the snakes covering Medusa's head.

"Evan, like me, didn't have the stomach for stealing and the like. Uncle Reiser regularly threatened to kill people or break their legs if they'd try be a witness when the cops caught him. Evan wasn't keen on it and he couldn't spend any time with me if he had been."

She explained that Evan often accompanied her during their early courtship to help out at settlement houses. The places helped immigrants and others adapt to life in the city, learn English, get jobs, get food, get away from abusive husbands. Evan also learned barber techniques from a man from Southern Italy in exchange for English lessons.

"I like to think that service goes both ways," Margaret said. "By giving of oneself, we receive."

Aiden sat in silence, unable to smart off if he wanted to.

"Your father didn't turn away from safe-cracking altogether until he angered my uncle by helping out a teenage Dean O'Banion," Margaret continued.
"O'Banion tried to rob your pa in the Kilgubbin area of

Chicago. Faced with a knife, your pa knocked him on his arse. O'Banion tried to flee, but his foot got run over by a horse-drawn cart."

Uncle Reiser didn't like that Evan took O'Banion to one of her uncles safe houses to bandage him up, Margaret explained. Evan and she had to move away, to where the three of them lived at present.

"The wrench I threw at Uncle Reiser dissuaded him from bothering us," she said. "Pa and that Italian immigrant started the barber shop he now owns."

Aiden sat with a lips parted in awe, prompting his mother to continue.

"Your father doesn't want you to end up like a young O'Banion who needs saving," she said. "O'Banion repaid the favor to your pa at Colosimo's Cabaret. But we are the only ones who'll help you without need for payback."

"I won't put you in pickle like that again," Aiden replied. "Though I might be missing chances to make good money helping those who twist the law—"

"You wanna make yer ma and pa proud and make the real dough, you keep your arse in school," Margaret said. "No need to rally around with hooligans, keeping the company of violent men and driving your poor mother batty."

At least for the foreseeable future, Aiden decided to not cause a ruckus. He wanted his father to heal well; however, he could never let go of a need for revenge on the bastards that led to his shooting. The first thing to do was get Pa up and walking again.

"I'll try to stay outta trouble, Ma," Aiden said. "I've

shown I can keep my mind in my books and not trouble the schoolmaster with needless guff."

Margaret put her hands on her hips and sighed.

"Don't sell me blarney, son," she said. "I'd hate to have to lower the boom on you."

"I'm not about to sell you blarney. I said I'd try."

"I hope you're saving up for law school or to start a business. I'm not bloody giving you anything to become a ward boss, I don't give a damn if you are family. First, you better hand me some potatoes while you peel the onions. Don't worry. The fumes'll help you get ready for your first campaign."

Aiden had to chuckle before giving a grin.

"Yes, Ma," he said. "But please don't worry about me fussin' with those degenerates."

Margaret went to him, swatted his behind, and eventually pecked him on the forehead with a serious look.

"You're damned right, you little cuss."

9

Setting off to Summer

John Torrio sat his oak table at the Four Deuces Club. It was pleasant Sunday afternoon in the first June of Prohibition, and the rum he smuggled from Cuba made it that much more peaceful. His favorite new hire, a red-headed prostitute who sheathed herself only in a silk robe, kept drinks flowing for the clientele and knew better than to offer her charms to the boss. He appreciated her knowing he had no interest in whoopee for cash. She only offered to fill his drink when it was empty.

The sight of Alphonse Capone approaching the table also made him happy. The new protege was more calm and calculated than his reputation suggested. Capone even took off his newsboy cap, smoothing the simple brown suit over his stocky body before joining his boss.

"What are you drinking, Capone," Torrio said. "I got a shipment of Havana Club two days ago. I reserve a case for so-called dignitaries such as Mayor Thompson, Feds on the take, friends, and up-and-coming workers like you. The rest gets cut for the customers. It's a big item for those who can afford more than the tenement house-distilled strike-me-dead from Little Italy."

The redhead pulled out a chair for Capone, taking his cap. He handed her a quarter before getting to business.

"Mr. Torrio, I'll have what you're having. What can I do for you? I've gotten all the Maxwell Street vendors to carry your cigars. Some speaks south of Chicago Avenue are still buying from the North Siders. You want me to make demands or bust heads? You give me the word, boss."

Torrio ordered the redhead to bring Havana Clubs and Chicago-made Cohibas for them as he thought a while and finished his first rum. His new subordinate had to do something about his attire. The ill-fitting monkey suit and cap had to go. He waited until they were served to continue.

"My boy," Torrio said, "I got big plans for you. But before we get started, take this twenty dollar bill and get yourself a proper suit and a proper hat. A fedora says you're the right-hand man for *il Capo* instead of a newspaper peddler. After that, here's what I need you to do."

The Outfit boss talked about his concerns with his previous lieutenant's son, Vincent Golino. The boy showed he may be a loose cannon, so Capone had to keep an eye on him as a side project, in addition to dealing with customers who needed convincing. He told his new man to offer speakeasy holdouts another chance to change moonshine suppliers or expect "a sucker punch with a lead fist." If speaks and vendors south of Chicago Avenue stayed with North Side Gang suppliers after the threat, Capone could hurt them.

Torrio didn't think anyone would be that stupid.

"Thank you, Mr. Torrio," Capone said. "You don't gotta worry about anything. I'll take care of it."

Torrio smiled before ordering another rum for his new protege. Before calling a Cadillac to take him home to his wife, he gave a sawbuck to the redhead and told her to keep Capone company.

- - - - -

The redhead drank rum with Capone until he was drowsy. In her room on the third floor, she put him to bed and exhaled opium cigarettes in his direction until he was asleep. She knew better than to rip off anything more than his pants, being smarter that the average hired company. She took a nap while he snored.

"Easy money," she said to herself before her eyes closed. She missed her husband and the life he was going to provide until her current boss had arranged for his death.

- - - - -

Aiden walked to Bughouse Square late Monday morning, free of classes at Holy Name and other watchful eyes from either his folks or any boss. With no thoughts on what he ought to do, he remembered dalliances with daydreams as he saw birds twittering in the trees above.

The nature in the middle of the city made him remember the last time he'd felt drawn to a beautiful stranger. The olive-skinned girl from winter popped in his head, and his memories ran over the events of the day.

Aiden had shadowed the gal to listen to two Italians

talk about a hit and he recalled John Torrio, Frankie Yale, James Colosimo, bootleg, and too much comfort with company-for-hire. The overheard info lead to a sense of trust from Dean O'Banion to be a snoop, which ultimately led to carelessness, Evan being shot in the knee, and a dead Italian.

The dead Italian had hazel eyes, olive skin, and wavy dark hair, reminding him of the pretty gal who'd had a moody after listening that day in the park. Aiden hadn't seen the beauty since, but he had a sense as to why not. He'd found it difficult to get to Bughouse Square, and everyone from his family was still living.

He smiled when he saw Harriet Rosenstein preaching from a soapbox, just beneath an ash tree flush with several bird nests. The view reminded him that throughout the tumult, forces of nature endured.

Aiden stopped for a spell and listened.

"The great Emma Goldman urges us to be 'foolish enough to throw caution to the winds to advance mankind and enrich the world,'" Harried howled. "I'm not the idealist she is, but, my fellow Bughouse dwellers, we only reach satisfaction through action."

Aiden's lips curled into a grin as he continued west from the park toward home. Margaret's stories, Harriet's words, and thoughts of the olive-skinned gal swarmed in his head.

The world would carry on before he could take his next steps.

10

November Frost of Prohibition

The two leaders sat down in the public saloon at Carrie's Ax, well within the North Side Gang's territory. Early evening showed itself in the night sky, which brought gray coolness not seen since the earliest days of Prohibition. Dean O'Banion and John Torrio took off their dark gray fedoras at the same time. Lieutenants of their gangs attended affairs on the opposite sides of the Windy City as the bosses sat among dozens of thirsty customers.

Five months after Torrio's Outfit and the Genna brothers dipped their toes into the moonshine business, gangs were thriving. Profits multiplied in exponents once they all took advantage of the Eighteenth Amendment, even with payoffs to the Feds, police, and local ward bosses. All was well save for the inevitable friction between Italian and Irish competitors.

O'Banion ordered himself and his so-called guest a dram of Old Bushmills, direct and undiluted from the old country. He had the best routes to smuggle the genuine article for Carrie's Ax and other friendly speaks.

Through meeting with Torrio, O'Banion wanted to flaunt the superior quality he could deliver, but also show formal, if not-quite-hostile, hospitality to his Italian Outfit counterpart. He maintained a quiet calm that showed the poise expected of him, hoping the peacefulness would make his questions more jarring.

"So, Mr. Torrio, now that you're here and drinking my high-caliber product, let's be honest with each other," O'Banion said. "What strings were you pulling when Colosimo died? I hear someone bumped off your man, Silvio Golino, as well. Was he collateral damage?"

A flash of red rushed to Torrio's cheeks.

"I had nothing to do with Colosimo or any other poor guy that day," he said with a glare that said otherwise. "Don't you North Side boys know that the guys from Naples would never be connected to killing a Mafia boss. Why is it that neither you nor the Feds believe me?"

O'Banion just returned an immediate smile. After some months of monitoring the competition, he figured that Torrio had hired Frankie Yale to take out Colosimo, with help from the Golino mook he shot last May. The Outfit and Genna Brothers wasted no time getting into the making, selling, and trading of hooch after the big funeral. He tested his main competitor's reaction and got deference.

"The collateral damage is my main concern here, Mr. Torrio. It may be word-of-mouth right now. Your new boy, Capone, might be expendable, but I prefer to keep my men safe," O'Banion said, thinking of the

McCarthys.

Aiden hadn't been around the flower shop for months, and he figured the lad was playing it smarter than he by keeping his nose out of trouble during a last year at Holy Name School for Boys. O'Banion didn't like how talent felt threatened, so he pressed on.

"I'd like an agreement where you keep the Outfit boyos south of Chicago Avenue and the Sicilian Gennas in Little Italy. In return, we North Side lads will stay in our territory. Let me know if we can make a deal."

Torrio grimaced with a pause, red remaining in his face in what O'Banion took to be bloody anger. Dean gulped down his Irish whiskey before nodding to a server for another. He offered Torrio a cigar, which the Italian declined.

"I'm glad we can look to the future to make business; we all want a larger sales count than body count," Torrio said. "You oughta remember none of our guys is interested in harming bystanders. I'll just need your word on not expanding."

Torrio scratched his throat and shot his whiskey. Tears welled in his eyes despite keeping his lips in a cordial-enough grin. O'Banion accepted his fresh dram and flashed a grimace.

"I'd like for peace as well," O'Banion replied. "But I don't know what you mean by any 'word on not expanding.' You and the Outfit appear to have sights on less-enforced land in Cicero. The North Side boys may want to take advantage of new markets."

"We'll have to take a look at that won't we?" Torrio said, with a fake smile in a laudatory attempt to hide his anger. "A future, more formal agreement on territory and profit is in order."

O'Banion admired the man's attempt to keep affairs copacetic and gave a genuine smile.

"I'll look into your recommendations," Torrio continued with an apparent, resigned affect.

"It's all up in the air, ain't it, Johnny?" O'Banion asked with a grin before giving a condescending, if cordial clap to his competitor's shoulder. He signaled for another Old Bushmills for Torrio before he finished his dram and excused himself to leave.

"I appreciate it if you'll allow me to keep another appointment," O'Banion continued. "Please give the missus the highest regards from me and my wife."

"Certainly," Torrio said.

When served with the second Irish whiskey, the Italian smashed his first glass on the table before gulping down the next. A Cadillac waiting on Milwaukee then took him home.

Once there, he kissed his wife, Anne, and headed upstairs to bed without any interest in dinner. Anne threw out the rack of lamb and lit a Murad cigarette after taking a seat in their study.

She didn't bother to shoo off the urchins she watched outside of their house. Anne Torrio let them help themselves to the discarded dinner in trash bins left out in the cold.

11

Adapting to the Wilderness

Aiden McCarthy awoke to the clank of pans in the kitchen sink the Saturday morning after O'Banion and Torrio met at Carrie's Ax. After tugging on a set of gray wool trousers and a starchy button-down he'd scrubbed clean the day before, he rushed out of his cool, drafty bedroom to see what was the matter in the heart of his family's house.

Margaret was hovering over their dining table, scrubbing it with a fraying rag as sweat ran down her furrowed brow. Her jerky, abrupt movements showed she was scared, angry, or a bit of both. Aiden went to the sink and started scrubbing the pans inside, not knowing what else to do. He figured she had no reason to be angry with him, but t was best to appear helpful.

When Margaret was done with the table, several scratches appeared in the finish. Still, she didn't stop fidgeting. Aiden flinched when she grabbed the broom, relieved when she attacked the dirt on floor like a dope fiend whirling dervish. Fresh from scrubbing the pans, he put his forearms into cleaning the sink, not bothering to utter a word.

The two continued their compulsive cleaning for a half an hour. When Margaret was about to race to clean the already spotless water closet, Aiden tapped her on the shoulder. He had prepared himself for a hostility, but not the less than cordial clip she gave his cheek.

"Can't you see I've chores to do?" she scorned. "I've no time for small talk."

Aiden didn't utter a sound in reply. He just put the kettle on to reuse some tea and put a piece of stale soda bread on a plate before sitting at the table with a bit of breakfast. He grabbed the rustled remains of the *Tribune* to keep him company, knowing better than to talk back, at least for the moment.

When Aiden had finished being enlightened by the latest on president-elect Warren G. Harding and a feature on Mayor Bill Thompson's views of women's suffrage, he brought his plate to the sink and began to scrub. His mother soon stood near him and told him to make up his room so she could sweep and dust. He dried his hands on a towel before he used them to cue for a stop.

"Something the matter?" Aiden asked. "Or are we expecting the mayor to drop by?"

This time, he dodged when she struck out. He met her reddened face and clenched jaw with a wide eyes and a heavy sigh. Margaret responded with sulking shoulders, stress lines on her forehead, and tears welled up in her eyes. He sighed again before he shrugged in exasperation.

"I haven't been hanging around gangsters, I've gotten good marks in school, and Pa's been up back at work,"

Aiden said. "What's crawling under your skin?"

Margaret swallowed, blew her nose in a tissue, nodded, and gestured for him to sit. After boiling water to steep the reused tea leaves for the fourth time, she joined him at the table and served them both before taking a chair.

"Been some rough looking characters hanging about, they knocked on our door this morning. Say they're collecting on bills, and I know Evan's having a bit of trouble with his bum leg and all."

Margret wrung her hands and continued.

"I told 'em they had the wrong house and shut the door, locking it. They seem to have gone, but I've been keeping my hands busy and my worries at bay."

Aiden wasn't shocked in the least. He"d noticed leaner meals, with little meat since the family stopped dipping into their savings after summer. They had less coal to keep the house warm as winter slowly approached. His mother's desperation moved him, as her usual personality was the opposite of vulnerable. He realized he had to make a change.

"I've stayed away from O'Banion since the shooting," he said after a while. "I can make money arranging flowers for him and stay away from the rough stuff. He's liable to be looking for help since most of his men have their fingers in bootleg."

Margaret sliced the air with her right hand. It was a signal to be quiet, but Aiden had more to say.

"I trust the man," he said. "He's part of the reason Pa and I are still around. I'll explain the need to stay out of bootlegging. He'll understand."

Aiden was about to continue, and then Margaret stood up, walked to the stove, and grabbed a wooden spoon. She returned to the table and smacked it.

"O'Banion and you oughta know what you'll face if you find yourself on the other side of the law," she said. "Pa and I'll post bail to get you outta jail, but once you're out, you may feel safer with the ruffians inside. If you get killed, I'll find you in the afterlife."

"Understood, Ma," Aiden said. "I'll keep safe. I'm in no hurry to get on anyone's bad side, least of all yours. Would it help if I proved my work with flowers?"

"You're damned right," she said. "Flowers will help, but I'd prefer your word."

"You got it."

Aiden hugged his mother, helped her sweep, and then ducked out with his newsboy cap and jacket after locking the door. Despite whatever he told himself about staying on the level, the lure of dough, drama, and dames called to him.

12

Back in the Thick of it

Just a half block north of Schofield's, Aiden watched a scene unfold as the sun warmed the cool autumn asphalt on State later that afternoon. A police officer walking south on State from Holy Name Cathedral waved at Dean O'Banion as he stood on the stoop of the flower shop. The North Side Gang boss nodded and waited until any authorities were absent before returning inside for a moment.

O'Banion then led out two fellas, one with dark skin and the other wearing a torn dress. He passed a brown paper bag big enough for whiskey bottle to one. The one in drag tried to give him a hug, but the North Side boss only took a slight step back, smiled, and offered a hand to shake. The two fellas took it before leaving with smiles of their own. He wiped sweat off his brow before returning to flowers and bootleg.

Aiden approached and hesitated before knocking on the door. He had his mother's contrived blessing to arrange flowers, but visions in his head of a fist-shaking Evan still sat like lead in his gut. The earning potential of more illicit dealings in the gang called to him despite all sense to the contrary. He didn't want to burden his parents with more worry.

Evan wasn't yet able to take on a full day of customers at the barbershop, and wouldn't accept higher payments from longtime, sympathetic clientele. The McCarthys didn't take charity.

Aiden rationalized that making money was what his family really needed. What harm could come of him agreeing to help arrange flowers? He may have to get more involved if that's what the nature of business required...wouldn't his father agree?

"What my parents don't know, won't hurt them," Aiden said to himself before he knocked on the door. "I gotta be smart about it."

O'Banion looked at Aiden with widened eyes of surprise. He asked, "What can I do for you, McCarthy? Your pa okay?"

"On the mend, thanks to your quickness with a Colt," Aiden said. "He's working again, but business is slower with his bum leg."

"I'd gladly send him more customers as one businessman to another, but I'm afraid he'd see through it if a bunch of gang-connected guys show up looking for a haircut. Tell you what, I'll—"

Aiden held his right hand out to call for a pause.

"I'm looking for a job, not a handout."

O'Banion stopped and peered into Aiden's eyes, taken aback either by the interruption and the lad's gumption. He cleared the doorway and swung an arm inside, which Aiden followed. He could only think of one thing to say:

76

"What'll your pa think of that?"

"I'm not in a hurry to tell him," Aiden said. "Ma will come to terms with it if I stick to arranging flowers. I'm close enough to being an adult, might as well start making my own mistakes."

O'Banion put his left hand on his chin before showing a slight shrug and turning to a hidden cabinet in a nearby desk. He pulled out a fifth of Canadian Club and poured a set of small drams in two lowball glasses. After loosening his tie, he took a seat on a bench and gestured for Aiden to do the same.

"If you want work, I'll start you with flowers," he said. "Bootleg is booming, so if you want to get in on that racket, you'll take all the heat from your folks. I also ain't one to bail you out if you land yourself in a jail cell."

"I just want to help with flowers for now," Aiden said. "No plans for a limp or time in jail if I can help it."

O'Banion gave chuckle before he took a sip and responded.

"I'm making deals with the Outfit dagos, even if there's some bad blood," he said. "We all got to move ahead, rally together, and work with Feds to make us all a hefty amount of dough."

"Sounds good to me boss. By the way, got any tea?"

O'Banion looked in the desk, took a few spoonfuls of tea leaves and put them in several bags, gesturing where the kettle was. He dumped Aiden's share of whiskey in his own glass.

"Right, so after you're done steeping your tea, we'll finish up some of these arrangements for Mass tomorrow. The Church takes a different payoff than the coppers."

Aiden chortled, made a cup of tea, and got ready to work with carnations and chrysanthemums. He savored the more freshly brewed tea and the company of his boss.

Thoughts of wreaking vengeance on those responsible for his father's limp floated beneath the surface, but now it was time to tend to flowers. Aiden and the boss found peace weaving peonies, petunias, and perennials. He collected the excess tea afterward, and both him and his boss made it home for supper.

- - - - -

Evan McCarthy hobbled to the front stoop of the house after a meal of boiled potatoes and cabbage. He propped his cane to the right of the door and sat on a step, sticking his empty corncob pipe between his lips. The family ran out of lard the previous week, having used up nearly the last of the salt tonight, and Evan didn't dare waste money on tobacco. The feel of the pipe still relaxed him as he watched the sliver of light reflected from the moon in the fall sky.

Breathing the tobacco-flavored air, his thoughts drifted while watching the firmament above him, which wasn't yet completely polluted from city lights. His day had gone well, thanks to a slew of loyal customers, one of whom had crafted a stool for him in exchange for credit for four free haircuts in the future. Evan tried to offer more, but the customer wouldn't budge. He was happy with the profit he'd brought home, with promise of more to come, and the barbershop banter was just as important.

Still, there were worries. Margaret had told him about the bill collectors. Pressure from them and worries about his family's lack of comfort swarmed the back of his mind as he saw Aiden join him to sit on the stoop after helping Margaret pick up the kitchen. His son held two cups with steaming liquid.

"Argh, son," he said, "thanks, but I've had enough watered-down tea to get me to swear allegiance to the Queen of England. Why don't you combine the two and get half the flavor?"

Aided took a drink from his own cup before giving a hearty smile and passing his pa a cup. He persisted with a wink.

Evan took the cup, expecting to have to work hard to fake a smile. Instead, a full-bodied flavor hit his mouth, with hints of citrus and bergamot. The corners of his lips tilted toward the stars in approval. He loosened his bow tie and exhaled a full breath.

"Bless you, son," he said. "It's a damned fine cup of tea. How'd you come across it?"

Aiden swallowed another gulp of tea before responding. He met Evan's eyes and offered a piece of the truth.

"Helped with preparations for Mass tomorrow at Holy Name Cathedral. I got more questions than answers, but isn't that's what faith is all about. I received tea with a bit of that wisdom."

Evan took a sip and nodded, knowing there was more to the story. On such a nice evening with his son and real tea, he decided to tread with ease.

"Months ago, while starting the recovery for my bum knee, I spent a lot of time in prayer when not being a pain in the arse for you and your ma. I prayed to not be a cripple, to be able to provide again, and for you to see how everything can change in an instant."

Aiden's cheekbones flinched as he returned a gaze.

"I know I've been bullheaded," he said. "I'm in no hurry to push my luck. I wish—"

With his hand raised to call for a pause, Evan gestured for his son to help him up. Standing at about the same height, he put his left arm to Aiden's shoulder while clutching his cup of tea in the other hand.

"I've heard you apologize plenty, and Margaret already told me about you arranging flowers at Schofield's to earn dough and help us out. I have to have some faith you've learned something; otherwise, you oughta remember consequences can hit harder than a wooden spoon."

Aiden got his father's cane for him before taking his own cup and offering an arm. Evan took it and gave a soft sigh as they opened the door to home. They looked forward to more idle chit chat and playing cards with Margaret at the kitchen table to help draw down the day.

13

Mid-Month Reunion

Harriet Rosenstein walked west from the Chicago Loop along Randolph Street in the cool breeze of the afternoon, taking a left on Peoria to the Golino household. She hoped to see Sophia and get her away from the house. Celia continued to grieve over Silvio in the months after his death, and the two friends had only seen each other on the few weekdays Sophia had snuck away to meet for tea.

Harriet knocked on the front door with a gentle hand.

When Sophia rushed to the door, anxiety ran through her mind. She knew, by eavesdropping on her brother, Vincent, that John Torrio was paying some of their bills. Just the other day, Sophia had intercepted a note from Torrio to Vincent that future funds depended on her brother helping out the Outfit. Bills were getting paid later and later, with some falling through the crack, and she expected someone to collect.

After hesitating for a second, Sophia opened the door to her own relief. She and Harriet exchanged broad smiles.

"Excuse me ma'am, I hail from the Blessed Virgin

Mother Mission , I seek grace and benevolence through service," Harriet said in a well-rehearsed voice just low and measured enough to pass as solemn. She dressed in the black, long-sleeved dress and veil of a novice. "Of particular need is young women like yourself, who long to serve the Lord and His community."

Sophia had to pull the sleeve of her gray cardigan over her mouth to stifle a chuckle. She was glad to see the wiliness of her friend in action. The mischievous shine to Harriet's eyes left no doubt that her intentions didn't lie with religious piety or social order.

"I must confess that I would enjoy hearing more about the Blessed Virgin Mission , Sister, but our house is in no condition to receive you," Sophia said, with a twisted, wry smile. "If it is amenable to you, would it be possible to meet later this evening with your ministry?"

"As a matter of fact, my humble Sisters and I will meet in front of Holy Name Cathedral tonight," Harriet replied. "It is in an important vicinity to the needy characters in Washington Square Park off of State Street. Our ministry aims to turn hobos and tramps in the park from their dreams of revolution and social upheaval toward sober progress envisioned by our sisters in the Women's Temperance Union. The Union has done such wonderful work toward the Eighteenth and Nineteenth Amendments."

Sophia had to suppress a giggle to maintain the seriousness of the charade. The climate of clandestine camaraderie comforted her.

"I must first tend to the needs of my household, Sister," said Sophia, acting as a stranger. "But it shall be both my and the Lord's pleasure that I find the direction needed to assist your mission. I must now bid you well until we meet later."

Harriet did the sign of the cross before leaving with a knowing smile. Sophia rolled her eyes before giving the air a quick, chaste kiss goodbye.

- - - - -

Celia seemed not to notice that anyone had come to the door when Sophia returned to making soup with the last of the vegetables in their pantry. The burden of running the household weighed on Sophia, despite a desire to keep the air positive.

"Here ya go, Mama," she said, happy that Celia returned a grin before they ate. Unpleasant thoughts still stewed in her head.

Sophia knew that she would soon have to bring in money to help keep them all afloat. She also figured that Vincent would follow in her father's footsteps and risk violent work for the Outfit. Her worries as an older sister tempered anger toward her brother and his *maschilismo*.

After eating, Celia retired to the living room with a Bible while Sophia put the remaining soup in the ice box, washed dishes, and made a decision. Her worries over her brother, her family's livelihood, and propriety could wait. She needed to meet a dear friend, Harriet, for some levity and perhaps a way to earn dough.

Sophia took a couple hours to first get dolled up, making do with some minor adjustments. She didn't have time to sew pleats into a knee-length, skirt, but could hem the cut off sleeves from a dark blue blouse.

After putting on the clothes and glancing in a mirror in the water closet, she smiled. She would've preferred a cloche hat to make her look pop, but settled on a string of pearls borrowed from her mother.

"It'll have to do," Sophia said to herself before donning a wool overcoat and heading to the door.

"I love you, Mama," she said before leaving.

"I love you too, sweetie," Celia replied, which wasn't her custom. "You'll be home for prayers, won't you dear?."

"I'll meet you for prayers, Mama."

Sophia didn't know what Harriet had planned for them, but she vowed to be a devoted daughter when she returned to reality.

- - - - -

When Sophia saw her friend in front of the Holy Name Cathedral, she embraced her without hesitation. Harriet had changed into a knee-length dress more fit for dancing than a night of prayer and missionary work. She returned a bear hug that Sophia needed.

"That was a wonderful presentation you did this afternoon," Sophia said. "Ma doesn't keep many tabs on my comings and goings as of late, so you didn't need to put on a show for her. I still enjoyed seeing you wear religious habits to respect our dear Blessed Virgin Mother. You must tell me: how does an improper lady serve the Lord?"

Harriet responded with a swat to Sophia's behind, adopting a rigid, stiff face of mock sincerity. She pointed her index finger as if she were about to scold a delinquent student.

"To be a successful revolutionary, one must know the bourgeois game and play it well," Harriet replied with the cadenced tone of Bolshevik schoolteacher. "Well, my child, if it seems I overplayed my hand, I did it with no intention to disrespect your mother. With good Catholics, I spin a good yarn to save otherwise damned souls from their fears of purgatory."

"Oh, dear," Sophia replied with a chuckle. "I await whatever guidance you can give my young, lost soul, be it for utopia, my character, or my position in this life. If nothing else, we could have a few drinks to enliven our spirits. Your choice."

Harriet took her friend's right arm and smiled. They walked north on State Street toward Tooker Alley, cutting jokes along the way. She reiterated that she hadn't the intention to disrespect anyone's mother, Jewish, Catholic, or otherwise.

"No worries, my dear," Sophia replied. "No worries at all."

Before turning right on Dearborn, Harriet told her friend to remove her wool coat, taking it and gently ushering her forward toward a club.

Sophia already had a hint of happiness, carrying a sense of adventure to wherever their desires led them. She knew it her friend wouldn't steer her wrong. It was a promise they always made to each other.

- - - - -

Outside the club, the syncopated honk of trumpets swirled over the march-like tempo of a tuba. The twittering of a clarinet and the sliding of a trombone clashed with the staccato tap of a snare drum,

85

welcoming Sophia and Harriet. The friends walked arm in arm up to the bohemian club's mocking, ominous entryway. Over the door of the Dil Pickle Club, one simple word warned all those who entered: "DANGER."

"Step high, stoop low, leave your dignity outside," Sophia said as she read a sign on the door. "Hmm, I think you've brought me to just the right place, my dear. Shall we?"

She stepped up to the door, where Harriet nodded a smile to two dark-skinned guards and introduced herself and her charge to them and the regular host. All three welcomed them. The host wore a flapper dress and a dangling pearl necklace like an experienced madame at a brothel, save for his Adam's apple.

The host in drag ushered the two gals inside and gave a wolf whistle as the guards remained outside. He gave Sophia a playful wink and a kiss to Harriet's cheek that left a smudge of red lipstick. Sophia returned the wink with tempting timidity.

"Now, now, my child," Harriet deadpanned. "You've barely even been inside yet and you are already making friends."

The ladies waltzed toward the front of a raised platform, where club-goers danced to dark-skinned men playing the instruments heard from outside. Men, women, and those in between held their rapturous applause for a break in the melody.

Sophia felt more comfortable at the Dil Pickle than at home, at school, or at church. She relaxed despite the cross-dressing staff, leering eyes, and not-so-subtle, so-called accidental brushes against her arms, bust, and behind. The interest in her and the pretense of manners despite such close quarters was exciting.

"This is exactly what I need," Sophia said while giving her friend a kiss on the cheek. "It's a welcome respite from life's doldrums. You always steer me right, my dear."

"Sophia, you've been a doll and my only connection to legitimacy," Harriet told her. "This place may be filled with all number of bohemians and misfits, but you can use your talents to break free of the bourgeois lifestyle you've had to endure. You only have to serve drinks and tease; gentlemen of leisure pay other gals for a *little extra*. You interested in a job?"

Sophia embraced her friend, making few around them notice.

"I'll give it my best shot," she said, batting smoky eyelashes to hide any reservations. "I'll pamper the boys and get to their pocketbooks, but just enough for the professionals to take over."

Harriet gave a wink before taking Sophia by the hand and leading her toward a table.

"Oh Mrs. Jones!" Harriet called out to a handsome lady in a glittering silver-sequined frock. "I want to introduce you and 'Wobbly' Jack to a dear friend of mine. I hope you think her innocence and charm will make the boys pay more to the girls of lesser virtue."

Jack and Venicia Jones listened as Harriet made the case for Sophia to serve drinks and tease the dough out of well-heeled trousers. They had discussed the job before that night, but it was only then that Harriet presented a worthy candidate. Someone had to "put on the tease before the squeeze."

Jack introduced himself. He got the nickname "Wobbly" from his time as an organizer for the International Workers of the World. He founded the Dil Pickle to host labor activists, the arts, and Marxist dialogue; however, he found jazz acts, prostitutes, and bootleg fueled more customers and revolutionaries. His North Side Irish hooch supplier turned a blind eye to the prostitution as long as the Joneses looked after the girls.

At first, the Joneses didn't like Harriet's rule that a server never "never give up the goods." Sophia's charms and innocence put the proposition in a better light.

"A little pure-blooded bait never hurt the fisherman's drive to make his catch," Jack said. "Sophia, what would you say to a warm-blooded man who can pay for whoopee? He can drop a sawbuck for a few hours."

Sophia straightened her knee-length skirt before responding.

"Sir, I'd love to dance with you as long as you wish. But you see, I've promised my virginity to a man who can take care of me for life. I'm sure you're capable, but I don't know if I'm ready. Since you're looking for a good time, might I recommend our finest companions? What do you say, big man?"

Jack's mouth slackened before he gave a hearty grin.

"You're a natural kid," he said. "We can make the official start next week Friday. But first, let's have a bit of whiskey and see what you can do."

14

There She Is

Aiden came from the South on State Street from
Schofield's, leaving for home at around eight in the
evening. He had been helping Dean O'Banion arrange
bouquets. The shop provided roses for wives and lovers,
carnations for mothers-in-law, and funereal wreaths for
victims of violence. He tried to assure himself that
funeral flowers had nothing to do with North Side
Gang activities.

His step quickened along with his breath when he saw
the same olive-skinned, dark-haired gal he'd seen from
months ago in Bughouse Square. Communists,
nationalists, homosexuals, and Bible-thumpers alike
made it a colorful place, but for Aiden, it was where
he'd noticed the lovely gal amid gangland gossip. Visits
to the park ever since just hadn't been quite as
interesting. Any sense gave way to other urges when he
decided to follow her north, past Chicago Avenue.

Minutes after seeing the gal and and Harriet
Rosenstein step into Tooker Alley and then the Dil
Pickle Club, Aiden stepped past muscular guards and
nodded with a polite grin. Through a doorway

announcing "DANGER," he gave a wary smile to the host, dressed as a woman despite the hairy arms and lack of bust. He didn't expect the flirty smack on his backside, but didn't raise a fuss about it.

The young McCarthy wasn't in the club for five minutes before the olive-skinned gal bumped into him, wearing a thin, sleeveless top and a simple skirt above shapely calves. The outfit showed the subtle curves of her shoulders, bust, and hips. She ran her left index finger around one of the black tendrils of the cute bob of hair framing her face. He was dumbstruck.

"Oh, excuse me, sir. I've just come here out of my studies with the Sisters of the Blessed Virgin Mother," she said. "Would you mind buying me a drink with me. You look a bit familiar...have I seen you supporting social revolution Bughouse Square?"

Aiden was taken aback, but happy. He nodded with a pause, happy that the gal appeared to have noticed him too.

"I believe you have, miss," he said. "Whiskey work for you?"

A bystander knocked her into him before her cheeks blushed and she gave a nod. She darted her hazel eyes from his glance in what he read as a mix of excitement and novelty. The view brought a smile to his lips.

Aiden ordered two Canadian Clubs for them, rationalizing that if he wasn't putting himself at risk, and wasn't at home, he'd cut himself some slack. His father had always told him to treat any gal he fancied. Sophia soon led them to a table with Harriet Rosenstein and a couple who looked important.

"I hoped that I would see you again, Miss...?" he asked with a pause.

"Sophia. And you, handsome? What should I call you?" she asked before shooting her whiskey with two measured gulps.

"Aiden. I'm pleased to meet you," he responded before pecking her hand and shooting his Canadian Club in order not to appear square. He didn't have to work too hard to suppress the tears from his eyes. The booze was watered down, if genuine.

After formal introductions with the Joneses and Harriet, Aiden gave the politeness required of him before he asked Sophia to dance. They swayed and shimmied to jaunty ragtime melodies, drank diluted whiskey, and only stopped to watch when burlesque ladies danced. The Dil Pickle whirled as customers, working gals, and guys who dressed like gals bumped shoulders and behinds with the two.

Harriet went to the stage between sets to protest the "capitalist war machine," earning applause before dark-skinned musicians started again. Her eyes shifted to watch Sophia from time to time.

After two hours of inebriated, teasing, semi-debauchery, Sophia asked Aiden if he would care to pay a maiden-for-hire for the night. Much to the pleasure of the Joneses, their new hire was working as they'd hoped

"Miss Sophia, I would only take you home if I could pay for a drink for your friends," Aiden said, before he put down the most of his night's earnings. "I would just like to make sure the lovely lady stays safe from hooligans of lesser repute."

Under Harriet's watch and the Jones couple's delight, Aiden draped Sophia's coat around her and they went from the club arm-in-arm. The guards outside bid them a cordial *adieu*.

- - - - -

Aiden walked west on Randolph with Sophia after they took the last streetcar south. They spoke of their studies, ambitions, and the jazz scene as they took a slow promenade together toward her house on Peoria. An occasional laugh peppered the cool air, letting off spurts of steam into the night.

"I never caught your last name," Aiden said.

"Golino," she said, "but I wouldn't mind changing it sooner rather than later. My pop got gunned down last spring and I'd rather just forget about it. I'll be taking care of my mom until she makes sense of it all in her head."

Sophia stopped walking with the realization that her new friend, the late evening, and the tingling of bootleg spirits on the brain made her loose in the tongue. She continued by changing the subject: "Never mind that, let's just talk about Joe Oliver. That cat's showing how great southern music can be."

Aiden recognized the last name from news reports and chats with his boss. He realized the possibility he'd considered in the park before summer was likely true. It was probable O'Banion had killed Sophia's father and her father had tried to kill his pa. Mentioning this seemed like a poor way to end the evening.

Aiden continued about Joe King Oliver.

"Oliver's found this new guy, Louis Armstrong, with

some real New Orleans style." he said, trying to show off what he read about in the weekly rags.

Sophia stumbled all of a sudden, grabbing his arm as he held her upright by the waist. She smiled and nodded sleepily as they continued to walk. He admired her svelte, muscular stems in silence.

"At any rate, I'm helping my old man," Aiden said, with a sudden discomfort from the quiet. "He got nicked in the leg some months back. I'm making a little dough arranging flowers as he gets back on his feet, so to speak. I've never wanted to know so much about carnations, roses, lilies and which occasion calls for which flower."

"I'm impressed" she said, welcoming the change of subject. "A lot of fellas wouldn't know the difference between lilacs and lavender, let alone know what to do with them."

"I'm pretty sure Schofield's Flower Shop won't be keen forever," he said as they reached the Golino household, "but it helps with bills for now."

"I needed a good time with a charming fellow like yourself, Aiden. I'm afraid it's getting late and I must check in with Mama," she said as her soft face shone in the moonlight. Her hazel eyes looked into his.

"Then I bid you good night," Aiden said, caressing her cheek before kissing it goodbye. "I hope you don't mind if I pay you a visit around town."

"Not at all," she said before squeezing the area left of his rib cage, pecking him on the lips, and going for the door of her house.

Aiden stood with his mouth agape as he watched her

fidget with a set of keys. She gave him a polite nod before entering.

- - - - -

Vincent sat in the Golino kitchen, knocking back a watered down brandy. He sat in the dim light, a single candle illuminating his boyish face as he loosened the tie on his white-collared shirt. He leaned back against the blue-white pinstripe suit jacket that hung behind him on his chair.

"Where in the devil's name were you?" he asked his sister with more than a bit of menace as she padded through the entrance to their house. She didn't face him right away as she took her time to close the door and hang up her coat. She then stood by a chair opposite and answered.

"I was meeting with the Blessed Virgin Mother Mission at the Holy Name Cathedral. I learned of their service to assist lost souls and followed one of their novices to help with her great work. They uplift so many spirits," Sophia said with a sincerity that appeared rehearsed. "Do you wish to join us sometime?"

"I heard a man's voice outside our house," Vincent replied, gazing like a feral cat to a crafty mouse. "Is he with the mission as well? Clergy usually don't kiss laypeople."

Sophia didn't like the questioning, but didn't feel like fighting after such a good night with her best friend, her new employers, and a dashing young admirer who not only knew about flowers and music, but could hold his drink. She answered with a measured tone that tempered her impatience.

"My dear little brother, the gentlemen is training as a deacon to assist lost men who depend on our mission," she said "Surely, you'd rather have a man escort me with the perils of Chicago's late night streets. I would have informed you and asked for your permission to go out, but you've been absent as of late. I gave him polite pecks on the cheeks, nothing more."

A pale reddish tint rushed through Vincent's face under the dim light He stepped up and peered into Sophia's eyes. At five-foot-nine, he was four inches taller than his sister, despite being a year younger.

When he realized that his added height caused her no fear, his anger simmered. Sophia just peered back with a stiff lip and scrunched brow.

"Just don't let me catch you hanging around any of those North Side boys; I don't want to break any heads on your account," he sniffed. "Make sure Mama's settled and say your prayers before you get to bed."

Vincent returned to his brandy as Sophia left him before any further argument broke out. He was annoyed, and she assumed that his posturing would only grow with continued back-talk from any little woman.

Sophia crept into her room, changing into her long wool nightgown before tending to her mother. She felt overwhelmed with compassion at what she saw. Celia had nodded off in an upright position in bed, the Bible in her hands as a fading candle flickered the shadow of her silhouette.

The daughter eased her mother over to rest on her side and blew out the candle. Sophia curled up beside her, whispering the *Ava Maria* as she calmed the muscles from her temples to her toes. In due time, she joined her mother in sleep.

15

Halfhearted Truce

Schofield's Flower Shop wasn't as busy before Thanksgiving as in other years. With the cooler winds coming in from Canada, the demand for flowers dropped. Thirst for shipments of whiskey from the northern neighbor sustained the North Side Gang as demand for winter necessities rose.

Dean O'Banion scurried around the flower shop as George Moran and Earl Weiss ordered barrels of bootleg over the telephone with Ontario-based middlemen. Among the associates, Aiden stood at his work table, trimming yellow chrysanthemums and violets for Thanksgiving and weekend Mass across the street. Per usual, he cocked his eavesdropping ear toward any banter.

O'Banion and his lieutenants were expecting a call from Italian competitors. A telephone ring pierced the air before George Moran answered.

"Schofield's Flowers," he said and listened for about a minute before putting his hand on the receiver. "Boss, it's an associate of Torrio. He says Torrio and Sam Genna want to lay out the new boundaries in Cicero later today."

"If they want to to cut down violence and keep their rotgut out of our businesses, we'll meet them later this afternoon" O'Banion said.

Moran relayed the response, adding the politeness required. He took down the meeting time and nodded as Torrio's associate agreed to meet. He adopted a sudden, pensive look, paling a shade before he hung up.

"It's all set, boss," he said. "But they ask that we leave guns at home."

"That's a load of bunk," O'Banion said before calling Aiden over and addressing him. "You've no doubt been listening in, lad. How about driving for us and carrying a gun in your boot? The Italians are prone to keep the meet copacetic, but we'll need you for backup."

Aiden didn't have it in him to protest. He felt he should have, but the boss was moody. Aiden figured he would likely see some of the bastards responsible for his father's damaged leg. Staying only in the business of flower arrangement was not an option.

He shrugged and gave a nod.

"Don't worry, lad," O'Banion said with a wink before handing Aiden a gun. "Torrio isn't the type to shoot a gun, and I gather he's got the brains to keep any lackeys from doing so. He'll be more interested in keeping the booze flowing than the blood."

"Good to hear," Aiden muttered as they all grabbed their coats, caps or hats, and headed out the door.

- - - - -

Aiden pulled the Packard onto 22nd Street in Cicero. Slavic and German immigrants made up most of the population of the small suburb; however, Outfit Italians controlled local government. Aiden, O'Banion, Weiss, and Moran had chatted about these well-known facts during the ride west.

As they drew near the Hawthorne Inn, they spotted two Cadillac sedans parked in front. Each was large enough to carry three passengers armed with Thompson machine guns, along with the drivers. Aiden felt the weight of the Remington Derringer in his boot as he slowed to a stop and tried to gulp away his unease.

The Hawthorne Inn was one of the more elegant buildings in town. The gray brick and arched windows with art deco trim signaled a touch of modernity. It stood out from its otherwise old-fashioned, working-class surroundings.

Aiden reasoned that the Outfit had taken the building to show off a new headquarters. Its presence loomed over the townsfolk to portray the growing status of organized crime from Chicago. It was the only building to have metal window shutters to keep out the bullets of any competition. When his passengers exited the Packard, Aiden was relieved he didn't have to join them.

From the car, he watched as Weiss walked to the door of the Hawthorne Inn in front of O'Banion and Moran. What he then witnessed aroused something other than fear.

A comely blonde in a crimson, knee-length flapper dress and a long string of pearls answered Weiss's knock, greeting the gang with lips curled in a simper containing the cute coyness of Greta Garbo. Girlish giggles peppered the gray air after O'Banion whispered in her ear.

A six-foot-three gorilla in a pink and brown pinstripe suit interrupted any sense of ease when he stepped out from behind the doll. The cocksure grins on the three gangsters' faces faded at once when the tough guy frisked them with sandpaper hands.

Aiden stepped outside the Packard when everyone took off their hats and disappeared inside. Pacing back and forth, he realized that what scared him more than the potential of getting hurt was that he liked the rush of adrenaline that flushed behind his ears.

He still hoped the Outfit and Genna tough guys wouldn't pull any fast ones, as he hadn't much experience with guns. He told himself to make it a priority to learn how to shoot. It was bound to be a good skill with the company he kept.

The blonde beauty from earlier made him think of Sophia. He recalled their delicious kiss and the shake of her hips at the Dil Pickle. The not-too-distant memory was a warming, if temporary distraction from worries about whatever was going on in the Hawthorne Inn.

He reminded himself to focus.

- - - - -

Inside the Outfit's Cicero headquarters, O'Banion shook hands with the two Genna brothers present, Torrio, and Torrio's new lieutenant, Alphonse Capone. Weiss and Moran followed suit, so as to show no disrespect in person. The North Siders and the Gennas, however, couldn't have hated each other more. A petite redhead and the blonde who had answered the door came out in nothing but silk robes, offering cigars and beer.

"These ladies look like they belong in school rather than a gangster's den," O'Banion whispered into Moran's ear.

Despite any dispute about prostitution or the potential for poisoned spirits, O'Banion had to show respect to Torrio, who was a shrewd businessman despite his ethics. Showing manners to the Genna brothers, starting with the leader, Sam, extended the respect and friendship O'Banion had with Mike Merlo, a leader in the *Unione Siciliana*. Merlo helped direct the Sicilians nation-wide and was the main reason Genna hatred didn't lead to more Irish bloodshed.

O'Banion took a cigar and gave the redhead a tip after declining the likely diluted beer. She looked uncomfortable before he explained himself.

"No thanks, darling," he said before pouring himself two fingers of Canadian Club from a flask he had in his suit jacket. "I can hardly refuse your charms, but I brought my own hooch."

The redhead returned a smile before sauntering out of the room.

Torrio's pinstripe suit-clad lieutenant, Alphonse Capone, had a noticeable wish to appear more diplomatic than the reputation that preceded him. With a tenor voice, Capone mapped out the traditional boundary between the North Side and the Outfit. The bootleg boundary between both remained along Chicago Avenue, with Torrio's gang to the south and O'Banion's gang to the north. He also laid out protections for liquor and moonshine production for the Sicilian Gennas in Little Italy.

Capone added that any agreement on boundaries in Chicago didn't preclude the Sicilians and North Side Gang from partaking in the Cicero rackets. That was the main condition on which Torrio deferred to get O'Banion on board. The good lieutenant also gave generic overtures to respect and good business over violent disagreement.

"It's equal opportunity here," Capone said. "We give the public what they want at the best price. Those who have the most to offer at the most efficient rate, drive growth."

"Apart from the low price, comes quality of the goods," O'Banion interjected, glancing at the Gennas. "I'm not one to sell my buyers cut-rate poison."

The younger Genna brother, "Bloody" Angelo, almost lost control of himself, nudging forward with clenched fists at the jab. Sam put an arm across his brother's chest, giving a nod to Torrio and then to O'Banion at his own pace.

"*Si*, that's something on which we can all agree," Torrio said. "Since we in the Outfit are the main owners of local breweries, we can sell you beer at fifty-five dollars a barrel if you sell some of your higher quality bootleg to us and our Sicilian friends, say for seventy bucks a case,"

The gang leaders haggled for a good ten minutes before settling on a price.

"If you respect Mr. Torrio's and the Gennas' territories, Mr. O'Banion, we'll all be copacetic," Capone said. "But we also can help each other out."

"I ain't one to disagree," said O'Banion. "It will all be good if respect's mutual."

They all shook hands, save for Angelo, who skulked in the corner of the room and just gave all parties curt nods. They agreed to cooperate for profit, with little interest paid to vagueness on enforcement and Cicero.

O'Banion tipped the redhead a dollar after she returned his hat and those of his two lieutenants. She gave him a chaste kiss on the cheek before returning to the bedrooms upstairs. The North Side boss and his two lieutenants made their way back into the cool Cicero evening.

- - - - -

As the horizon beyond the Hawthorne Inn began to eclipse the sun, O'Banion, Moran, and Weiss strode toward the Packard. Aiden was thankful he didn't have to use the Remington, but was put on edge as John Torrio walked out the door with a short, clean-shaven, muscular henchman in his wake.

Aiden recognized Torrio as the Italian he saw conversing near Bughouse Square with the late Silvio Golino. The lieutenant with the Outfit boss looked only five years older than Aiden, but was dressed in a sharp pinstripe suit and wore a black fedora that gave an iota of class to his mischievous mug.

O'Banion seemed cordial enough with the two, so Aiden tried to remain calm. He still figured the older Italian had played a part with his father having a life-long limp. The two gang bosses were about fifteen feet away from the Packard before their discussion could be heard.

"Torrio, I'm inclined to think that you will keep your word," O'Banion said. "But if those Gennas don't respect my bootleg routes and supplies, don't be surprised if I get angry. Agreements go both ways."

Aiden tensed as Torrio took O'Banion by the shoulders, put little at ease by the lazy, lopsided grin. O'Banion responded with a toothy smile, a reminder to project poise under pressure.

"Dean, as an immigrant to the son of an immigrant, I say we all work together against the Protestant, racist, nationalist bastards who support the 18th Amendment and Volstead Acts. To spill blood would be a curse."

The gangsters shook hands again before Torrio and his lieutenant walked back into the Hawthorne Inn and the North Side men continued to the Packard.

Aiden drove back to Schofield's while the three others chatted about the meeting. Weiss seemed the most ill-at-ease with their future, but he agreed with Moran and O'Banion that the new order of things might be best for business.

Unease remained with Aiden after returning to the flower shop.

With a stiff lip, Aiden returned the Remington Derringer to his boss after Weiss and Moran had left for the evening. O'Banion gave a smile while flipping open the chamber to show that the gun hadn't been loaded with anything but a sense of foreboding.

"You look rather green there with that gun, lad," O'Banion said to Aiden's tense gaze, clapping him on the shoulder. "But you did good. You kept your cool. Get on home to supper with your mother. I'll need you at work earlier tomorrow, gotta make sure the archbishop has his flowers for Mass."

"With respect, I'd ask you to keep my family's wishes in heart," Aiden replied. "I thank you for helping out my pa. Though it's his preference that I not work for you at all, I'll only help you with flowers for now."t

"And what's your preference, lad?"

"I like the money and have no qualms about breaking the law to piss off the arses in charge. However, I'm still seventeen and respect my ma and my pop.."

"Family comes first, lad."

"That, and I've difficulty pretending to work well with any Italian who might harm my family. It's best I'm not put in that position."

O'Banion sighed and put his hands up in resignation.

"Business is business," he said. "Torrio's more into making money than more dead bodies. We shouldn't have to worry about much more from the dagos. You won't have to worry if all you'll be doing is arranging flowers."

Aiden didn't let on that he was looking to court a dead dago's daughter.

"Evening, then," Aiden said, "and don't give me a bloody gun till I know what to do with it. My limit's with threats and fists."

"You're a little piss-head," O'Banion muttered. "You know how to face a man twice yer size, do I have to teach you how to handle an arsehole with a gun?"

Aiden feigned a kick toward O'Banion's right leg before he skipped away, shaking his head. He grabbed his cap and jacket, giving a wave before heading out the door.

"Cocky, bloody hellion," O'Banion chuckled after returning to his work desk. He calmed himself with Canadian Club and arranging chrysanthemums before heading home to his wife, Viola.

16

Bitter Bedfellows

It was the day after Earl Weiss went to Cicero with Dean O'Banion, George Moran, and Aiden McCarthy, whom he considered a glorified flower boy. Weiss enjoyed being in the inner circle negotiations, and the boss ordered him to spread the gospel of superior North Side Gang hootch. He wasn't thrilled to supervise an associate, Danny Keagan, but had to remind himself that running the rackets and serving a thirsty public wasn't always a hoppin' time.

In the overcast afternoon, Weiss led the lollygagging Keagan north of the flower shop, a few blocks east of Bughouse Square. New speakeasies on Michigan were ripe for North Side Gang sales. Many so-called pansies and pantywaists frequented the area. Weiss couldn't understand why the boss had problems with prostitution, but not the poofs, but he deferred to demands.

"Those funny-acting boyos are good customers," O'Banion had told him. "The ritzy class, holy rollers, and Protestants won't do business with them, but then again, the same bastards won't deal with most Irishmen outside of Chicago. We gotta give fellow misfits a

107

chance, Earl."

Weiss noticed Keagan seemed just as agitated, if not more so, as they walked east past the Water Tower, then north on Michigan. His charge slumped his shoulders and his eyes became angry slits. Weiss couldn't stop him, even if he had wanted to, when they came across two figures in tuxedo shirts necking in an alley outside a cafe called the Elephant's Eyebrows.

Keagan, being tall, but svelte, slammed his right fist into the side of the head of one of the two strange lovers, using the full benefit of his height to maximize momentum. The scream that came out of one of the tuxedo shirts was more high-pitched than either North Side man expected.

Weiss grabbed Keagan's arm before he could land any more blows.

Not prone to pity, he felt a rush of embarrassment when he realized that the tuxedo shirted figure that now lay on the ground had a noticeable bosom, rising and falling with sobs. The other one didn't have an Adam's apple, and he could now see that her hair was pinned up on the back of her head.

Weiss took Keagan by the throat, squeezing to threaten, but not kill.

"Dammit, I don't give a rat's hair whether you come to blows with a fairy on your own time," Weiss yelled, "but you damned well do not hit a woman."

After throwing Keagan to the ground, Weiss jerked the gal in the tuxedo shirt upright and handed her over to her lover. He gave the lover a few clams before his subordinate got to his feet.

"You damned well better apologize if you work for Dean O'Banion," Weiss snarled at Keagan.

The two women's eyes widened in astonishment at mention of the North Side boss's name. Keagan shifted on his feet and kept his lips shut, reluctant to admit fault. His eyes and mind appeared to open a bit more when Weiss gave him a look that could have turned Medusa to stone.

"Sorry," Keagan muttered before turning and following Weiss with a stiff gait toward the Elephant's Eyebrows.

"Just keep your damned hands and words to yourself," Weiss growled. "If you strike anyone else, lad or lass, you won't have to worry about losing your job. I'll put you within judgment of St. Peter."

Dealings at the Elephant's Eyebrow were copacetic as Weiss got back to playing salesman. He set up North Side Gang orders for it and two other speaks along Michigan before dismissing Keagan to return to "whatever hellhole you call home."

Danny Keagan didn't mutter any cocky remarks before walking northwest. It was a wise choice.

Weiss sauntered south to Schofield's and took a nip of Canadian Club before reporting on business to O'Banion. He kept quiet on the associate's scuffle with the lesbian lasses. He wasn't in the mood to get into a talk with his boss about the rights of pansies to buy bootleg and didn't want to relinquish any more leisure time than required.

The lieutenant wanted to keep a date, of which he knew his boss wouldn't approve.

- - - - -

Minka Summer lit Earl Weiss's cigarette that evening as they lay together in bed at the Four Deuces Club on South Wabash. Her best customer had bypassed the hooch on the first floor and craps, poker, and blackjack games on the second floor. He seemed content while he ran his fingers through her reddish mane in the comforts of her perch on the next floor up.

After Colosimo's death, Minka had been a regular, and then a working girl for John Torrio. She figured her new boss was somehow involved in her late husband's death. The newspapers hinted at it, Torrio was chummy with Colosimo's ex-wife, Victoria Moresco, and she never like the Outfit leader to begin with. At any rate, she needed money, and it was easier to make it off of sex than singing.

To add fantasy to her liaisons, Minka hung drapes with golden dragons dancing along red silk, bought from a burgeoning Chinatown just to the South. Her ivory skin, subtle curves, and other touches made johns forget the club's other attractions. Minka Summer strove to be one of a kind.

Weiss puffed on the opium-laced tobacco as his hand drifted over his compensated companion's taut, bare stomach. The view from there to her thighs and rest of her stems intoxicated him.

"These are great doll-face," he said. "But they make me more stupid than a fifth of Chicago's best whiskey."

"The girls and I have no problem getting the dope in Chinatown," she said. "You don't need a prescription like you do for laudanum or medicinal hooch, but it

110

gives more of a kick. An extra bonus is that my employer doesn't make a dime off it."

Minka appreciated that Weiss not only enjoyed their pleasure-filled liaisons, but held a mutual distrust of Torrio. It was also a good thing he was as good in bed as he was generous with gratuity. She dared wonder sometimes whether what was happening between them was more than just a pay-for-service transaction.

"A little meeting yesterday with Torrio went well enough," Weiss said, interrupting her thoughts. "But I don't trust the old guinea any further than I can throw him. He's got this new monkey, Capone. You heard of him?"

"Darling, I'm a big earner for Mr. Torrio," she said. "I like your style. And if you keep up the good performance and kindness, I'll make sure you don't have to worry about whether you can trust old John. You'll already be on top of affairs."

She wrapped her left leg around his left calf, further drawing his body and mind to her. Her easy money off of Capone remained unmentioned. She didn't consider it noteworthy.

"Heavens, you're beautiful," Weiss whispered with the intensity of opium racing through his veins. "We'd get out of this hellhole if I could afford it."

"I'm sure you would," she purred before nibbling his lips as if they were an *hors d'oeuvre* to her last meal. "We can make Chicago and its rackets work for us. You and me will make our own ticket out of here."

Minka climbed on top of him before she nuzzled his neck, brought her bosom to his face, and made sure they both enjoyed a sensual interlude before drifting toward unconsciousness. They both were out of breath, her crimson locks in a mess, before they caught a good night's slumber.

17

A Prohibition Thanksgiving

Sophia Golino hadn't been looking forward to Thanksgiving. She figured the first one since her father had passed away would be hard enough if her family didn't have good food and drink.

She used earnings she had made serving at the Dil Pickle to buy two turkey breasts. She then stuffed them with porcini mushrooms and fennel bulb, adding garlic roasted potatoes as a side. The scents of meaty stuffed turkey, peppercorn, and mild anise filled the air as she led Celia to their simple table. Late afternoon was drifting into early evening.

Vincent appeared in a good mood, which was unusual. To his sister's misfortune, his mercurial mood grew malcontent when she answered their door to a guest.

Harriet Rosenstein brought two bottles of Cabernet Sauvignon to their door as Sophia embraced her and led her inside to take her coat. Sophia introduced her as a Catholic novice overseeing mission work with recent immigrants. It was an easy lie to cover for her best friend's role in getting her a job.

Celia gave a cordial nod as Vincent's face drew sharp at his lips, chin, and cheekbones in an unpleasant grimace. His narrowed eyes bore into Harriet. The atmosphere inside the house became cool, but in a way less pleasant than the autumn air outside.

"How did a novice get her hands on a bottle of wine?" he asked. "She looks more hebe than Catholic."

"We Catholics are still allowed sacramental wine. Our religious freedoms are still protected despite the Volstead Act," Sophia replied. "A guest is always welcome in our household."

Vincent grew quiet, but blood still pumped to his face in defiance.

"We should take a bit of the Lord's wine and enjoy this splendid feast," Harriet said in a rare bid to calm the atmosphere. She served the wine to Vincent before getting to Celia, Sophia, and to herself. "Sophia, please lead us in prayer."

Sophia led them in grace after they took their seats. Her brother took his chair with a huff but stayed because his appetite overtook his anger. Celia and Sophia made up for his lack of hospitality. Sparse conversation permeated the chewing and savoring of the cuisine.

Only when Sophia finished her third glass from the second wine bottle did she reveal her frustration. It was not only Vincent's current discourtesy; the fuse had been lit since the first night she came home from the Dil Pickle Club. After that night, he had the nerve to establish a curfew and yelled when she broke it on a regular basis. The male chauvinism persisted despite her older age and ability to vote soon.

"Well now, Vincent, in about a year or so you'll be big enough a man to become a full-time gangster, just like dear old Papa. You'll no longer just be able to be a tough guy around the women of your family, but you can rough up Irishmen and Polacks. Harriet, join me in a round of applause for how far my brother has come along."

Celia and Harriet didn't make more noise than the sounds of their breath, much less say anything. Blood flushed into Vincent's face before he threw forth a bunch of Italian epithets and stood up from his chair. Sophia stayed silent, knowing she had hit a nerve.

"You are a *puttana* who doesn't even deserve to eat with those gathered around this table," he said after he stood. "You oughta learn your lesson one way or another."

Harriet rushed to lead Celia into her bedroom as the two siblings confronted each other, both out of earshot when Vincent's right hand cracked on Sophia's left cheek. Vincent watched with rabid triumph as his sister shook and gained her composure. He failed to stop her from grasping an empty carafe while she got from her chair to her feet.

"Leave us," she said, holding the improvised glass club in her right hand as if ready to swing. "I think I'd rather strike you myself than let you continue to bully this family. The women will take it from here. Come back when you're able to not be a stubborn *stronzo*."

Vincent stepped back, stumbled, and fell, being both flustered by his sister's bravado and set off-balance from his own wine intake. The smack of his head hitting the ground alarmed Sophia, and with the speed at which she'd lost her temper, she reverted to her role of worried sister.

Harriet joined her friend on the floor next to the unconscious Vincent within the minute. They were both happy to see his chest rising and falling. Sophia elevated his head and put a blanket over him before she checked on her mother. Celia was going through her bedtime routine, mercifully oblivious to the goings on in the kitchen.

Sophia joined her mother in evening prayers before going to Harriet and Vincent's side. Her brother had full breaths and only seemed in a deep sleep, which assuaged her guilt and helped her focus. She got off the ground and hugged her friend, holding back any tears of frustration or panic.

"Can I do anything, my lovely?" Harriet asked. "You want me to stay the night?"

"Darling, you're the cat's meow and don't ever forget it," Sophia said. "I'm glad I can count on you, but I have to handle this on my own."

Harriet hugged her friend and kissed her on the cheek before she left.

Sophia brought a blanket and a pillow to lay next to her brother. Her worry outweighed her anger as she tilted his head to the side and listened to the click of the kitchen clock mirror his pulse. The regular rhythm lulled her body and mind to sleep.

Pleasant dreams of Celia's smile, Harriet's laughter, and Aiden's allure were not enough for a serene slumber unaffected by worry and red wine. In six hours, Sophia stirred when Vincent flinched awake and asked for coffee. Thankfully, he didn't mention the night before.

"I'll boil water and wake up Mama," Sophia said through gritted teeth. "You'll have to fix your own breakfast while I tend to the house."

Her brother grunted and only drank coffee before he headed out the door. Sophia was quiet with the patience she could muster. She made oatmeal for her mother and herself, eating with a silence that masked the thoughts swirling in her head.

18

Black Friday

Aiden sipped tea as he finished helping Dean O'Banion with ledger books detailing the legitimate business at Schofield's Flower Shop. After O'Banion and Moran had finished their third drams of Canadian Club, they insisted their young associate partake. Aiden couldn't have declined, even if he'd wanted. He marveled at how his superiors worked with the efficiency of an elevated train through Downtown traffic despite their apparent buzz.

The three toasted the air before getting back to work. Liquor flowed freely as the day's last rays of sunshine. Any further attempts at bookkeeping proved a lost cause as O'Banion and Moran finished their sixth drams. Aiden donned his cap, chuckling to himself before leaving.

The one dram was enough to warm him as he marched north to the Dil Pickle Club. Thoughts of who he was about to meet pumped blood through his veins. Upon seeing the entryway of the Bohemian escape, he readied for a scene change, reading the impish sign above that announced "DANGER!"

"Hiya, candy-cane," said the effeminate fella at the door of the joint. "Stop by later if you want me to help you explore other ways to make whoopee."

Aiden caught the hand that tried to smack his backside.

"I don't want you to get any ideas," he said with a grin. "I'm not into the fellas, and you oughta keep your hands to yourself."

"No worries, sweetie," the gent said, venturing a coquettish grin and a wink.

Aiden grabbed a diluted Canadian Club before looking for the gal he fancied. It would be their third meeting since he'd walked her home the first time. He relaxed as dark-skinned men played trumpets and a trombone on stage, all muted. A sequin-clad Mamie Smith look-alike purred above the cheeky melody.

He nodded his head with the music, sipping liquid heat while gals in multicolored dresses and pearl necklaces danced with guys and gals ranging in clothing from tuxedo shirts to rags. He finished his drink when he spotted Sophia rounding the edge of the small stage.

She swayed in a red dress that clung to her hips and hung just above her knee. He admired the white feather boa caressing her bare shoulders as he snaked through the moderate crowd to meet her. After joining her to dance in tempo with the trumpet, Sophia draped her arms around his neck, brought her body to his, and kissed him on the mouth while shaking her hips. Warmth flushed to his ears, cheeks and other areas before he paced a slight step back to conceal his excitement.

"My, you're a choice bit of calico," he said to her ear. "Join me for a nip of bootleg when you get a moment?"

"How long are ya willing to wait?" she whispered to him before leaning in and kissing him with a flick of her tongue. "I have to tease other daddies for dough until I let my hair down with you, my sheikh."

Aiden pecked her on the cheek before retaking his place at the bar. He ordered a watered-down beer as the next song started. He wondered if he was batty for being so patient, watching Sophia shake her hips at other guys. She didn't kiss anyone else the way she did with him, but discomfort hit him as he looked on.

The cool beer didn't keep him from getting hotter under the collar. He tried to keep her job in perspective while observing the Pickle's owners, Jack and Venicia Jones. They seemed happy with the way Sophia flirted and got people to drink or take an interest in the professionals. The other thing that kept his temper in check was that his red-clad gal came up to him every few songs to kiss his neck and ask for patience.

"Can I get you company for the evening, sugar," said a dark-haired gal who Aiden recognized as Harriet Rosenstein. "That lovely gal you're eyeing doesn't want to lay her goods down for some mick gent. But I know a nice selection of Oriental or Bolshevik gals that could tickle your fancy."

"I know you're a friend of that beautiful lass, there," Aiden said, finishing his beer. "I like your speeches, but I'm not interested in paying a gal for company. Sophia is worth more than a session in sin."

121

"There's frustration in your eyes."

"A little, but I tend not to be short-sighted."

"I hope for your sake that you're a man of your word," Harriet said. "Sophia is like a sister...If I find you have any bad intentions, I'll kick you in the balls so hard you won't walk straight for a year."

Aiden ordered another beer before nodding to Harriet and watching her get to work to weasel weak men out of their wages. The next time Sophia worked her way to the bar, he sent an Old Bushmills to Jack Jones. He ordered a soda water for himself and a Tom Collins for his crush. He sighed after she shot her drink and got back to dancing.

It was nearing 10:30 in the evening when Aiden finished his soda and decided to call it a night. He donned his coat and headed for the door, only for Sophia to chase after him. Outside the club, her first move was to throw herself at him. She clawed at his clothes and grabbed at his waist before he stopped her. He put her mascara-lined cheeks in the palms of his hands.

After kissing her on the forehead, their breaths returned to normal before he took her back to the Dil Pickle, past the alarmed guards, to get her coat and cloche hat. A chilly wind hit their faces before they caught a late streetcar south toward her house.

She held his hand on the way and gave him a smile to warm him during the rest of the walk west. Upon reaching Peoria, Sophia's steps slowed and her face grew more stiff.

He felt cold again. Anxious.

- - - - -

Sophia shivered upon seeing her house. She had left the house with her mother in a pleasant mood, yet her brother's slap still resonated on her cheek and in her soul. A tear ran down her left cheek. Creases formed around Aiden's eyes as they peered into hers. She embraced him and sobbed.

Aiden pulled away with a slight jerk of his chest, unsure of himself and what he should do. He gnawed on the inside of his cheek, waiting for inspiration or a clue.

"Dammit, I need just one man in my life who is gentle and thinks about what I need," she said. "You're swell, cute, a good time, and are more man than I'm accustomed to, Aiden. Could you just hold me and not ask questions?"

He grabbed her by the hips and brought their bodies together, not uttering a word as she buried her head into his shoulder. He didn't know what else to do, so he kept his mouth shut.

"My brother's almost as big a monster as my father, except Papa was better at hiding it," she said after a while. "Tell me you're not a monster, Aiden. I won't have another one in my life if I can help it."

Aiden shuffled his feet, kissing her on the cheek before responding.

"Doll, I've done some tough guy stuff, and found myself not being keen with it" he said. "As of now, I only go to Holy Name, arrange flowers, and fancy a hostess at one of speaks my boss supplies."

Sophia nuzzled his neck and kissed his earlobe as they

both took a deep breath. The warmth of their bodies together gave a buttress against the cold surrounding them. She whispered about her family's Outfit connection, Vincent's slap the night before, and her fear that her younger brother would be another wise guy.

They shivered together before Aiden cobbled together words he felt he needed to speak, even if he wasn't sure how to phrase them.

"I might have seen your pa get shot," he said after stepping back and looking in her eyes. "I've said before that my boss has his paws in a lot of business. It was self-defense, I swear— ".

Sophia pushed him away from her, tears rolled down a face that grew more agitated by the second. He watched with a gulp in his throat, realizing that he should have just listened as she stepped away from him, keyed her door on Peoria, and went inside.

Aiden stayed and watched the shadows in the house as lights and movements extinguished. He then marched north toward home. The walk was long enough for him to speculate and dread a fitful rest.

For Sophia, sleep never came.

19

Calamitous Compromise

Alphonse Capone picked his teeth in contrast to anything that society types could consider dapper, not that he gave a damn. He was picking out shards of beef while waiting for a Saturday meeting with John Torrio on the first floor of the Hawthorne Inn.

The cold of the Cicero winds made Capone want to be back with his Polish prostitute on the second floor, but the steak lunch had warmed his spirits enough. The sight of John Torrio and Sam Genna approaching to take seats at his table quashed any sense of leisure.

Capone's face became as firm as a Catholic nun's ruler when he stopped with his teeth. He brushed his hands on a kerchief and stood. After joining Torrio and Sam to sit, he ordered them all a bitter espresso without sugar, cream, or brandy. Any comforts took a break for business.

"*Signore* Genna, *Signore* Torrio, I'm honored to be in your presence," Capone said, forcing a grin. "To what do I owe this prestigious pleasure?"

He watched as Sam Genna spoke in Torrio's ear in a Sicilian accent. Torrio tapped the hand of his Mafioso counterpart from Chicago's Little Italy. He nodded assurance that Capone was to be trusted.

"We want a more direct relation between Sicily and you fellas from Naples," Sam said. "These micks can only feel like they're competing with us on an equal level. But we gotta stick together if it's us against them."

Capone was silent until Torrio signaled for him to speak.

"*Signore* Genna, I think we can all understand that our countrymen take precedence in bootleg, moonshine, or any other rackets from which we profit. The agreement we made several weeks ago with the Irish is a mere formality. Even if those prick Feds try to undo us, I am an Italian first, American second when it comes down to business."

Torrio ordered Capone, Sam Genna, and him a dram of Old Overholdt to toast their understanding. Bonded by nationality, drink, and disposition, they agreed to favor each other over the North Side Gang. This despite any other verbalized treaty with so-called foreigners.

Sam Genna interlocked his fingers in front of his chest. Anyone who didn't know better might take it as a sign that he was praying. He exhaled, then lowered his gaze to the top of the table before moving it to Capone and setting on Torrio.

"Let's say my brothers happen to notice our moonshine supplies are a little light and we got reason to believe the micks are involved. We gotta make a little rough stuff in our interest but don't wanna disrespect you, *Signore* Torrio."

"I can't keep an eye on everyone," Torrio replied.

"What I don't see, don't offend me. But I can tell you, your brothers, and all the micks that we'll all find a solution that's copacetic."

He then gave a wink before continuing.

"If your boys try to rip off anyone on the North Side, keep the violence and any noise to a minimum. We still gotta keep up appearances. If it looks like I'm giving you a slap on the wrist or lump you in with the Irish competition, you gotta make like it's a surprise, Sam, *capisce*?"

Sam nodded to Torrio and Capone, returning the wink.

Torrio ended the meeting with a round of handshakes between the three of them, telling his lieutenant to get their guest some company.

Capone snapped his fingers at a blonde, Slavic prostitute who then sat on Sam's lap. Within minutes, she led the Genna upstairs, wiggling her behind until he grabbed it.

Torrio ordered some Scotch for him and Capone as the two finished business. After a few hours, the Outfit leader left for home back in Chicago for a well-prepared meal with Anne and an evening of marital bliss.

Capone didn't return to his wife, Mae. For the evening, he preferred the paid company of the Polish gal, and his suite upstairs was much closer. He decided take another day at work before getting to his family.

20

The Promise of Advent

A week after last seeing Sophia, Aiden's steps made an *allegro* tempo with the frosty Chicago ground as he walked the short distance from his last afternoon class at Holy Name to his job at Schofield's. His sweetheart's rejection after Thanksgiving still weighed in the back of his mind, but he tried to divert his thoughts to his studies and making dough before a small break. Focusing on life's practicalities several weeks before Christmas was depressing enough, so the scene outside of the flower shop provided Aiden with a welcome distraction.

Just to the south of Schofield's, a gang of three light-skinned hooligans were picking on an olive-skinned, dark-haired lad not yet old enough for secondary school. The blonde-haired leader held a brick above his head, ready to strike. Aiden stepped across State Street, happy for the chance to yell at someone.

"Hey, you bastards oughta pick on someone who can take three blockheads," he said. "Just as well, three against two seems rather unfair. Wouldn't you say?"

The leader steadied the brick and turned toward

Aiden. His underlings did the same as their prey held his breath. Blondie lifted the brick above his head as Aiden took out his Schrade knife and released the blade, relishing the testosterone in the air .

In that moment, Aiden's heart fluttered as Sophia joined his side and dared the ruffians to throw what they wanted at them. The three blockheads weren't looking to hit a girl, but they wouldn't dismiss the idea from a sense of chivalry. All five boys stood at attention when she bunched her fists.

"Come on, *bastardi*, if you want to pick on some street urchin, you gotta fight me, my man here, and any of his friends at Schofield's!" she shouted. "Just give us a reason to act. I got no problems with blood flying!"

Dean O'Banion took a step out of the flower shop at all of the shouting and leveled a Colt at Blondie's head after seeing the threat toward Aiden. The thug's two accomplices fled before Sophia kissed Aiden's cheek and ran north on State. The boss cocked his gun and fired. The remaining ruffian peed himself after having the brick shot out of his hand.

"Make for home before someone meaner than I comes after you," O'Banion shouted.

The hooligan obliged with no argument.

Aiden took the hand of the olive-skinned lad and led him into the Schofield's. He then excused himself and motioned in the general direction of where Sophia had fled.

"So, boyo, what are you doing on this side of town by yourself?" O'Banion said to the lad, while waving for Aiden to go on and leave. "What's your name? You've got some stones traveling on the North Side, you looking Italian and all."

Aiden grinned at his boss before he left to go after the gal.

- - - - -

Aiden sprinted north on State Street, his cheeks red with both the speed he was running and the anxiety of where he stood with Sophia. When he reached East Delaware Place, just to the North of Tooker Alley, two arms yanked him to the left and put him against a brick wall. He was worried until he realized his eyes were opposite a lovely set of hazel.

Sophia brought her lips to his before she rested her head on his right shoulder. Her breaths were steady while he waited for her to speak. He figured he should keep his mouth shut since the last time he had opened his mouth to her, the results hadn't ended to his liking.

"I regret I ran away from you since our last time together," she said. "I just watched you and your boss act strong, but still with honor. It's something I'm unaccustomed to"

Aiden weighed what he wanted to say in his head, wondering which parts he should leave out to keep things on an even keel.

"Sophia, you're a doll-faced vamp," he said. "You got looks, smarts, and you put me in a mood. But courting the competition's daughter is new to me too. It gets under my skin to watch you flaunt your goods at other boyos to lure them to the professionals."

She responded by putting her hand on his chest and looking him in the eye.

"So...what now, my sheikh?"

Aiden didn't answer, furrowing his brow and attempting to think through their dilemma. He kept his eyes from hers, thinking about an answer before she grabbed his chin with a solid, if silk-like, grasp to make him pay attention.

"Look, I gotta make money," she said. "I'm not the least bit interested in any frisky faces at the Dil Pickle, but I still gotta make customers think so. Let's meet mostly on my days off. I'll get your attention while passing outside the flower shop. We'll rendezvous when we can, *capisce?*

"*Sto ancora imparando*," he said. "I'm still learning, so please be patient."

Aiden shifted in place from one foot to the other before continuing.

"There's a cafe on Michigan. They bring out the firewater later, but if you'd be kind enough to join me for a while, we could make like teetotalers before we both get to work. I'm buying."

"I'd be delighted, *signore*," Sophia said, holding out her arm so Aiden could take it.

They walked the short distance to the Elephant's Eyebrows, where he held the door for her. She pecked him on the cheek before he pulled out a chair for her. A gent wearing lipstick took their order and returned soon with oolong tea and biscuits. The waiter's blonde finger waves brushed the side of his cheek. He winked before sashaying away in platform shoes.

"I'm not a regular here," Aiden said. "My boss says it's a place to escape Protestants and see degenerates, his best customers. I say they make a good cup of tea and what they do in the bedroom is none of our damned business."

Sophia gave a snarky smile. After tea and friendly chitchat about dandies, Bughouse Square, jazz, and the so-called Bohemian fringe, they got to logistics of how this courtship might work. They decided they could meet at the Dil Pickle after his shifts at Schofield's on occasional Saturdays. She could also visit him after Mass on Sundays, reminding him that she had school as well.

Aiden gave her a smooch on the cheek after she'd taken charge. She excused herself to the powder room before they would have to part ways. Upon returning to Aiden, he stood ready to go with her coat. Chivalry, if old-fashioned, happened to suit him well.

"May I escort you to your employ, my lady," he asked with a hint of mischief in his eye, expecting a raucous reply.

"Uh, well, that is genteel of you, my good man," she responded with a wink and a poke to his gut. "But a lady in this day and age can take care of herself. I'll call upon you later."

Aiden admired the audacity, sneaking a glance at the curve of her behind. He took to it like the bait is was. Sophia's soft, olive-skinned neck and her feminine bob of black hair caught him hook, line, and sinker. He was still smart enough to bide his time.

She turned around and blew him a kiss as they parted ways.

Part II

Chicago 1921

1

St. Patrick's Day Preparation

Before the sun showed in the East over a disparate group of paperboys, hobos, and speakeasy patrons stumbling home, Dean O'Banion directing traffic for bootleggers and delivery boys from one of Torrio's breweries. In the months since the Cicero agreement with the Italians, the North Side Gang had gained a warehouse on Ashland and Division. Allen's Storage was an official greenhouse and wholesale intake for Schofield's Flower Shop. Any drys were paid to either believe that or look the other way.

Business buzzed before Chicago celebrations of Ireland's patron saint. Politicians, Protestants, Catholics, business owners, Feds, and police; no one seemed to care when a few million drinkers were ready to put money down. The market allowed O'Banion to find a wealth of new workers among the hobos between Bughouse Square and the crossroads of Clark and North. Thugs thieved and profits soared as the public quenched its thirst.

Not that all those working were pleased.

Danny Keagan had already shown his unhappiness to

137

Earl Weiss about North Side Gang dealings with homosexuals and Negroes. But until today, he hadn't yet brought those concerns to the boss. He was thick enough to make his preferences known before one of the busiest days of the year.

"Oh, they can't help how they are any more than you can blame your dingbat father for how goofy you are, Keagan," O'Banion said. "As long as they pay their tabs and work with us to keep the Feds at bay, I don't pry or want to get in their business..."

O'Banion then gave an exaggerated nod and stroked his hairless chin with his right hand as if just figuring out some news.

"...Say, since you're so interested, does that mean you have something to admit? I have to say I'm flattered, Danny, but I'm not into courtin' the fellas. I don't think my wife would like it either. Or are you looking to join those well-dressed, but repressed fellas with the Ku Klux Klan, Keagan? They're name is from the Greek, 'circle of brothers.' I hear they're looking for young lads like yourself downstate for whatever nonsense they like to do to each other."

Keagan swore under his breath. He decided to keep his mouth shut rather than get into further argument.

"Never mind, boss," he said. "I don't care as long as they stay away from me."

"You oughta worry more about anyone who wants to steal from your boss than any man who wants to bed other fellas," O'Banion said. "Now carry on and don't worry your pretty little head about other lads."

The North Side boss made like he was wiping grime

off his face before continuing to address everyone else.

"Alright, boys," he said. "Let's get these four leaf clovers and dye these white roses green. We gotta bundle of orders to fill before we celebrate good ole St. Paddy!"

Keagan brooded as he got to work.

- - - - -

Aiden woke up around six and meandered to the kitchen to see Margaret carrying a two pound flank of beef to their icebox. She had a stunned look on her face, noting to her son that it had been delivered ten minutes ago courtesy of Schofield's Flower Shop.

"I told the delivery man we don't take charity, but he wouldn't listen," Margaret said. "We can't just waste it though. I suppose we'll invite friends who've been down on their luck to dinner tomorrow. There's no shame in filling your plate if you're a guest."

Aiden's face scrunched with unease upon seeing the gift. He had worries about future expectations of his boss, but tried to shrug them off after seeing his mother's face.

"Ma, as far as Pa knows, our guests chipped in for a fine community dinner," he said. "It's about time that roast we ordered came in."

The crimson color of embarrassment on Margaret's skin gave way to a smile of bewildered joy stretching from cheek to cheek She showed her complicity with a quick wink as Evan stumbled in the kitchen shortly after a quick morning shave.

Evan tousled his son's hair before giving Margaret a peck on the cheek and sitting down at the table with a copy of the *Daily Tribune.* He sipped the undiluted breakfast tea she set out for him before she returned to the stove to mind the oatmeal.

Margaret rebuffed Aiden's offer to help cooking and ordered him to the table with a flick from her wrist. He joined his father at the table with a fresh cup of tea.

"I hope you're just arranging flowers for O'Banion and not losing track of your studies," Evan said to his son. "Word in the barber shop and in the papers alarms me about people goin' loony for bootleg."

"Well Pa, I said I was picking up more hours at Schofield's " Aiden said with truth. "I'll just miss the first part of my day of class to help the boss to prepare for tomorrow. But I'll catch up on my own. One of my mates lets me know about the assignments."

Evan sipped his tea and managed a smile despite the seriousness in his eyes.

"The real money tomorrow will be in beer and spirits," he said. "I trust you won't test God, nor our luck, with poor choices."

Aiden shrugged his shoulders and returned a gaze to his father.

"No one can help it that O'Banion has his hands in making a profit," he said. "I can earn for my family and get good marks in school. I've earned your trust this past year, haven't I?"

Evan raised his eyebrows before he returned to his paper. Aiden retrieved a history of the Roman Empire from his book bag and thumbed through it between sips of tea. They awaited the oatmeal in silence.

Margaret gave a Aiden a look to mind his father before

she set down the oatmeal and they ate. Tense glances flew across the plain, but clean, table as Evan shook the newspaper and Aiden spooned oatmeal to his mouth. The mood found a match for the shade of dark gray in the sky outside, only tempered when Aiden brought a smile to his mother's face by thanking her for breakfast and taking his bowl to the sink.

"I suppose you'll be eighteen soon enough," Evan said after a while. "You can't have your pa always looking out for you."

"I respect that, Pa," Aiden replied.

Margaret attempted to stoke more warmth by humming "The Irish Emigrant." While clearing any plates, she explained the beef roast to Evan. He agreed it was a good plan to make guests of those less fortunate. She kissed her men on the forehead before they left the house and went separate paths.

Aiden looked back at his mother and took off his cap in salute before he continued.

- - - - -

Before Sophia Golino left the house for her studies, she didn't say a word beyond the etiquette required of her as she made breakfast for her mother, herself, and her brother. Her morning greeting to Vincent came out in a monotone voice as she cleaned dishes. The only sign of warmth was her pause to peck Celia's cheeks and say goodbye, leaving her mother to blush.

The apparent domesticity disappointed Vincent more than if they'd had a confrontation. The events of Thanksgiving still pecked at his pride; however, neither sibling brought up the subject. The Golino household appeared quieter since, but unease lingered beneath the surface. He decided to direct any angst toward following his father's steps in the Outfit.

Vincent gave his mother a tepid goodbye before heading to the Four Deuces. He was happy to have given up school in hopes of actually doing something. Duty to help provide for his family wasn't his primary concern. He resented his absence from John Torrio's inner circle. Relatively recent realities recoiled in the rear of his mind during his walk southeast.

Vincent's father had been an idea man within the Outfit and had urged John Torrio to let Colosimo get bumped off. Despite Silvio's efforts and murder, which paved the way for moonshine profits, the Golino name wasn't getting the respect it deserved. The boss relegated Vincent to the status of average thug and errand boy, and his father's murderers ran free.

There were many reasons to not get on Torrio's bad side. Not only did Vincent not want to get a shiv to the throat, but he didn't want to disrespect Silvio's memory. As the new man of the house, he had to make his own way in the rackets, marry off Sophia, and have his own *figli* with a cute little wife. Angering Torrio wouldn't help.

As for the Outfit's affairs, he got word of the November Hawthorne Inn meeting and reconciliation between various providers of giggle water. Vincent inferred more from the meeting than the farce of cooperation.

The *diablo* who had shot his papa partook in it, for one thing. He was pleased to hear of cooperation

142

between the Outfit and Little Italy, but Italian brotherhood couldn't halt his thirst for vengeance. He kept an ear attentive to those taking care of business.

Silvio's replacement, Alphonse Capone, was more candid about Outfit activities than Torrio. Vincent appreciated Capone's *coglioni,* despite any envy regarding his status. He shut up and cleared his ears to listen when Capone had gossiped with lackeys the day before. Liquid happiness loosened tongues for a fortuitous exchange.

"That mick lout, O'Banion, oughta just stick to arranging flowers," Capone had jested to a few Outfit moonshine runners. "The fairy-lover doesn't mind hiring his same kind to ship bootleg. Tell you the truth boys, it wouldn't take a lot to knock him off, 'cept that Torrio'd rather not waste the money on bullets."

Back in the present, Vincent adjusted his black newsboy cap atop the dark locks on his head. Glancing at his reflection in the windows of a butcher shop, he remembered Capone's words. He tried to put off his thirst for revenge, but Capone had mentioned a flower shop across the street from the Holy Name Cathedral.

Vincent first had to be a lackey for Torrio on the Four Deuces Club. After work, he could head north to Holy Name and light a candle for his father at the cathedral. He rationalized that there was no harm picking up flowers across the street. It would give him a chance to study Silvio's murderer and any friends.

- - - - -

Aiden arrived at Schofield's Flower Shop more than half an hour after leaving his folks. He had wondered about his father's worries. He knew his father's intentions lay out of concern, but again rationalized that what his pa didn't know wouldn't hurt him.

"Good to see you, lad," Dean O'Banion said, appearing ripe with a bit of spirit in the morning. "Will you only be dyeing flowers and arranging shamrocks today or could you help me and the other lads with the libations to celebrate our dear St. Paddy?"

Aiden thought a few seconds before he responded:

"Since we are under the gun, I'll be glad help out at Allen's Storage tonight after class. I wouldn't want to leave my boss short-handed. Business is business, even though one is illegal, but pays more."

"Atta boy, Aiden." O'Banion said. "We'll be just doing warehouse work later on. The dagos want to keep things peaceful as long as demand stays high, so drop by after school to see what we do on Ashland and Division."

Aiden nodded and went to work arranging flowers.

An hour before noon, Aiden watched as Sophia walked in the door with a sway in her hips. She wore a plain gray, wool coat and white cloche hat that didn't quite cover the dark waves atop her head. Her crimson lips curved in a wry grin before Aiden addressed her.

"My lady, may I say you look like as beautiful as a blooming bud today? May I interest you in some white roses for you and the Sisters of the Blessed Virgin Mother?"

Sophia and Aiden's courtship had been coy since confessing their mutual connections to gangsters. Celia wouldn't likely see any problem, but they both figured Vincent would raise a fuss. They didn't venture toward each others' homes for now.

"Thank you, but I need something else," Sophia said. "I would like to buy one half-dozen pink roses for delivery to a Margaret McCarthy. You know the address, I think. I need to show her my appreciation for raising her son so well. A lady appreciates the fleeting gesture."

"The lavender roses that the young Irishman sent to Mrs. and Miss Golino were his pleasure," Aiden replied, playing along. "Though I shall make sure that Mrs. McCarthy's half-dozen are delivered this evening, post-haste, at no additional charge."

Sophia nodded after winking and pursing her lips. She then slipped a note to him before leaving Schofield's under lecherous glances from some of O'Banion's regular customers, both those buying flower-arrangements and those ordering crates of beer and whiskey. Aiden unfolded the note and read:

> *If you can steal time away from your family and duties tomorrow afternoon, I would like to meet you for lunch at the Dil Pickle on St. Patrick's Day. Jack and Venicia Jones are providing free ham sandwiches and potatoes before a night of spirits and dancing.*
> *Kisses, Sophia.*

Aiden decided. He would take a leave of absence from school and O'Banion tomorrow to not to miss the rendezvous. Despite the realization that his absence would seem conspicuous on both fronts, he tried not to pay much mind. He was too busy for that.

145

Aiden had to leave his untidy work area to rush to afternoon classes across the street. A dirty table could wait. He'd then check in at home with Ma and finish his evening with work in a bootleg warehouse. Evan's lingering disapproval stirred Aiden's Irish Catholic guilt, but not too much so.

2

Spoilers

Vincent Golino arrived via streetcar to State Street and Chicago Avenue as the sun drifted toward the western horizon. He'd spent his day roughing up deadbeat johns, gamblers, and drunks at the Four Deuces and was ready to spy on his father's murderers. He was itching for eventual vengeance.

After lighting a candle for his father at Holy Name Cathedral, he kept telling himself that he was just collecting information for now. He looked west across the street to Schofield's, and his left hand ran over Silvio's stiletto switchblade, nestled in his front jacket pocket. His cheeks flinched with fatigue and the effort he put forth to suppress anger

Three important-looking figures, each clad in a wool blazer, soon exited the shop and walked to a Packard parked along State. One of them, the mick he saw shoot his father, had a limp. Another mick, taller and more serious, joined a young-looking Polack to flank the murderer. The Polack surveyed the street with a furrowed brow, glancing over at Vincent. The young Italian took both hands out of his pockets to make them visible as the other flunkie started the car.

Vincent gave the appearance of only admiring the cathedral. He stole a glance as the Polack let his guard down and opened the Packard's door for the gimpy mick. With eyes back to the cathedral, he fought off any stray tears while listening to the killer talk to his men before entering.

"Alright boys, we're short on time, so let's get a move on to the warehouse," he said. "The shamrock delivery is coming fresh from Detroit. Police had to take a percentage to keep the Feds off our backs. At least we don't have to worry too much about the dagos."

"Sounds good, Deanie," the Polack said before shutting the door and getting in the back. The Packard then drove north and hung a left onto Chicago Avenue.

Vincent fumed as he frisked the stiletto. He'd get a closer look in Schofield's and buy a flower to remember his father. The swiftness of his pace matched his fervent convictions as he showed himself into the shop. No blood could be shed today, but it was only a matter of time.

- - - - -

Aiden crossed State Street from classes back toward Schofield's to check in as evening approached. He had just seen someone enter the shop. He followed, figuring he could at least help a customer out before stopping home for supper and then helping at the warehouse.

The stranger was the only other person inside, apart from O'Banion's recent hire, a dark-skinned porter in his early thirties named William Crutchfield. The porter stopped sweeping the wooden floor on for a moment to acknowledge Aiden's entrance and wave his hand to the customer, who was standing by a work table with arms crossed.

"Evening, Crutchfield," Aiden said to the porter, receiving a nod before turning toward the customer. "Good evening, sir. How can I help you?"

Aiden extended his hand in greeting. The olive-skinned face looked familiar. The handshake wasn't returned as the young man's arms remained crossed.

"I need a single black rose with some baby's breath."

"I'll just have to step in the back," Aiden replied, noticing that his unpleasant guest found something familiar in him as well. "Sorry to hear about your loss. Can I get you a cup of tea while you wait?"

"I'll take a brandy if you got it Though some spade-lover gin would do the trick. Them darkies don't mind showing a gal her place. The problem is boys with fairer skin won't do what's needed."

Crutchfield stopped sweeping and grunted as a warm sensation climbed to Aiden's ears. They both maintained their poise in spite of the olive-skinned lad's lack of manners.

"The deacons across the street swear by our tea; it's an import from Ireland," Aiden continued. He tried to coax more information by meeting intensity with innocence. "I'm afraid we don't carry anything that the devil would hand out, Mr...."

The young man didn't give an immediate answer. Instead, he leveled a tough guy stare that was an almost laughable cliche. Aiden returned a fake grin before he nodded his head and went toward the back of the shop.

The callous customer stayed put.

"I know damned right you got giggle water back there. You think you're the only business with cops on the dole?"

Aiden shook his head, grabbing three black-dyed roses and a few sprigs of baby's breath. He returned toward the cocky, olive-skinned wise-guy. He wanted to tell the guy to piss off but figured it wouldn't help.

"I haven't a clue what you are implying," he responded as he wrapped the small arrangement. "I can throw in these two flowers as well since inventory is so flush. Such flowers and arrangements are selling well this time of year and will only pick up after Lent."

The young man responded by paying Aiden the money for one rose, glaring with a challenging *maschilismo* as Aiden tried not to react with any wise cracks. The tough guy walked toward the exit.

"Please stop by again, sir, if you've anymore need for flowers for yourself or your family," Aiden called out. "We can always muster up black roses for our clientele."

"You Irish keep up with your games, I'll be sure to take out the last of yours."

Aiden had to wince as the putz headed out the door. He turned toward Crutchfield, noticing the porter had taken a break from his sweeping. He only returned a bemused gaze as they both shrugged their shoulders.

"There goes one ornery ofay," Crutchfield said.

Aiden guffawed with the porter before cleaning to his work table. He put the remnants of trimmed flowers in a waste can, wiped the wooden surface with a rag before preserving it with linseed oil, and gathered more refuse to dispose of outside. Thoughts of the rude customer stayed in his head as he worked. He remembered that he'd last seen such a similar display of *maschilismo* the day Evan had taken a bullet.

Before leaving Schofield's, Aiden checked in with Crutchfield. The porter said he had things under control, and they bid each other a good night before going separate ways.

- - - - -

Harriet Rosenstein wandered north on State from Superior, her thoughts on Sophia and her new sweetheart. That Aiden hadn't sought the company of looser gals impressed her. And although Harriet thought the he was a bit of a brown noser for sending Celia flowers, she had to agree that the gesture was well-done.

She had said to Sophia a few days ago that she could see why the gent ruffled her feathers. As a *de facto* older sister, Harriet just reminded her friend to use a rubber if they got to spooning. One had to avoid Cupid's Disease.

Sophia had just returned a mock glare in response.

Overall, Harriet held cautious optimism for her friend, whistling as she walked. The sight of Sophia's little brother, Vincent, put a quick stop to her gaiety. She recalled the memory of him mussing up Sophia's hopes to have a proper Thanksgiving. Even though the putz wouldn't recognize her, she decided to follow him with the stealth of an alley cat after a rodent.

She cursed the stench of male chauvinism Vincent

151

gave off, even though it made him easier to follow. The sight of Aiden leaving a flower shop soon thereafter made her uneasy. Sophia's sweetheart looked put-together, if not content. She followed the brother, even though she'd consider the link between the two.

Vincent stomped the ground several times while walking north toward Bughouse Square. He seemed to have a lot of hatred burning his short fuse, but managed a gentle hand for a small bunch of flowers in his right hand. Harriet had no doubt the thug would take frustration out on whichever dandy dared disturb him.

Harriet watched as Sophia's hell-bent brother slugged a fella in drag who had bumped into him. After throwing the flowers to the ground, he continued to smack the nancy around. With no intervention from police, he eventually stopped when a crowd of hobos began to circle around.

Vincent continued to snarl at people while retreating and heading back south. She followed until he could soothe his senses with paid company south of Randolph in the Loop. Ducking into a nearby speakeasy, she stewed.

Having earlier only wanted to snuff out *maschilismo*. Harriet came to realize her snooping could help warn Sophia and make sure she knew what she was getting into. It looked like her brother and her sweetheart were on a course of conflict.

"I may have to protect Sophia from her brother, her lover, and the Outfit," Harriet said to herself after shooting a dram of rum. "No one said playing the role of an older sister would be easy."

She continued with her rum well after twilight set in. When cool raindrops peppered the ground, she decided to skip meeting with one of her latest male companions and head west to her boarding house. Harriet wasn't in the mood for whoopee, company, or even a laugh. Tomorrow was going to be busy.

- - - - -

Aiden read the nervous pressure in his chest as a mix of happiness, passion, and trepidation. The ruffian from earlier and the guilt from disobeying his parents still had him on edge, but less so after checking in with Margaret. He felt well enough to continue to the North Side Gang warehouse as quickly as he could through a late winter drizzle.

At the corner of Ashland Avenue and Division Street, Aiden knocked the solid metal door that towered at least two feet above his head. The warehouse was built of rusty brown bricks and sported fading white letters proclaiming "Allen's Fireproof Storage." It was one of many such warehouses erected west of downtown since the Great Fire ravaged Chicago. The only distinguishing mark on the Schofield-leased building was a three-foot-by-three-foot Allen family crest. On it, three brown hounds stood at attention within circles under roaring red lions.

"Courage, vigilance, loyalty," Aiden muttered to himself as he waited with his thoughts. The chill to the air and freezing damp drops from the sky made him less than comfortable. He steeled himself against the elements, pondering the crest

A swarthy, rose-cheeked fellow with a flame of orange around his round, freckled face opened the creaking door. The man would pass as the archetype of a leprechaun had he stood shorter. Shining green eyes made the man's face seem more cordial than combative.

"Allen's Storage, home of Schofield's seed house and floral stock, my good sir," said the man. "Are you proposing a delivery, hoping to order, or pay an overdue fee? If you got my name by the count of three, you may get part of your parcel for free. But only if Mr. O'Banion likes you will I let ya be."

"You must be Robert Mullen," Aiden replied. "You may be the only man who can toss O'Banion by his legs across a room and still live to talk about it, but I'm the youngest to have given him a kick and not be limping myself. I seek to give my service, so we can do without any sense of avarice."

"Our reputations precede us then, Aiden," Mullen said with a smile. "Come in, we're trying out the new green dye and are having trouble unloading it all."

The two shook hands with a firm grip before Aiden tilted his newsboy cap in respect and stepped into the warehouse. It was the first time he met Robert Mullen or seen his boss's operation to prepare booze for sale. The clandestine operation inside rendered him speechless.

Inside, Aiden saw a Chevrolet ERTL truck. It was packed with Canadian Club brought through Detroit, which was now being unloaded so it could be processed, colored, and diluted on an assembly line.

Before heading to an underground cellar, whiskey was mixed with caramel color and municipal tap water to make a product with about half the original potency and twice the profit potential.

O'Banion came up behind Aiden, giving him a firm pat on the back.

"Dilute our stock, double our profits," he said. "At least we don't sell stuff riddled with rat waste, wood alcohol, and poison, like the dagos."

Aiden nodded, withholding any verbal sass with a gulp and a grin.

A boy of fourteen years handed Aiden a small shot glass filled with a brownish liquid. The fumes of potent, but drinkable, ethyl alcohol released notes of oak and vanilla. Aiden glanced at O'Banion before taking a sip.

"That's the unbastardized version, my boy," the boss said. "I give every man here two ounces daily to keep an understanding that their hard work helps sell a better product."

"*Slànte*," Aiden replied, raising his glass as he took a glance at the two dozen workers unloading and cutting bootleg whiskey into unmarked bottles. He gulped down the liquid, not letting a grimace form on his lips.

"Plus, the extra kick from the real stuff makes workers leery about stealing," O'Banion added in quieter confidence. "And should they try, they aren't as quick."

"I would never try to pull a fast one on such a scrupulous businessman," Aiden replied. He flashed a slanted smile and raised his left eyebrow to show how he took his boss's diatribes against lesser bootleggers. "How can I help the cause, then?"

155

O'Banion chuckled as if he hadn't killed a man for having less of a mouth.

"Agh, get to work, you smart-arse," he said before knocking the newsboy cap on Aiden's head. "All I gotta do is let your pa know what you're up to, and you'll find yourself in a pickle."

Aiden nodded with the respect he reserved for Evan and Margaret when they were angry. After straightening his cap, he joined Moran and Weiss to help unload crates of whiskey. O'Banion returned to keeping a close, but cordial watch on every aspect of the warehouse. They all labored as Rob Mullen kept an eye out for competitors and visitors, both wanted and not.

As the hour hand approached ten on the clock, Aiden tried to duck out, unable to avoid talking to the boss.

"I understand your pa wants you to get a proper education, even if that ain't in the rackets," O'Banion said. "You can't go cheating those you depend on. After tomorrow, keep us both outta trouble and spend more time in school. Go on home now like a good lad."

Aiden smirked to O'Banion and nodded with a grin to Mullen before heading home.

3

Prohibition's Second St. Patrick's Day

Aiden walked east on Division the next day before heading right on Dearborn toward the Dil Pickle. His steps were quick as he looked forward to meeting Sophia. His enthusiasm to seize the day remained, despite conflict with his father in the morning for missing school. He had skipped out of Allen's Storage in the hour after noon.

At least O'Banion and his mother didn't give him much grief. Margaret had loved the flowers from the anonymous gal. His boss seemed to understand that St. Patrick's Day was more a day for fun than work. The warehouse was quiet, save for several stray staff and Robert Mullen guarding the door, leaving only to take a few nips of beer and whiskey.

Because Margaret had told her son earlier in the morning they had enough for another person, Aiden was to invite a friend to dinner later. Aiden thought of two fellas he wanted to get to know better. William Crutchfield already had plans with own family and Mullen said he'd be delighted.

When Aiden arrived at the Dil Pickle at half after one,

the usual host in drag greeted him. The sequin-clad fella withheld giving a slap on the behind and just gave a polite nod. Aiden much preferred their encounters that way and tilted his cap in response.

Aiden smiled when he exchanged glances with Sophia from within the club. She looked marvelous in a knee-length, red-hued flapper dress. A green clover tucked in her hair over her left ear set off the dark locks that framed the dimples in her olive-skinned cheeks. He sauntered over to her, taking off his cap once they were at the bar.

She handed Aiden a ham sandwich as he ordered two whiskeys. They brushed lips before chasing passion with liquid fire.

"*Mama mia*, that's got quite a kick," Sophia exclaimed before she slapped Aiden on the behind and joined several other ladies to dance an Irish jig.

Although it wasn't what he remembered seeing his family dance, Aiden grinned as he tapped his shoe to the bouncing cadence. The crowd clapped in time as a tempest of fiddles and flutes filled the club. A row of gals kicked their legs with the beat. His eyes drifted from those of Sophia only when his gal's friend pulled him to the side.

"I need a word with you, buster" Harriet said, trying to lead him toward the exit of the Pickle. "It's a matter of your intentions with my pal, Sophia."

Aiden knew better than to argue with a strong woman, but pulled his arm away with quick jerk of his shoulder before he followed Harriet toward the entrance. He forced out a sigh of exasperation when she pushed some dancers out of the way.

"What's this about?" he asked, trying to be calm as he and Harriet stood in the alleyway outside the Dil Pickle. "It's a day for celebration with my family and a beautiful lass. I'd rather stay outta your scuffles."

"You're working with the North Side Gang," she said. "The brother of that 'beautiful lass' seems to have something against you micks. I watched him cause too much trouble yesterday to let it get back to Sophia."

Aiden's mind flickered back to the Schofield's the evening before. The curmudgeonly character to whom he had sold the black roses came to mind. In particular, he remembered the bile-filled final comment:

"I'll be sure to take out the last of yours," the thug had said.

"Get off it now, Harriet," Aiden said. "I'm in no rush to rough up Sophia's brother."

"And if the putz should put a death mark on you?" she asked. "What will you do then? Why are you hanging around her anyway, if she has to choose between loyalty to her brother and a good time?"

Aiden tensed as he saw Sophia step outside to see about the scene Harriet had brought about. She gazed at them from about twenty feet, viewing their stern faces.

"I'd never ask Sophia to choose between me and family," he said. "She's a kindred spirit, who I had only met by chance. I've hidden nothing. There's no beef with her brother. If he wants a fight, I'll figure something out."

As Sophia rushed toward both her best friend and her

sweetheart, the olive-skinned young man, who Aiden realized was Sophia's brother, came staggering down the street. His wavering steps signaled that he wasn't well.

"There you are, sis," Vincent slurred louder than a Bughouse loony. "Followed you from home this morning. Not only are you not helping the dregs of society, but your getting zozzled with them. Time to go home, now—"

"Vincent! Go back home before you get hurt!" Sophia shouted

The little brother made his way to Sophia with glassy eyes unfocused on anyone else next to her. Aiden and Harriet both stepped in front of her when Vincent reached to take her arm.

"Isn't this just precious, then?" Vincent said, standing in place. A look of recognition shined through his otherwise slackened face. "My sister is a lying *puttana*, protected by a hebe and a mick. Do you know this *bastardo* works with Papa's murderer?"

Within a few seconds, he pulled out his stiletto with his right hand and swung it wildly toward Aiden. As Harriet held Sophia back, Aiden dodged the knife, stepping away from the ladies.

The two tall, dark-skinned guards from the Dil Pickle rushed to the scene. One tried to grab Vincent, but was too slow and received a slice to his forearm. The other was quick enough to knock Sophia's brother to the ground with a left jab.

Aiden jumped into the skirmish, but instead of landing any blows, he pulled aside the uninjured guard.

The man had just knocked Vincent out with a punch to his temple and was about to continue. Aiden used North Side Gang diplomacy instead of his fists to keep Sophia's hot-headed younger brother out of the morgue.

"Sir, I'm sorry for the wound your friend received," he said. "But I'm afraid that my brother-in-law was too drunk to have his head on right. Please know that Dean O'Banion will cover your partner's injuries if you let me take the loony lad back to his mother."

The guard stood up straight and backed off. He tended to the other guard while addressing Aiden.

"If Mr. O'Banion will take care of it, I'll let it slide this time," he said "The name's Silas, and this here is Jeffrey. If I see that dago around here again, we won't be responsible for any damage. But Mr. O'Banion's got my word I never did see anything this time."

Aiden put his hand out to offer a handshake to Silas.

"Mr. O'Banion and I appreciate you being discreet, sir," he said, receiving a firm grip. "If you call an ambulance, we'll be out of your hair by the time you get off the telephone."

Silas made sure Jeffery had pressure on the cut, gave a nod, and left to call for help before Aiden got on the ground with Vincent.

With Sophia's help, they propped Vincent up enough to drag him away from the club, back toward State Street. Harriet then helped them load him on a streetcar headed south. Aiden gave the operator a small tip to not pay the three any attention.

- - - - -

Dean O'Banion toasted his wife, Viola, kissing her hands with pursed lips. In a hall closed to the public at the Drake Hotel, he then raised a toast to "the continued prosperity of my friends." A few aldermen from Downtown Chicago joined police and a few local judges at the table to drink Old Bushmills and other superior contraband.

O'Banion never thought that cheaper, but more polluted, rotgut would make headway, let alone gain a leg up from the Outfit. Lines still formed outside speakeasies south of Chicago Avenue, where the hooch was not only cheaper, but deadlier. His guests demanded optimism, so like any salesman, that is what he showed.

"I've mixed feelings about the Feds and Puritans who've made our business illegal," he said to the small group. "On one hand, they're restricting our freedom. On the other, we're making a pretty penny off the Fed's stupidity. Make something illegal and demand soars, especially for the real McCoy."

As guests chatted and clapped each other on the back, O'Banion took a gulp of Bushmills. When George Moran tugged at his side and whispered in his ear, the message jostled him even more than its delivery.

"Mr. O'Banion, I'm afraid that an incident demands your attention," he said.

Before O'Banion could wave him off, Moran continued,

"Aiden has volunteered you pay for the injuries of a guard at a club you sell to. It seems there was a young Italian kid."

"Little gobshite," O'Banion cursed to himself before putting down his Bushmills and addressing everyone. "Well friends, eat, drink, be merry with what God gave us. Please excuse me. Good business never rests."

He and Moran moved away from the guests into a back room, thinking they would be out of earshot of any hangers-on. Words spilled out before they could be sure.

"We'll pay for the guard's treatment. We've got to keep our retailers happy. But you make damned sure that Aiden gets here to explain how he got wrapped up with any Italian bastard."

"Officer O'Neill made sure that Aiden, the Italian, the two gals they were with, and whatever happened between them stays out of the papers," Moran said. "The guard, Silas Robinson, and his brother, Jeffery, sure got a rosy disposition toward Aiden. They seemed to think that he was helping his brother-in-law."

O'Banion mulled this over for a few minutes. The scuffle from last December outside Schofield's involving a feisty dame flashed through his mind. A small grin hinted on his face before he shook his head.

"I remember that grimy goombah, Silvio Golino, having a son and a daughter," he said. "Young McCarthy's been grinning a lot this past few days, ordering and paying for the flowers of a gal who lives south, near Randolph. I'm not sure that this'll be good for business."

O'Banion shifted from foot to foot and continued before returning to his guests.

"So Aiden's sweet on a Golino dago's sister."

- - - - -

While O'Banion and Moran chatted. Aiden's rival associate, Danny Keagan, heard everything in his duties serving bootleg for his boss's celebration. His earfuls from the previous week, being mocked as if he was a damned fairy, made him think how could use this tidbit about Aiden to gain favor from the Outfit or the Gennas.

He watched as O'Banion and Moran rejoined the jubilant group to indulge in evening festivities. After stealing two fifths of Canadian Club, he headed out on his own. One of the bottles would go to whichever group of Italians wanted his information. He stowed the other away for himself.

- - - - -

Aiden raced home in time for St. Patrick's Day dinner after making sure Sophia and Harriet had Vincent safe and sedated. Sweat dripped down his faced as he opened the door to their small house. With the excitement of the early afternoon, he'd almost forgotten that the McCarthy's were hosting company.

With the extra beef, Evan, Margaret, and he had invited several guests from their life. One of his father's poorer customers and his young son, a widow Margaret befriended at Holy Name, and Robert Mullen joined them. Evan had to move a desk to the cozy kitchen so that all guests would have a place at the table.

"Hurry and sit down, son," Evan said to him as Margaret brought out two loaves of soda bread, followed by about a dozen boiled potatoes on a platter. "Your mom's been slaving at the stove all day."

Mullen gave Aiden a nod as everyone feasted their eyes on the large beef brisket that Evan was thirsting to carve. Margaret led everyone in grace before they passed the food from person to person. The air was cordial, if quiet.

Aiden noticed Mullen was showing an interest in the widow, Shannon O'Grady, seated just to the gentle giant's right. He expected the lack of subtlety from the guard's gaze, so he moved events along with a nod to pass along food.

When Mullen spooned potatoes onto Ms. O'Grady's plate, she stopped him on the third potato and flashed a soothing smile. She wrinkled her nose before giggling.

"Ah sorry, ma'am," he said. "Suppose I should'a asked you first. Did you want some 'tatoes, Ms. O'Grady?"

"That's quite all right, Mr. Mullen," she said. "For the best fellas, manners can get mussed with generosity. I just hope we've saved enough for everyone else."

Aiden and Margaret joined the two with a polite chuckle. Margaret and the guests carried on with the others as grateful chewing mingled with inane banter.

Aiden's mind drifted elsewhere.

- - - - -

Earlier that afternoon, Aiden had helped Sophia and Harriet take Vincent to the Golino household. After taking a streetcar south, he and Sophia dragged him the rest of the way while Harriet thieved two baguettes and cheese from an outdoor market.

The three put the hot-headed brother into his bed with a concoction of hot tea and laudanum to ease his anger and pain. Celia didn't seem to be worried about her roughed-up son. She'd seen it all before.

Harriet's view of Aiden improved enough to join a conspiracy to keep the romance between him and Sophia on the down-low, telling Celia that the stranger helping out was a deacon. Celia didn't seem to pay that much mind to that either, giving salutations in Italian before returning to her room.

"I hear Gertrude's on Ohio and Damen has wonderful tea and scones," Sophia said before Aiden excused himself to head to his family's feast. "Gangsters have no love for tea."

Though the shop was just within the Outfit's territory, Aiden reasoned that his profile wasn't yet high enough in the North Side Gang for anyone to pay much mind. It was a date.

With plans in mind, Aiden gave Sophia a squeeze on the hip and a peck on the cheek. He followed with a nod to Harriet. He hurried home to not worry his mother and father as the ladies enjoyed the looted food.

- - - - -

Back at the McCarthy dinner table, Margaret gave Aiden a furrow-browed look of concern as she noticed him staring off. She followed with a noticeable kick from her foot to get his attention, followed by a polite grin. He gave her a wide-eyed, self-deprecating glance and a shoulder-shrug.

"Ma," he said after taking a bite of his brisket, "I don't know how you keep such a lovely home and make such a feast."

"God blessed me with a good work ethic and the mind to get things done," Margaret said. "I appreciate that you're grateful, but quit rubbernecking and pass the roast to our guests, won't you?"

"Yes, Ma," he said in a low voice before passing the food and returning to his beef and potatoes. While eating, he thought about introducing his pistol of a mother to his spitfire lady friend. The thought made his cheeks flush.

Aiden later pulled away a more-than-willing Mullen from helping Margaret and Ms. O'Grady clear the table so that the dishes could soak. He was afraid that the giddy, well-built doorman would break a dish by accident. It wouldn't end well for anyone, and Margaret thanked her son with a knowing nod.

"Pa's got a corncob pipe he likes to show new guests," Aiden said, taking his oafish new pal by the arm. "He's always dying to show it off. Won't you join the men by the front of the house?"

4

Hangover

Shock hit Vincent Golino harder than the loud knocks on the front door in the late morning several days later. He was still blurry-headed about St. Patrick's Day, and why he had slept most of the day after. He didn't see his sister or his mother as the knocking continued, so he answered the door in a robe to an Outfit associate.

"Mr. Vincent Golino?" the man asked. "Mr. Torrio wants a word with you."

Vincent, still a bit blue in the gills, wasn't sure if that was good news or not. As he had no idea what else to do and figured refusing the boss bore the potential for lethal repercussions, he responded with conjured confidence.

"I'll be with you in a moment," he said. "Just gotta get cleaned up, long night with the ladies."

Ten minutes later, Vincent emerged in Silvio's suit and his hair-combed with a part down the middle of his head. He knew better than to don his father's fedora and got his own door to take the passenger side back seat of the Cadillac. He tried to compose himself as he rode south.

Memory led him to having followed his sister to a club called the Dil Pickle. After hitting the sauce himself at a straighter dive, he was about to give her a piece of his mind when he ran into the mick working for Dean O'Banion and the hebe from Thanksgiving. The last thing he remembered was getting hit upside the head by a darkie. He couldn't remember how he or Sophia got home.

When he arrived at the Four Deuces club on South Wabash, a middle-aged flunky offering to open the automobiles door was a good reminder to observe his gang's hierarchy. Avenging his father and watching his sister might have to take a backseat to Outfit endeavors.

A less-hairy, but more muscular man escorted Vincent into the club's saloon. He let out a large breath before taking the seat Torrio offered. The two of them shared an oak table.

"Vincent, my boy," Torrio said as a topless blonde vamp the same age as Sophia filled both their glasses with a round of brandy, "just like your papa, you've made yourself a valuable player among us Naples businessmen."

Vincent listened as Torrio recommended that he spy on a North Side fella by the name Aiden McCarthy, whom he and Torrio had connected as one of Dean O'Banion's errand boys. Torrio also talked about how Aiden was sweet on Sophia. There was no need for Vincent to let on that he had figured this out. He accepted that Torrio was exploiting his family connection to take care of competition and reveled in the chance to climb up the Outfit ladder.

Shoving his sister under a rail car if he could make thousands of dollars for himself and his ma tempted Vincent for several seconds. However, he figured such actions wouldn't help him get the reputation he sought.

"What happens to my sister if any of this spying should go sour?" Vincent asked. "My responsibility to her and my ma is at least equal to my love for the broader *famiglia*."

Torrio gave few clams to the attending blond server before sending her to get him a coffee. He then returned his full attention to young Golino. The Cheshire cat grin on his face was just kind enough to put Vincent at ease.

"I'd never order anything against loved ones," Torrio said. "Where would our organization be if we played loose with our base moral principles?"

Vincent returned a smile before downing his brandy, content with new orders. The booze, flattery, and barely-covered bosoms intoxicated him with a sense of grandeur. Keeping an eye on his sister and her mick fella had a larger motive than personal vengeance. He gave Torrio a firm handshake to emphasize a new sense of purpose.

- - - - -

From a wall across the room, Alphonse Capone glared at his boss and the Golino kid as the two took Cuban cigars. Other worries than a potential loss of status ran though his mind. His primary predicaments weren't as serious as a demotion in the Outfit, but they still chaffed him.

Capone had sores beneath the belt that he blamed on liaisons with loose women and paid company. Not only but did they look strange, but they threatened to sow discord at home. His wife, Mae, had the audacity to complain about sores spreading to her. He had to keep assuring her that he was taking care of it.

Whores were business and his wife and son were private life, and Capone had to separate the two interests. After visiting a doctor, he started getting injections of something having to do with arsenic. He assured himself that he was feeling better already.

Capone smiled, figuring the Golino kid wouldn't have the wherewithal to keep family and business separate. Johnny Torrio had talked to him first about the McCarthy-Golino connection, so he wasn't worried about the runt. He beckoned a gal with the flick of a wrist.

"Hey there, toots," Capone said to an alabaster-skinned dame with ebony hair running down to cover her breasts. "I got coke if you're up for a good time. The first hit is a freebee. You may get more if you impress me."

The lady-for-hire took his hand and led him to the fourth floor of the Four Deuces. The stairs were a good warm-up for any forthcoming exertion.

- - - - -

Sunshine disappeared beyond the western horizon of Chicago's East Side as warmer breezes of the coming spring yielded to the evening wind. Aiden used the chill to shield his unease as he moseyed along Augusta to meet his boss. The need to report to Dean O'Banion after the St. Patrick's Day predicament wasn't surprising; he had used the North Side boss's name to diffuse a powder keg.

Outside Carrie's Ax, Aiden could hear commotion from the crowd within despite the relative earliness of the evening. He dreaded hearing what the boss thought about Silvio's disappointing son, let alone any rumors of an illicit relationship with his daughter. The sight of Robert Mullen somehow made it easier to bite the bullet.

"Evenin' lad," Mullen said as he saw Aiden. "The boss would like a word with you; I reckon he is in a bit of a mood. I ain't working tonight, so all I know is what I see."

Aiden tugged his newsboy cap down in greeting as he saw Shannon O'Grady step out when Mullen held the door. The off-duty, muscular Mullen tapped her behind, jostling it with his palm. She giggled before Mullen gave a low, yet friendly, growl. His eyes glanced to where his hand had been before he gave a sly wink.

"I'm sure the knowledge you get by what you see is better than what most men get by listening," Aiden said with a grin before they shook hands goodbye. He chuckled to himself as he watched his friend get frisky with Ms. O'Grady.

Inside of the main saloon, O'Banion sat in a leather-upholstered chair at a table shared with Earl Weiss and George Moran. He smoked a Cohiba as he sipped on a dram from a bottle labeled "Tullamore Dew." The grins on his lieutenant's faces showed that they were helping with the bottle. Aiden marveled at how his boss worked his connections to get the genuine article while everyone else in the speak drank diluted Canadian Club.

"There's the little pain in my arse," O'Banion said just above the din of the room. "Have a seat with the big boys, if you know what's good for you."

Aiden took off his cap before sitting down. He ordered a watered-down lager, courtesy of deals with Outfit breweries, and nodded to O'Banion's 'big boys.'

"I could make hay out of you necking with the daughter of the dirty guinea who shot your father, but the doll you fancy is your own damned business so long as long as it doesn't impact *my* business." O'Banion said with characteristic aplomb. "The lass's boneheaded brother is making that a difficult proposition."

O'Banion sipped his whiskey and gave a poker face.

Aiden reminded himself to not be put in a corner. He had handled Vincent with as much tact as he could muster. He had to protect his own interests, as well as those of Sophia, his boss, and to some extent, his parents.

"There's no reason to question my loyalty," Aiden said. "I not only stuck up for the stupid bastard to help my gal, but also to keep any beef he has with me or the North Side Gang out of the press. A wise man once said, "'tis better to impress aid to a rival than cut his bollocks off.'"

O'Banion gave a hearty laugh while he struck his right knee with the palm of his hand. He gave a toothy smile before he gulped down the last of the whiskey in his glass.

"You did the best you could on account of the hot-headed dago," O'Banion continued. "Just remember you gotta stick up for what's most important to you. Even better if you don't run afoul of the North Side Gang."

As Aiden listened, a drunk at a nearby table grabbed the blouse of a slim server girl, tore at it, and slurred like a drugged rooster to his friends. Her arms flew up to cover the slope of her shoulder and any torn cloth that would reveal the curve of her bosom.

"I tell youse guys, these Irish gals are so much looser than they let on," the drunk said to the embarrassed lass as she tried to maintain her modesty. He grabbed her brown locks with his hairy, ape-like hand and brought her face to his. "How much does a kiss cost, strumpet. Why don't you sit on my lap and I'll buy ya a stout?"

Seconds after the thug said it, O'Banion gave him an upper-cut punch that landed him on the floor. The stragglers with him stood up, but Weiss and Moran jabbed two of them in the chest with hard fists, sending them back down. When O'Banion patted the Colt revolver holstered underneath his jacket, the others held up their hands. The North Side boss only flashed his teeth and held a finger to his lips until the speakeasy crowd went silent.

"Laddies, we need you to get your friends out of here before there has to be more roughhousing," the barman said to the unwelcome ruffians. "Mr. O'Banion here is welcome to leave the coppers out of it if you keep pushing your luck."

The bullies soon cleared out with help from the

doorman. O'Banion handed the accosted lady two one-dollar bills. He also called over another gal to escort her to where she could regain her bearings.

"So, my boy," O'Banion said after he returned to his seat with his lieutenants and Aiden, "I won't ask you to put off your youthful pursuits, but you gotta keep your damned priorities straight."

Aiden stared with sober eyes at O'Banion, mesmerized with respect. The room at Carrie's Ax soon returned to normal as whiskey flowed again. He sipped his beer as an entertainer started with a flute and limericks in the background.

"You've my word then," Aiden said before the accosted server returned to their table to peck his boss on the cheek.

"That's mighty good to hear, lad," O'Banion said after returning the server's smile and asking for another bottle. "You'll join us for a real drink from the homeland before returning to your mother."

The server soon poured each of them a fresh dram.

Aiden smiled and obeyed with pleasure, taking in the laughter, limericks, and spirits around them. The warmth in his veins made him take his time heading home. He didn't want to go looking for trouble.

5

Palm Sunday

A group of twelve men and two women raved about
the sexual exploitation of women outside the Four
Deuces Club at four in the morning. Unlike the more
uncouth charlatans and preachers from Bughouse
Square, the ladies and gentlemen lining along South
Wabash smelled and acted as if they'd bathed in holy
water. They dressed in their Sunday best, in dark suits
and formal, white, ankle-length gowns.

The dozen or so "Soldiers for Salvation," as they called
themselves, marched along Wabash. Undaunted by the
stench of human waste, opium, and hashish that
peppered the air, they held their righteousness with the
same efficiency and fervor as their cadenced march. It
would have impressed the last Kaiser of Germany.

"Sons of the devil and followers of the wicked one,"
the clear leader said, "as a soldier for the Lord's will,
know that we will liberate the women you've taken as
white slaves. The fight for purity will free them from
unnatural lusts."

Danny Keagan snickered soon after he meandered
outside the club to see what the ruckus was about. John

Torrio wasted no time employing him full-time after Danny linked the Golinos and the McCarthys. The greatest loyalty test for Torrio was disloyalty to O'Banion. Keagan showed that freely.

The tall, cocky, curly-haired turncoat was more interested in wiles of women than a sense of honor among thieves. He snuck up to a young lady with chestnut-colored hair who was also watching the missionaries.

The gal's hair was wrapped up under a ruby-colored cloche hat that teasingly shielded her face from the glow of a nearby street lamp. Her swan-like neck led to a vee-neck blouse that hinted at a moderate-sized bust. The stocking-clad calves jutting beneath her hemline showed she was too liberated to be a holy roller and too sophisticated to be a prostitute.

"What're you lookin' at, love?" Keagan asked.

The gal gave a demure smile and tried to brush off his attention, pulling a jacket to her chest. He pressed on.

"I'd ask if you needed an escort, but I'm off to work soon in what those well-dressed preachers consider a den of sin."

"I ain't interested, bub," the gal said. "I'm just here for the show before I head to home and bed. Alone, for now."

"Well I didn't mean to suggest that you were selling your wares." he said. "I'm a bit of an outsider myself. Only work to make sure the boss and the girls get their fair pay. May I call you a ride? It's dangerous this time of morning"

The gal gave a slight blush when he whistled for an

Outfit-leased car. The rouge in her cheek stood in even brighter contrast due to the chill in the air. Despite his usual ineptitude with women, Keagan's found some confidence. When she held out her right hand, he felt obliged to take it until she held out her finger and poked him in the chest.

"I ain't anyone's good-time gal," she asserted with a grin. "So what's the skinny, buster? I'm between boyfriends."

The dame struck Keagan as rather pushy. On any other day he would have given up by now, but the mixture of moxie and beauty attracted him like a moth to a flame.

"*Mademoiselle*, I'd love to ask you to dance at a speakeasy or blind pig of your choosing," he replied, "but as any good gambler knows, it's better to play the slow game. Care to tell me where the driver should take you?"

Chestnut hair laughed and curtsied as her ride home arrived. He bowed with exaggerated graciousness and asked where she was headed. The dame pecked him on the cheek before she whispered the address to a Near West Side boarding house in his ear. When he tried to kiss her on the lips, she put a finger to his and rolled her eyes.

"At a later time, you should pay me a visit," she said. "By the way, what should I call you if you show up at my door?"

"Danny. And you?"

"Just call me Harriet."

Keagan gave the address to the driver and kept his

eyes on the car until he couldn't make it out in the distance. He strolled back to the Four Deuces, happy about his recent luck and new work for the Outfit.

Keagan then went to the Four Deuces club before his shift started. He tamped down any lascivious stirrings in his head about the fiery dame with a small breakfast of dry toast, week-old pastrami, and a slug of moonshine from Little Italy tenements. The sting of ethanol, with a hint of rat urine and wood alcohol, put him in the right mood to deal with delinquent johns before they rushed home to their wives at dawn.

"Out, you bloody bastard!" Keagan shouted, descending from the second floor as he chased one of the clientele who didn't want to pay for his fun in the cat house.

"You stiff the owners of this club one more time, I'll cut off the rest of the fingers on your bloody hand," he said as he waved a bloody pinkie finger above his head.

A few goons sympathetic to the john approached the Four Deuces, so Keagan shot off a Remington shotgun. The unwelcome company fled along Wabash to get away from gunshots, cops, and any other inconvenience.

Police soon surrounded the building, only to be paid off and make a quick exit. The protesters had left well before then, so there weren't any trustworthy witnesses available. The only thing that hung around the clearing streets were the entrepreneurial racketeers, along with the graft and passions that made them money.

When the morning rush slowed down, Torrio and Capone sent an espresso to Keagan. He declined the offer of a gal-for-hire. He preferred to separate business and pleasure, whenever possible.

- - - - -

The shotgun blast and the police sirens awoke Minka Summer, who had slept alongside Earl Weiss at the Four Deuces since 11 pm the day before. Her body flinched against him with genuine surprise as he gained consciousness. She felt cold despite of the heat of his body, the trappings of the sheets, and the beads of sweat on her brow.

"It'll be alright," Weiss said with greater conviction than a well-pleased john. "Owners of all the speaks, including your dago bosses, have a handle on the coppers and many of the Feds. What do you got goin' on in that pretty head of yours, anyway?"

Minka felt his hand on her waist as she rubbed the sleep from her eyes. She gave him a peck on the cheek as she gained her bearings. She pulled her emerald silk green robe around her before propping herself above her lover on one arm and lighting an opium-laced cigarette with her free hand.

"I try to separate pleasure from worry, but I'm frazzled tonight," she said. "There weren't any problems with you."

Weiss got up on his elbow and put a steady, calm hand on her shoulder as she handed him the cigarette and reclined in the bed. She sighed as she nestled herself against him and he pecked the space between her cat-like eyes. Waves of opium wandered to take hold.

"I heard Torrio talking with somebody about a dead dago and his son," Minka said. "I figured, based on the accent and what was said, that the fella used to be in with your boss, O'Banion."

Weiss put the dope on the side table, releasing her for a moment after they had both taken a drag.

"Thanks love," he said. "If there is a double-crosser, I need to know. See if you can find out more about this new fella. I'll see what I can do to probe into what's going on. I like to keep my house in order, you know?"

"Sure," she said.

Minka took a drag of dope and edged closer to Weiss. He put his hands on her hips before she opened her robe to him for a second round of whoopee. She preferred his arms over anyone else's, but their tryst ended with the disdainful reality of her having to trade pleasure for money.

"I wouldn't mind you being my only man." she said, placing his hand on her chest.

Rouge flushed Weiss's cheeks in response. He was otherwise dumbstruck.

Knowing that she would have to shoo him out and get to work gave her a bitter taste, so Minka ended their time with a touch of sweetness. She washed them both with cool, cleansing water before she dressed him and got herself into an outfit meant to tease. They parted with a kiss before both going downstairs toward separate paths.

6

Good Friday

With the cosmopolitan swank of post-impressionist paintings and art deco trimmings, Gertrude's interior seemed larger than it was with its high-loft ceilings. The hardwood floor, earthy-sweet, mocha-tinged scents and light chatter echoing through the smoke-laced room created a space for anyone, big or small. Businessmen and tramps alike sipped coffee and tea to help them take a break either from work or continued panhandling on street corners. Although they shared the homey ambiance of the salon, neither group deigned acknowledge the other. The air inside was shielded from cool, early-spring air flowing through the Ohio and Damen crossing.

Aiden McCarthy and Sophia Golino sat by one of the large, transparent shop windows in the late afternoon, grinning at each other. The banter between them signaled to anyone who cared overhear that their rapport blossomed beyond mere infatuation.

"The first time you got zozzled sounds rather different than mine," Sophia said to Aiden as they sipped Irish Breakfast Tea laced only with a teaspoon of honey. "Am

I cavorting with a delinquent?

"I wouldn't say that," Aiden replied, taking in her hazel eyes. "A pal, John Davis and I snuck some of Pa's whiskey while him and Ma where away. We were fifteen and we sang limericks until midnight. We were asleep when the folks came home, but the hangover was hard to hide."

Aiden explained about how he didn't have trouble with school because a snowstorm had postponed lessons. He still had a rough time of it, having to clear snow for his parents and older neighbors down the way. He added that he loved his mother too much to be considered a ruffian, expecting Sophia's grin.

His parents knew about the drinking because not only did he and John look rough, but a noticeable amount of his father's favorite whiskey was gone. Evan played a trick on the "little pissers" by putting a dram of cheap moonshine in their tea before they stumbled to the table for a breakfast of oatmeal mixed with sour milk.

Aiden admired the smirk on Sophia's crimson-hued lips as she ran a hand though her black locks. He blushed as he continued, using a lower voice for his father:

"'You look sick lads,' Pa said, pretending to be none to be the wiser. 'Take some of this spiked tea before you head out with the shovels. It'll keep you warm as you get to work.'"

Sophia laughed as Aiden explained that his pa put his arm around Margaret and grinned, watching as he and John and forced themselves to gulp the rancid liquid. The two turned an unhealthy shade of white before scurrying outside to make a mess of the sidewalk. His parents gave the lads a gentle green tea after they had returned the kitchen. They were then scolded to keep away from Pa's whiskey and to get busy cleaning up the mess.

"You can be sure I haven't imbibed as much since then," Aiden said back in the present with Sophia. "And I believe John has learned to not follow a McCarthy on a piss."

"Your ma and pa sound like a hoot," Sophia said before her face grew more solemn. "Thoughts of my pa and brother make me sick."

"Whatever their faults, I got to know you after all the run-ins. So it worked out."

It was Sophia's turn to blush as she held out her hand. He traced his left index finger over her right palm, causing it to flinch before he gave it a gentle grasp.

"I know that you've got troubles at home, and I'm not sure how I can help you," he said. "But I can always play the diplomat if your hot-headed brother comes looking for trouble."

Sophia took his hand and kissed it, returning a smile. They drank their tea and continued with the tale of her first time with too much wine at a family dinner when her papa was still alive. The conversation shifted from their shared admiration of women's suffrage, despite a shared dislike of Prohibitionists. After awhile, they just smiled and listened to the conversations around them, adding side commentary until it was time to head their separate ways.

"I'd like it if you met Ma and Pa," Aiden said. "Easter

will be too soon. Ma likely wants to just include family for dinner during holy week. But how about joining us the Sunday after?"

Sophia squeezed his hand and stood, prompting him to get to his feet. She nodded her head and pecked him on the lips. They parted ways, both grinning like fools, after he gave her directions to his house.

- - - - -

Vincent Golino watched from a block away at a newsstand on Damen. The mick and his sister seemed jovial after tea and a chaste kiss. Her good cheer fueled the opposite in Vincent. He ran his fingers over the stiletto switchblade in his pocket before he grabbed his lighter and lit a Lucky Strike. A fellow thug told him the smokes would help him relax.

Thoughts of Silvio ran through his head, and he assumed the worst about his sister.

"I'm only watching now, McCarthy," he muttered to himself. "But I'll shoot you before you take my sister away from her family."

Vincent shielded himself against a steady breeze as he breathed sharp smoke into his lungs. Watching Aiden, he fantasized of a chance to tear off the mick's limbs. His lungs burned along with his temper and the part of his neck behind his ears.

The cool breeze helped keep the hot-head in check. Vincent reminded himself of his duty to observe and report to Torrio. If not for the desire to make his father proud and keep a low profile to the coppers, Vincent would've drawn blood as red as that boiling underneath his thin, olive-toned skin.

Cigarette exhaust drifted like a smokestack from his lips as he looked on. He waved away a drifter begging for scraps in a tongue from Eastern Europe. Severity seduced him as he stood alone and noticed Sicilian eyes across the street. Hostility held Vincent's attention as much as curiosity about who he saw.

Little Italy's Angelo Genna appeared on his own mission to keep an eye on possible North Side Gang weaknesses. Just north of Gertrude's, the malevolent Mafioso gave a bum a wad of dollars and a knife. He stood back and watched, using a stranger do the dirty work.

Both of the Italians waited to see if Aiden had a knack for dealing with hard fellas. The bum was taller than Aiden by a good two inches, but his halted gait implied that he took much less care of himself. A blade and the brawn were supposed to be advantages.

The bum came up behind Aiden and punched him in the left kidney, demanding money. Pain was clear in Aiden's face when he spun around and shook his head. Aiden kept enough wits about him to unleash a surprise right hook to the palooka's solar plexus. The thief dropped his knife and stepped back, falling to the pavement after a jab to the jaw.

Aiden took the stiletto, the blade reflecting the sun's rays like a punch to the eye. He shook his head and staggered with a slight grimace toward the wannabe thug.

"What's a tramp like you doin' with this fine weapon?" he wondered. "It's a bit too nice. I'd say you've got someone putting you up to this robbery."

Aiden threw the knife to a stabbing halt before his assailant's upper left thigh. The bum only shook as his eyes grew wide and he whimpered to himself.

Any potential witnesses to the scuffle kept on walking rather than intervene. Vincent and Angelo only observed for fellow gangsters. They listened to gauge Aiden's actions rather than to report to authorities.

"You oughta be more careful with that knife," Aiden said as he extended a hand toward the prostrate ruffian. "You might get hurt. Now come on and show me whatever you got paid to heckle some Irishman coming from a tea shop. I gather you don't have enough gumption to do it on your own."

After the man got up, he handed Aiden the two dollars that Angelo had given him.

"S...sorry," he stuttered. "I like America and want help my mother."

"Aye, you sap, that's what most of us want," Aiden said as he returned one of the dollars. He took the stiletto and kept the other dollar as his attacker still shook.

"Run along and get home to your ma now."

The bum nodded his head in deference before limping off.

Angelo watched, giving a slight shiver of agitated nerves as Aiden walked off the attack with some normalcy. He took back the dollar and put fear into the dejected bum rather than follow Aiden to the North Side.

Vincent Golino took in the entire scene on the eastern side of Damen, a cap pulled down to hide his face. He admired the Sicilian, who showed no mercy. In Aiden's lenience, Sophia's brother only found weakness. He didn't doddle on details. Torrio was expecting him

- - - - -

Aiden's mind had been on Sophia and both his and her families when he stepped outside Gertrude's. He hadn't expected to get rough with anyone before Schofield's to help with Easter. Fate, vendettas, and greed had threatened to change his mood. The stroll northwest calmed the pain around his kidney and soothed his nerves.

After dropping the dollar into the alms box at Holy Name Cathedral, Aiden marched across the street into Schofield's at about five in the afternoon. He figured keeping his hands busy would put his head at ease. He needed to unwind in the simple world of flower-arranging for celebration, sadness, or ceremony.

What Aiden found brought no peace. His jangled nerves served him well as he opened the door and dodged, evading a vase that Dean O'Banion had thrown just left of the entryway. After tossing his newsboy cap on a hook by the door, itself hanging over shards of fine ceramic, he watched in silence as O'Banion raised his face from a ledger book.

The boss let forth a number of curse words before getting a hold of himself. A couple workers, including William Crutchfield, went back to task after the porter let out a sigh and paced to get his broom. Aiden avoided the mess and approached O'Banion's desk.

"Agh, bloody sorry lad,'" the boss said. "I've my undies in a bunch about something my bookkeeper found about the St. Paddy's Day rush."

189

"Sounds like a bit of whiskey could help."

"Why don't you grab the bottle and join me for a sit?"

Aiden nodded, obeyed, and shrugged off any shock. He served two drams of Canadian Club before toasting. It helped.

O'Banion explained that some sales were not accounted for in the North Side Gang's inventory. Nor had any profits for said liquor been collected. Gossip reached back to the boss about new North Side customers buying at a lower price.

The well-oiled gears in Aiden's head cranked before he rapped on the table with his right hand to show he had a thought. Before sharing, he stopped to take another sip and asked the other workers if they were thirsty. Only Crutchfield joined them before Aiden poured him a dram.

The boss chuckled and took his own sip.

Aiden filled O'Banion in on his run in with the bum, showing off his new stiletto. He wondered aloud if an Italian competitor might have been attempting a swing at him. He watched as O'Banion shuffled further through the ledger books. After a while, the boss clucked his tongue and gave a wink.

"Cheap moonshine is big in Little Italy," O'Banion said. "That stiletto could belong to one of those Genna goombahs."

The boss went on his tirade again about how South Side Sicilians were dealing poison. Aiden and Crutchfield remained silent, sipped, and listened.

"We on the North Side won't sell wood alcohol that would make you go blind or distillate laced with the waste of dead rats," O'Banion said. "I think we oughta keep an eye on the Gennas and any rats they have..."

Neither Aiden nor Crutchfield bothered to give their boss any guff while he was on his high horse. Instead of talking back, Aiden busied his fingers with flowers. Crutchfield returned to organizing orders in the back. Again, whiskey helped the work along.

Aiden completed several Easter lily bouquets for Mass on Sunday before helping O'Banion put the ledger books and the whiskey under a hidden doorway behind a shelf of baby's breath. The sun's rays were fading when O'Banion decided their work was done, signaling everyone to finish their tasks.

After cleaning up his table, Aiden put on his jacket and newsboy cap and got up to leave, noticing him and Crutchfield were the only one's present except for the boss.

"Don't keep your parents waiting lad," O'Banion said, handing him a lily. "Give that to your ma. Enjoy your Easter. There's no time to waste on the Sicilians until after we celebrate our Lord's Resurrection."

"I'm not sure she'll appreciate the gesture," Aiden replied with a mocking sincerity. "Ma and Pa, as most devout Catholics do, observe the Devotions of the Cross today. But I'll be sure to pass on your good tidings after Mass this Sunday."

"You're a right piss head, you know?"

Aiden tugged his cap, tucked the stiletto in his pocket, and gave a toothy smile before he stepped outside with the porter. He and Crutchfield chatted about family and parted ways at Market Street, wishing a Happy Easter before one headed west and the other went south.

7

Tough Customers

Angelo Genna and his brothers, Mike and Vincenzo, drove to a two-flat on Damen and Ogden as the moon hid behind the evanescent shadows of clouds in the sky. A few evenings after Easter, the three were collecting moonshine they had missed from Holy Week. The over three hundred gallons the Gennas had collected for the week had brought in around $1,500, but any missing moonshine mattered. It was as much a point of pride as future profits to keep producers in line.

Members of the Amato and Salco families, who distilled and lived at the Ogden two-flat, were first generation Italian immigrants. Unlike the Gennas, they lacked Mafia connections. They lived together in their humble, red brick, tin-roofed abode, running a still in the basement to support four adults and six children. Putrid, often poisonous fumes hung in the air.

The loud knock of Angelo's fist on the door of the two-flat jarred anyone within hearing distance. He stopped when the door opened a few inches to the silence inside.

"Is Don Amato here, *Signora*?" he said to a stout

woman in her thirties who stood half a foot shorter than him. "My brothers and I are missing moonshine. There's a problem with the books, you see."

He spoke with a gentleness that masked his intentions until he stuck a black wingtip-clad foot between the door and the frame. He glared into her eyes and showed the outline of a Beretta pistol in his jacket.

Louisa Amato didn't understand much more of Angelo's message than the sight of the gun, so she went looking around the house as the Gennas let themselves in. After returning to the foyer with her eldest son, Gino, she feigned that she couldn't find her husband anywhere, responding in Italian that she had looked among all the men and boys of the house.

With her negative reply, Angelo Genna grabbed her arm and twisted it at the elbow. Gino tried to help her until Angelo's brother, Mike, caught and bent his arm behind his back. Angelo demanded in a roaring Italian and English where he could find the swiped spirits.

The youngest Amato, Francis, at six years of age, meandered into the foyer and pointed the Genna brothers toward the kitchenette. Mike released Gino, who pointed out ten gallons of alcohol tucked away behind a hidden panel near the sink.

Angelo let go of Louisa Amato's arm, shoving her to the floor. He leveled the barrel of his Beretta 9mm at her forehead before Vincenzo restrained his arm and shook his head. Angelo shivered and shot the wall out of frustration before the brothers took the moonshine to their Cadillac.

Vincenzo returned to the flat and handed Gino $5

while his brothers waited in the car. He and the eldest son helped Louisa to her feet before he dodged a kick from young Francis. Vincenzo dragged the kid to the door by his ear and left him outside the home before joining his brothers in the Cadillac. Angelo and Mike shook their heads in disappointment.

"Should'a shot the little *bastardo*," Angelo said.

"We can't kill our producers," Vincenzo replied. "After tonight's lesson and a week of hunger, I don't think they'll try to rip us off again."

A satisfied smile crossed Angelo's lips.

"Let's just return this firewater home so we can decide how much to sell on the North Side and how much to the South Side," Vincenzo said. "Swedes, Poles, and Irish are more than happy to buy the goods at a better price."

The three Gennas rode in the Cadillac in silence for only a few miles west on Taylor Street. Sam Genna looked on as his brothers arrived with the recovered product. He lit a cigarette for himself and Vincenzo, calling him over. Mike and Angel unloaded some of what they gathered before sharing a pint of barely drinkable spirits in the shadows separated from slivers of moonlight. For the most part, the sky stayed dark, shielding the world below with dark clouds and the exhaust of industry.

8

A Noble Experiment April Fool

Dean O'Banion spent the morning arranging daisies for his mother-in-law at his flower shop. He considered it a welcome break from fulfilling arrangements for funerals, weddings, and Mass the coming Sunday. He cut twenty percent off the price of funeral flower arrangements for struggling families who lived on the North Side.

"'Give to Caesar what is Caesar's,'" he said to a dumbfounded customer. "'But give to God what is due.' Since the 'meek will inherit the earth,' they oughta get their cut too. I think that's what Christ would want. But then again, I was never that great with catechism."

Whether to keep Archbishop Mundelein as a loyal customer or to contribute to community, O'Banion donated five percent of his earnings, illicit and not, as alms to Holy Name Cathedral. He gave another five percent of Schofield's profits to the United Charities of Chicago. Once in a while, he accompanied George Moran to help dole out food to those who couldn't afford it, and always did so with a crooked, if full, smile spreading from cheek to cheek.

However, when his tough lieutenant, Earl Weiss, came through the door of Schofield's Friday morning, about an hour before noon, O'Banion's became much less concerned with morality. Gangland dealings were different, in particular when it involved the Genna brothers.

"Weiss, my man, I've been a victim of theft," he told his lieutenant, "and you know that I'm more into 'an eye for an eye' when it comes our less-than-legal business. In private matters, I'm more about turning the other cheek. At least, that's what the wifey prefers."

O'Banion explained the bookkeeping irregularities he had found and the back and forth with Aiden the Friday before Easter. Frustrations with the often heavy-handed Genna brothers weaved their way through the gossip grapevine of Little Italy. A few neighborhood residents loyal to the North Side Gang confirmed rumors.

"The Mafia guineas are ripping us off," he said. "Sill, I don't think most Sicilians are bad."

"I'd say that if we don't react, we not only show carelessness, but weakness, boss," Weiss said. "What do you have in mind?"

"*Un amico* tells me a rotgut shipment will be moving from the Genna warehouse on Taylor and Ashland this Sunday after late morning Mass," he said. "Trucks worth double digit large will leave to be distributed. I'd like to be there to take some of that."

Weiss wasn't one to shy away from needed conflict. He had no compunction about keeping an eye on Outfit competition from a rented bedroom at the Four

Deuces, but worried that his time with Minka Summer would be ruined by brazen gang conflict. He spoke of his hesitations to O'Banion, leaving out any mention of Minka or the wonder of her womanly wiles.

"I've a few notions on how to keep our arses out of the fire," O'Banion said. "I figured to use more slight of hand than force. Those Gennas won't see until Monday that they might have been slipped a Mickey Finn."

Weiss listened as his boss described how disguises, planning, and Genna overconfidence would help them strike back. A few roughed up associates and an accounting error would be the only things to hint that something was off. The plan charmed the lieutenant and made him happy, in part because he wouldn't be involved in the works.

O'Banion shook hands with Weiss before he poured both of them drams of Canadian Club and focused on the chrysanthemums, roses, and carnations before him. After the whiskey, the lieutenant and the boss made their way to warehouse work.

- - - - -

After noon at Allen's Storage, O'Banion approached Aiden as the young man helped cut Canadian Club with caramel-colored water. The boss pulled him aside, pouring them both a small pull of unbastardized whiskey. They wiped sweat-beaded brows despite a tinge of overstayed winter to the air.

"Aiden, lad, you know what keeps the North Side Gang better than all the other bootleggers in the city?"

"Oh, that's a hard one," Aiden said with a sardonic smile. "We're committed to a better product that isn't diluted by poisons or rat waste. Also, we'll never prey off the innocence of Chicago's virgins for the hairy horny hands of goombahs—"

"Smart arse," O'Banion interrupted with deadpan. "You shouldn't think I don't practice what I preach, but I still gotta sift through rubbish. Any manager's got to get his hands in the dirt. A man is working hardest when his hands are filthy."

Aiden shot his whiskey.

"Why don't you let me know what you want?" he asked. "Not too much into politics, too much work to do—sir..."

O'Banion put a grip on the young man's shoulder that made him shut up.

"You can't put your loved ones in danger, and believe me, I don't want that to happen either," O'Banion said before he laid out what he wanted Aiden to do on Sunday. He watched his young associate mull through the idea before responding. He expected a smart-tongued response, but the lad was pleasant.

Perhaps it was the boss's grip. Perhaps it was the potential for a hefty bonus.

"Well, if I won't have to explain missing Mass and I won't have to harm anyone too much, I suppose it won't be a problem," Aiden replied. "By the way, how much do I make off this sabotage? Pa could use a new stone to sharpen his shears, and I like pay for groceries to help Ma out in the kitchen."

O'Banion smiled back at him.

"You'd be one of the North Side Gang's top deal-makers some day if you want," he said. "Until then, let me offer you a payment that'll be hard to refuse."

9

Sunday, Suckers, Sentimentality

Aiden waited outside the Genna brothers' Little Italy warehouse, thankful Pa hadn't asked too many questions. He tried to disregard some of the ethics his parents had taught him, but his orders still made him uneasy. He vowed to inflict as little pain as possible while he rationalized his boss's orders against the Genna brothers as Old Testament justice.

"I'm glad that the Gennas are good enough Catholics to wait until after today's services to ship their moonshine," Aiden said to his tough-looking, older accomplice as they waited west of Taylor and Ashland. "You got any problem cracking heads?"

"We could be rippin' off the Chicago Archdiocese and it still wouldn't bother me as long as we're about to shake down dirty dagos," the other hijacker said. "If you get in trouble, you'll have to limp away on your own gimp legs."

Aiden's partner, Bruno Lanski, had the olive-skin and black-haired features of an Italian, but he was a Polish tough guy. Aiden's initial impression was that the man's hate for Sicilians was as great as his fondness for money.

He was about to see things weren't so black and white.

Bruno's features softened as he continued: "I know I'm more than a bit sour for some, but the ounce of sentimentality I've left is saved for my daughter. Otherwise, it's just a job. Beg your pardon if I don't smile more."

"You've got no problems from me," Aiden said with straight-laced lips and solemn eyebrows. He ran a hand through his auburn hair to push off any jumpy nerves.

The two returned to their surveillance from Marshfield Avenue, about fifty yards away from the Genna warehouse. They watched as two of the drivers entered Chevy ERTL delivery trucks. The trucks were set to join several others containing moonshine for speakeasies and lower-class blind pigs around Chicago's Little Italy.

Aiden put a smudge of dirt on his face in hopes of better matching the driver that was his target. Lanski only twisted his beard and pulled the brim of his cap lower.

They both watched as Chicago Police, led by Officer O'Neill, came from the north on Ashland to inspect supposed complaints received from neighbors.

As O'Neill led Angelo and Vincenzo Genna to talk with the officers on patrol, Aiden and Bruno crept over to the two targeted trucks, pulling a stiletto and a pistol on their respective drivers. While almost all workers in the warehouse and the two Genna brothers focused on O'Neill and other police, Aiden's silenced his driver with a blindfold and a gag. Bruno knocked his out with a blow to the forehead.

"Alright then," O'Neill said in a loud voice, signaling Bruno and Aiden that it was time to go. "I won't report this to the Feds if I get two sawbucks each for me and my four colleagues."

Vincenzo paid each patrolman the bribe as Angelo memorized faces of the police for future retribution.

O'Neill then directed Aiden and Bruno in one direction as he motioned another direction for other drivers. The two North Siders headed to Allen's Storage, losing their police escort about halfway through the two-mile trek north. Police kept an eye on trucks that weren't hijacked as they made their deliveries to the West and South Sides.

Aiden and Bruno delivered the moonshine with vast applause from workers in Allen's Storage. After crates of the inferior quality booze were unloaded, the two drove the ERTL trucks southwest to Kedzie and Ogden. They left the hijacked drivers and trucks there.

Aiden placed a dollar in the front pocket of the driver he had left gagged. He took off the driver's blindfold just before he left. It was the Sabbath, after all, and he was inclined to show humanity to his mark. He was sure Bruno wouldn't extend the same charity.

After a North Side Gang driver returned him and Bruno to Allen's Storage, Aiden took a one hundred dollar bonus from O'Banion for the Genna moonshine. Although he had been nervous about the heist, he was happy to have earned a month's wages. In a few hours, he'd introduce his lady friend to his family. He had to keep a move on.

- - - - --

Bruno Lanski was grateful for the extra hundred dollars in his pocket but didn't stay for any of the fanfare. Upon return to Allen's storage, he collected his money and snuck out. He had to respect his young accomplice, Aiden, for having a similar ethic. They'd both done their jobs, got paid, and continued on to more important plans.

Bruno returned to his two-room, brown-stained, oak-shingled house two blocks north of Milwaukee and Damen around half after five. His otherwise dour features changed when his daughter answered the door. He gave her a hearty hug and they exchanged broad smiles that brightened otherwise soot-smeared faces.

"Well, darling looks like we'll be eating meat tonight," he told sixteen-year-old, Anna Lanski. Their living space was inviting with soft glow of a gas lantern and the fragrance of fried butter in the air.

Anna returned to the kitchenette on the other side of the room to add paprika and garlic to the potato and cabbage stew she was making. Her father helped her sear the chunk of pork shoulder he had brought home before it cooked at a relaxed pace with the vegetables and savory broth. The two sat by the lantern and talked about Anna's studies.

Bruno's wife had died in a struggle eight months ago with thugs at the Chicago Avenue border separating gangland influence. He had since built his world around supporting his daughter. He was in constant worry that some hoodlum would take her from him, not trusting anyone who spoke Italian. Dean O'Banion's speeches on protecting innocent girls from lecherous men won him over. The flower-arranging gangster also paid pretty well.

In just over an hour, he pushed away his worries and he and Anna took seats their simple, pine table. After she said grace, the two ate in pleasant silence. They enjoyed the stew before Bruno cleared the table and soaked dishware. They went to sit around the lantern afterward with tea for her and potato vodka for him.

Anna read *Gulliver's Travels* in her lap as her father wrapped himself in a quilt. Although he was himself unable to read, Bruno loved it when his daughter did so. He wanted to make sure she could afford to study at a university. He knew that he'd have to pull more jobs with O'Banion to make the dream a reality. Her marks in school were never an issue.

"Go on dear," he said with a gentle pride. "We've got time until you are off to bed to prepare yourself for studies tomorrow."

Anna smiled and read on.

> 'Ingratitude is amongst them a capital crime, as we read it to have been in some other countries: for they reason thus; that whoever makes ill-returns to his benefactor, must needs be a common enemy to the rest of the mankind, from where he has received no obligations and therefore such man is not fit to live,'

A tear welled up in Bruno's eyes as he sipped vodka and listened in silence. After another hour passed,

Anna would lead him to his bed and give him a kiss on the cheek. Her lips grimaced when she tasted the vodka herself. She decided to stick with tea and *Gulliver's Travels* before sleep also found her.

- - - - -

At about six in the evening, Sophia Golino showed up outside the McCarthy household. Margaret was excited at hearing that Aiden had invited a friend for dinner; however, she didn't expect the friend to be a young woman clothed in an ankle-length skirt and navy blue cardigan. She answered the knock with a slanted smile that exuded nervousness.

"Mrs. McCarthy, I presume," Sophia said, giving a pleasant nod. "Aiden has told many kind things about you and his father. I'm his friend, whom he for dinner. My name's Sophia. I brought some Naples-style bread pudding for a treat at the end of the meal, if it suits you. You're the lady of the house."

Margaret calmed her smile and took the bread pudding, extending her hand in greeting.

"That's darling of you, miss," she said. "Please step inside as I call the men."

Aiden had already entered the kitchen, wearing a white, button-down shirt and brown tie. Evan followed close behind, somewhat bewildered that their company was a lady. The elder McCarthy grew somewhat bashful upon remembering he had forgotten to shave. Sophia gave a polite smile when he blushed.

"Let me take your coat, my lady," Aiden said as he gestured for their guest to sit. Margaret brought out a honeyed ham and potatoes as her son introduced their guest to Evan. They all took a seat.

Margaret led them in grace before breaking bread and starting their dinner. To make their guest feel at home, Aiden's parents talked about family and poked fun of their son as they ate. It was something they'd do more often, if given the opportunity.

Evan explained how Margaret and he had met, and his eventual investment in the barber trade. They both took turns telling stories about Aiden standing out in school, such as his erstwhile exclamations back in primary school that "Me and St. Patrick are the only ones with power to protect against the asps!"

Sophia chuckled as a bashful Aiden smiled. She congratulated them on handling the drinking party Aiden had with schoolmate, John Davis.

"You gotta keep him in line, I imagine."

"Aye, it's been a right pain having to listen to teachers go on about his rebellious ideas," Evan said. "But he's our son and we'd rather him ask questions than be a dunce. Aiden wouldn't be a McCarthy if he didn't have a bit of piss and vinegar about him."

Margaret shot him a look about language, which prompted Evan's quick apologies to the ladies. Aiden gnawed on a piece of bread and kept his mouth shut for the time being.

"What about your family?" Evan asked. "What do your parents do, miss?"

Sophia appeared hesitant. She didn't want to lie, so she kept as close to the truth as she could. She wrung her olive-skinned digits as Aiden nudged her foot under the table in what he hoped would be a taken as a supportive gesture.

"My father had been working wholesale in the spirits trade, trying to make do after Prohibition," she said. "He hasn't been around for the past year, though. Mother and I keep house the best we can with money I make serving at a club. My brother is bossy, but I can't fault him too much."

Around the table lurked a quiet intensity before Margaret provided a needed transition.

"Oh dear, my uncle and I had a devil of a time when I was a kid after my parents passed," she said. "It takes a grown lass to make the best of it. Bless your heart and those of your family. You've brought us a wonderful addition to our table. I'll bring the sweet cream to enjoy with the lovely dessert you brought."

Sophia grabbed Aiden's hand in the one of the few open displays of affection they shared among his parents.

They all enjoyed the bread pudding Sophia had brought while Evan attempted mild-mannered banter about colorful "gobshites" who frequented his barbershop. Margaret reminded him several times to calm down the language. Aiden only rolled his eyes as Sophia gave soft smiles and urged Margret not to worry.

After the meal, Sophia thanked her hosts, being rebuffed from any offer to help clean in the kitchen. Aiden offered to escort her home. His parents approved.

It was about nine in the evening when Aiden and Sophia arrived at her house on Peoria and Randolph. Sophia took Aiden's hands in the warmth of her own when he brought her to the door. She kissed him on the lips, and he responded with his, wrapping his arms behind her waist.

"I think your first evening with the McCarthys was a success," he said.

She put her hand on his left cheek, caressing it as she replied,

"It was a wonderful and genuine escape I hope will happen again soon. Your family is lovely. If Ma get's more like her old self, it'd be grand if we could all join in a hearty dinner."

Aiden pecked her lips before they grinned goodnight and parted.

- - - - -

Inside the Golino house, Vincent watched from his bedroom as the two went separate ways. He could have been happy for Sophia. Either Aiden was proving to be a gentleman or his sister was showing herself to be more traditional than he thought. He wasn't looking to be content, however.

Vincent hadn't observed any of Aiden's earlier escapades looting the Gennas. He could only confirm what John Torrio already knew. The Outfit didn't yet sanction Aiden's killing, and he felt his sister didn't respect him. Sophia's smiles only angered him.

"I'll be damned if some mick makes off with my sister," Vincent said to himself before he returned to his bed with a diluted, bastardized bottle of brandy. "Pa would agree with that."

He smoked a Lucky Strike and listened as Sophia attended to their mother and got ready for bed in

Celia's room. A peaceful silence lulled the two to sleep while Vincent stubbed out his fag and relied on the tarnished spirits that coursed through his poisoned bloodstream.

- - - - -

Evan McCarthy washed his face in the small water closet of his Chicago Avenue house. He exited, talking about their dinner visit as Margaret tucked herself under the cotton covers of their bed. The wool blanket atop served to make them both snug as they got used to not waiting up for their nearly grown son.

"Sophia was a nice gal, wasn't she?" he asked.

"I'd say she was a doll, being a guest in my home and still offering to help clean. I also think that she's a good influence on Aiden. Anyone that can make him blush about his mistakes and compliment our parenting is good in my book."

Disquiet flashed in Evan's eyes despite the coziness of the room and their bed.

"She said her father was 'in spirits wholesale' and then disappeared for about a year," Evan added after a click of the tongue. "That's about the time an Italian shot me in the leg. I might add that our dinner guest bore a slight resemblance."

"Poof, keep your conspiracy theories to yourself, bub. She has Italian looks about her. But as it says in Ezekiel, 'The son will not bear the punishment for the father's iniquity.' I would add that neither does the daughter."

"You know scripture better than me and should know I'd never disrespect any visitor to our household," Evan said. "But our son is gone more often than not, and he oughtn't get involved with lawbreakin' influences."

"Evan David McCarthy, you know we may be the only ones who protect Aiden and ask nothing in return. But our boy's got a good head on his shoulders. That young lady is proof Aiden's using his noggin more often than not."

Nestled in bed, Evan pecked Margaret on the forehead before he extinguished the lamp and decided to let his notions be.

"You've always been the wise one," he said before he joined her to catch a good night's rest. "I love you, my Irish rose."

"You damned well better," Margaret said. "I've no time for blarney. I love you too, remember."

10

Wednesday After the Heist

Clouds blocked the sun from shining any spring warmth on the three-story brick house on Taylor, where Sam Genna lived with his family. He and his brothers were still fuming after two ERTL trucks, along with thousands of dollars of booze, had been stolen the Sunday before. Too busy leasing land and making deals with Mayor Big Bill, Sam tasked Vincenzo and Angelo to work out retribution.

Vincenzo wrung his hands while he listened to Angelo recall events and suggest ways for dealing with the missing profit. Being older and more mild-mannered, he still had to listen to Angelo's ideas despite any misgivings. If for nothing else, he wanted to keep things copacetic within the family.

Angelo raved about how he spotted a Polack driving one of the trucks heading north on Sunday. After having found the two hijacked trucks around Kedzie, he only found one tied-up, unconscious Sicilian driver. The other truck, was empty, save for a gag and some rope on the passenger side. He figured finding the Polack was the key.

"There's plenty of Polish shops west of Kilgubbin, in O'Banion's territory," Angelo said. "If we go smashing shops and asking about any neighbors helping out mick friends in the North Side, we're bound to come across the blockheads who stole several grand of our coffin varnish."

Vincenzo thought the suggestion brash, even if he enjoyed Angelo's chutzpah. His job was to direct the spark of rage to not burn down any semblance of gangland peace. More war meant less money. The older brother rubbed his hands on his temples, sighed, and took a shot of moonshine before responding in a cracked voice to match how he felt.

"And that would leave us in the pits with Dean O'Banion and his gang." he said. "Though I don't like those mick and Polack monkeys any more than you, Torrio wants us to keeping dealings more or less calm."

"I think we oughta hire help," Angelo said. "I got a bum to attack one of O'Banion's cronies the other day. It looks like the mick is sweet on a dead Italian's daughter."

Vincenzo was rapt with attention. He hadn't expected such foresight and footwork from his brother. He lit a Lucky Strike and inhaled as a stream of pleasant coolness coursed through his veins. The smoke relaxed him.

"This McCarthy character proved formidable. He not only knocked the bum on the ground, but gave him a dollar back out of pity," Angelo said. "But if we hire some recent arriving ruffians from the old country, they oughta do a better job than some worthless wino."

"As long as the Genna brothers aren't found to be reneging outright on the Cicero territory agreements , where's the harm in helping fellow Sicilian immigrants earn dough?" Vincenzo said. "We need someone at least as intelligent as us to take the lead."

"I'll brief and prep the boys I find, offering a few bottles of spirits from our backyard," Angelo said. "We'll know who screwed us soon enough. Me and Mike will be there out fellow countrymen. Even if we put a bee in the North Side Gang's bonnet, Torrio is more than willing to overlook Sicilians helping Sicilians."

Vincenzo clapped Angelo on the shoulder and they toasted with a shot of homemade medicine. He felt good about the plan of action before reporting it to Sam. The lead brother approved.

"We need *coglioni* to strike fear into anyone who would steal from us," Sam said to Vincenzo. "Angelo is often too quick to temper, but you and him will find a good balance. *Andate in pace, mio fratello.*"

11

Savage Saturday

O'Banion was in a decent mood, balancing ledgers at Schofield's over laced coffee and cake Viola had made. He and the help had fulfilled most of his flower arrangements, the porter was stocking supplies and organizing orders, and Moran had called earlier from Allen's Storage to report that "the boys are handling supplies as smooth as Siamese silk." He was considering catching afternoon Mass across the street and surprising the missus for an early supper.

Just before noon, Aiden and Robert Mullen busted through the door, putting off pleasant plans.

"Boss, there's a ruckus to the northwest by Wicker Park," Mullen said. "A bunch of hairy goombahs are going into shops and homes looking for stolen liquor."

O'Banion got off his chair, called to two men who were finishing flower arrangements, and turned a sign to say the shop was closed. He punched a table, told the porter, Crutchfield, to clean and keep a lookout, muttering words about "degenerate dagos" while putting on his coat. Aiden and Mullen went back out the door to a Packard parked out front, knowing better than to wait for instruction.

"Did they mention anything about missing moonshine?" O'Banion asked as they all assembled in the car. He made sure his Colt pistol was in his shoulder holster as the others checked their weapons, making the count three guns and two knives. "The Sicilian guineas are liable to rough up civilians since we outfoxed them last week."

"They didn't say," Aiden said from the back seat, "but they gave a rough description that could lead to our man, Bruno Lanski."

"Just keep on driving," O'Banion said to Mullen. "We got to make keep any bloodthirsty bastards from running amok."

- - - - -

Schloski's Deli, which catered to Polish Catholics at its location just south of Milwaukee between Damen and Division, was quiet on ordinary Saturdays. The occasional repentant Catholic mother, hoping to make a fine meal on the Sabbath Day, could be count on to pick up a ham. The group of strangers speaking Sicilian-accented English and Italian disrupted the daily grind around lunchtime.

"You know who might steal moonshine for a little extra silver?" asked one. "If you can't help us, we may be forced to put the push on your family."

Another pulled a Beretta pistol on the owner, Marek, who shook behind the counter top. The ruffian jabbed the barrel at his head to make a point

Marek knew a lot of his customers, owning the primary delicatessen in the neighborhood. He hadn't been willing to share much information with any goons until they threatened his family. The gun was persuasive.

"Mr. Lanski might know something," Marek said, giving the address. "It looks like he came into some dough last week. You fellas can't get too rough with a guy for making a living."

Marek went silent when the thug with the gun drew an index finger across his neck and snapped his fingers.

Two stocky Sicilians came up to the counter to stay with Marek before the apparent leader convened outside the shop with any remaining hired guns. The two helped themselves to bread, smoked ham, and smoked lox, both taking turns jostling their captive. Their severe, olive-skinned faces were as hard as the clubs in their hands.

"Let's head out and knock around some Polacks," Marek heard from outside as he stood numb.

Knowing the Lanskis were only blocks away, he was able to kick a silent alarm leading to the back of the shop. On any other day, the signal was meant to warn bootleggers when the Feds showed up for surprise inspections. Unable to move, he hoped that his stock boy, Jozef, was sharp enough to escape unnoticed to warn the Lanski family.

As it turned out, the boy was already on his way.

- - - - -

Fifteen minutes later inside the Lanski household, Jozef Kaminski had already warned Bruno and set up surveillance from an open window in view of the entrance. Having brought a Winchester carbine from

Schloski's, he trained his sights on the throat of an olive-skinned man approaching on foot. He had just seen the wiseguy pointing a gun at his boss, and enjoyed the change in circumstance. Three men followed the man in Jozef's sights, who promptly gave a loud knock on the door.

The seventeen-year-old stock boy felt compelled to pull the Winchester's trigger, but hesitated when Anna answered while her father loaded his Ruger pistol. Jozef held hope that common decency would rule out any danger. He relaxed his trigger finger, which was attached to a burn-scarred right hand.

It turned out the thugs had no compunction with threatening a young, unarmed woman. Her meek greeting was met with the barrel of a Beretta aimed at her chest.

"Can I speak to your papa, sweetheart?" the thug asked as three meatheads stood behind him. He amplified the anxiety by cocking his weapon. One of thugs, who looked related by blood, was the only other one to hold a gun. They all menaced with glares and clenched fists.

Bruno, having left his Ruger by his bed, came to Anna's side with his hands above his head.

"What are you doing pulling a weapon on my daughter?" he asked. "Hey, Angelo, Mike...My little girl hasn't been the same since her ma was killed south of Chicago Avenue. I didn't have any problem with Italians till that happened."

The fine hair on Jozef's neck stood at attention when Angelo shrugged and forced a lop-sided grin that was

222

cordial enough to skin a cat.

"You look like someone who's stolen from us not too long ago," Angelo said. "We got no qualms with your daughter, but if you can't find us several grand or that much worth in moonshine, we got problems."

Bruno held his hands high as his daughter stepped back. Angelo held his pistol toward them, moving it back and forth as if keeping time with a cuckoo clock from hell.

Jozef approached the scene from behind, holding his carbine to his side as Angelo trained his Beretta on him. The two shouted at each other in their mother tongues before a shot interrupted the babel of anger. The stock boy fell down before Angelo punched Anna in the gut, putting her the floor.

"Better move and help us however you can," Angelo said. "Otherwise, I can't say your people will get help in time."

Mike clipped his brother with fraternal hostility on the shoulder, raising his eyebrow.

"Let's get back before the coppers get a tail on us," he said.

Bruno didn't put up a fight as goons led him to a Cadillac parked down the street. In his mind, he wished death for Angelo. The goons who rushed him to the car, elbowing him in the ribs, provoked the same feelings.

As the Cadillac drove off, the lady next door to the Lanski family came over to help Anna and Jozef, finding both on the floor and him with a bullet wound grazing his shoulder. Her husband tried to call Dean O'Banion at Schofield's and got word "the boss is already on his way."

O'Banion and his associates came to the Lanski's door within minutes. The boss dialed for the ambulance and friendly police officers as Aiden, Mullen, and the neighbor attended to Jozef's shoulder and Anna's belly. Sirens blared in the distance until they could load the wounded for Cook County Hospital.

Alphonse Capone, having followed the Gennas and watched the drama, had already headed south in a Cadillac.

- - - - -

Parades of prostitutes, lines of gamblers and drunks, and clusters of otherwise respectable businessmen were itching to pay for vice at the Four Deuces Club as early evening approached. Yet John Torrio was in a bad mood. Despite evidence of profitable weekend evening traffic, his lieutenant brought troublesome news from the Northwest.

Capone had wanted to keep as close an eye on friends as on enemies, and had followed Angelo and Mike Genna after a moonshine deal. The two Little Italy fellas led a gaggle of Sicilians to rough up several businesses on Damen. The brouhaha wasn't cause for fuss until civilian casualties. The news grew worse when O'Banion and Irish-friendly police came to the scene. The Outfit had to act.

"I don't care as much about who started what as about who's going to pay," Torrio said. "Our friends in Little Italy were hitting hard enough to have been provoked. Those North Side micks are a shifty bunch."

"I'll say, Mr. Torrio," Capone said. "Just tell me what

you wanna do. I'll make it happen."

One of Torrio's longtime doormen interrupted the back and forth. Capone stood with uneasy attention, happy to follow orders.

"Mr. Torrio, a Mr. Dean O'Banion and his lieutenant are here and would like a word," the doorman said.

Torrio told the man the North Side fellas could enter after handing over their firearms. He urged Capone to take a seat as they waited tight-lipped and silent. Both put on their best poker faces, masking tempestuous thoughts with outward tranquility.

O'Banion and George Moran took off their fedoras and surrendered their firearms at the door. They followed an escort to Torrio's table, not bothering to shake hands, take a seat, or otherwise signal cordiality or comfort. They appeared neutral, if not humble.

"*Signore* Torrio, the Genna brothers and the North Side Gang have been breaking our treaty on territory," O'Banion said. "We each have our own version of events, but I offer truce. I think you'll agree it's better for business."

"I only heard there was a problem between the Poles and Sicilians," Torrio lied. "The Gennas have a right to punish rule-breakers."

"I gotta respect your point of view, *signore*," O'Banion said, not showing any frustration. "I just ask that you tell the Sicilians that we hope Bruno Lanski will come to no harm. He's a good man and his family has suffered. Where's the profit and goodwill in that?"

Torrio realized O'Banion was trying to appeal to his so-called better nature. Still, he had to maintain a facade of ignorance and impartiality. He relished his position with an inward grin, unnoticeable to anyone but Capone.

"And what sort of gentleman's guarantee should I offer the Gennas on your behalf?" he then asked. "I've never heard of this Lanski character, but I'm sure that a show of goodwill will encourage our friends in Little Italy."

O'Banion asked Torrio to allow the doorman to bring forth a leather briefcase, which had been checked at the door. The three allowed Moran to open the bag, which contained two thousand in cash and a fifth of French brandy. A few drunks around them showed interest before Capone flashed a revolver.

"The dough is for the Gennas' goodwill; the booze is for you if you set the exchange," O'Banion said. "The kicker is eight thousand dollars worth of diluted drinkable alcohol for the Gennas if they release our man, Bruno, without too much harm. We just have to load empty trucks back at our storage."

Torrio grinned. He nodded his head before looking at O'Banion.

"You or your boys may have started a ruckus," he said, "but I'll see what I can arrange for our future."

"I figured you'd be the man to see," O'Banion said.

"Your instincts are correct," Torrio said. "You got my word I'll talk to the Gennas. But before you leave, would you care to relax with a drink or a dame?"

"Please don't be offended if we refuse," O'Banion responded with gravel in his voice. After donning their fedoras and retrieving their guns, he and Moran left in peace.

Soon afterward, Capone watched as Torrio reached for the telephone and asked the operator to get Sam Genna on the line.

The lieutenant lit a Lucky Strike after getting his boss another brandy and eavesdropping on the back and forth in Italian. He had to work not to smile at how Johnny "the Fox" Torrio appeared to work his magic.

12

Tuesday Troubles

Danny Keagan sat up in bed with a start. The cool air hit him hard as a trickle of sunlight showed itself in the windows of the Near West Side boarding house where he had been sleeping. He remembered he had to check in soon with an Outfit goon. After rubbing sleep from his eyes, got up in his underclothes, opened the door to a hallway, and stumbled to a public telephone atop the staircase. He didn't want to wake the woman who'd been laying next to him, but he had obligations.

After clearing his throat, Keagan picked up the receiver and asked the operator to connect him to the Four Deuces. In less than a minute, he gave his last name in greeting to the other side of the line and was put in touch with Alphonse Capone.

During the back and forth, Capone reminded him about eruptions between the North Side and Little Italy. Torrio and he were to oversee negotiated terms between the two sides. Keagan was to report to the Four Deuces in an hour to help guard against drunk johns and other threats.

Keagan agreed to be at work soon and gave a nice-enough salutation in response to the boss's right-hand man. He still considered Capone an opportunist and a brown nose, but knew to keep any objections to himself. Once back in the bedroom, he got dressed.

Harriet Rosenstein groaned and rolled over since her bed wasn't as warm with Keagan not in it. She watched him as he put on his suit pants and jacket over his rumpled, white button-down and underclothes. Her lips curled into a grin.

"I have to say, I'm happy you don't expect me to make you breakfast," she said, propping herself on her left elbow to hint the bust tucked under a thin sheet and even thinner nightshirt.

"No time for coffee or sugar, sweetheart." Keagan said. "I'll just grab a little bread from a bakery on the way to work."

Harriet got out of bed and shuffled her legs into a pair of palazzo pants. He gave her a brief look over before she meandered over to him. She pecked him on the right cheek and batted her eyes. They had a smoky, spicy allure despite her recent slumber.

Keagan had to restrain himself and only pat her on the behind before putting on his new fedora. The only other accouterment of status he had was the small sparrow's feather in the brim. He had added it before spending the night with her.

"I don't know what you do for a living, and I'd rather keep things simpler by not asking such questions," Keagan said before brushing her lips with his. "Just so you know, I protect my boss's assets. I don't seek them out for company. With you, it's pure pleasure."

"'The best things in life are free. The second best are very expensive.'" she replied, returning a slap to his behind. "Coco Chanel is a wise woman."

Keagan tilted his hat to Harriet before he got on his way, blissfully unaware Harriet had overheard his earlier conversation on the telephone.

- - - - -

The exchange of Bruno Lanski for two trucks of hooch was to take place before noon behind a warehouse on Madison and Halsted. The red brick, fireproof structure was unimposing, despite taking up half a city block. It was also well inside Outfit territory, which suited John Torrio well in his role as arbitrator. He knew any police and otherwise nosy neighbors were paid to look the other way.

The Outfit boss showed up in a Cadillac at eleven in the morning with Alphonse Capone, Vincent Golino, and a Thompson machine gun-armed thug in tow. Torrio invited Vincent along because the boy didn't appear drunk, for a change, and he wanted to see if Dean O'Banion would bring along the fella dating Golino's sister.

To the left of Torrio and Capone, Vincent stood in silence and stared where the North Siders would soon show up with trucks to exchange with the Gennas for their man. Everyone was to be present at quarter after the hour.

"I don't know what these monkeys need, but since they seem to have both reneged on established boundaries, they all need to be treated as children," Torrio said to his men. "It's better to be feared than loved. That's even more important when it comes to making money."

After noticing Vincent flinch, he whispered to Capone,

"I'm glad you suggested the Tommy Gun. But it'd be a shame if I had to use it on one of our own."

Dean O'Banion soon showed up with Earl Weiss driving one truck of drinkable alcohol and Moran behind the wheel of another, accompanied by a young man with auburn hair. All four got out of the trucks, appearing ready to serve slices of humble pie for the Lanskis.

When Vincent spit on the ground and looked into the young man who'd been riding with Moran, Torrio had to stifle a grin. He figured they were in the presence of Aiden McCarthy. A brief introduction from O'Banion confirmed it.

Moran and Weiss showed their pistols, making their hosts aware that safety switches were engaged and that chambers were empty. Aiden and O'Banion showed they were unarmed. The North Side boss agreed his lieutenants would only use their guns if Torrio wasn't able to keep the peace.

Torrio stroked his hairless chin with the back of his hand and clicked his tongue in response. Capone nodded to his boss and then to the North Siders before motioning with his hand to the stoic goon with the Thompson machine gun. Vincent was left to steam.

The Genna brothers then came in two Cadillac sedans. Angelo, Mike, and Sam got out of one and presented their pistols, agreeing to the same terms as the North Siders. In the other sedan, Vincenzo gave the signal he was unarmed and exited to take Bruno Lanski out of the back seat. A handkerchief blinded Bruno's eyes and rough rope wrapped his hands. He had bruises on his forehead and right cheek.

All gathered maintained a semblance of civility. Torrio was moderately surprised and pleased that Vincent was keeping his mouth shut, even though blood still flushed the Golino boy's face. The Outfit boss got started.

"Alright, here's how it's gonna go down," he said. "Since the Irish put in two thousand cash and eight thousand clams worth of drinkable firewater, I expect the Gennas to examine and take what's theirs. If it is what O'Banion says it is, and that's what I expect, then Mr. Lanski will be handed over no problem. If there is any doubt on either side, it should come back to me. My fella with the Tommy gun can take care of any funny business, but frankly boys, I'm not in the mood."

As decreed, the exchange took place without incident. Both the Gennas and members of the North Side Gang remained as humble as gangsters could be. Sam Genna and Dean O'Banion shook hands with each other and Torrio.

"Any bitching and heat between competition in bootlegging, moonshining, gambling, or women will have to go through me from here on out," Torrio said. "You may not like it, I can make sure that all sides can make a buck without burning down empires. *Capisce*?"

Almost all those present, with the exception of Vincent, nodded ascent. Torrio pretended that he didn't notice as he led the little *bastardo*, Capone, and tough guy with the machine gun back to the Cadillac. All three gang interests left with unnatural quiet after firearms were returned.

- - - - -

Darkness enveloped the Chicago skyline as any light from the sun disappeared beyond the western horizon. As natural shadows became nonexistent, Earl Weiss brooded over the day's events, sighing with an air of dissatisfaction as he marched south. As he approached the Four Deuces, he stopped along Wabash when he saw Keagan outside.

"What in bloody hell is Danny doing here?" Weiss said under his breath, staying out of his former coworker's gaze.

Weiss slunk his way into the club, waiting until Keagan was otherwise engaged with winos too broke to pay for prostitutes, booze, or a spin on the roulette wheel. Inside, he blended in with more filthy philanderers before taking Minka's hand. She was waiting at the bottom of the stairs leading to the floor with her room, declining other eager johns. Weiss allowed her to lead him with a sensuous stride up the steps.

"I like it when you wait for me," Weiss told her as he watched her behind shift back and forth. "However, I'm not sure if I'm up for being anyone's steady yet. I've had thoughts of saving myself for a nice gal."

"Does a good girl do this," she said after taking an abrupt stop once they reached their floor. She spun around, grabbed the front of shirt, and kissed him on the lips. Weiss responded by putting her over his shoulder and running the rest of the way to her room.

Inside, Weiss got out a Lucky Strike after setting her feet to the ground. Before he could catch his breath and light his smoke, she unsheathed herself from her red silk dress and sprawled out on the bed.

"I thought we would've talked before giving in to more base desires, love," he said, "but you've rendered me speechless. Come here."

He returned his cigarette to its case for the next hour, jumping into bed to enjoy her body. They both lacked a coherent thought until their chests could return to a relaxed rhythm. The lingering body heat was all that kept them warm against the early-spring chill outside the clouded window.

"How about those apples, sugar?" she asked, draping her left leg over his in the afterglow.

"I'm rather keen," he replied as he got to the waiting cigarette and lit one for her. "I'm also happy your schooling wasn't in a convent. Other than impure fantasies of you, my head's been buzzing about traitors and bootleg.

Minka pulled the sheets over them. She propped herself on an elbow and flicked ash on the floor before meeting his eyes with hers. It was her signal for business after pleasure.

"Now you have my clearheaded attention," she mocked. "Did you learn about the Irishman who now has the same boss as me? Even a silly girl like me can figure out truths about tough, serious gangsters."

Weiss smacked her on the behind and pecked her on

her pouting lips before running his hand along the covered curve of her hip. He nodded and peered in her eyes.

"Do you want me to bump him off? Because I can do it if you want me to," she said. "I'm willing to kill to get out of this place with you. I can make it look like an accident."

Weiss laced a sliver of hair behind her ear. He admired the soft arch that connected her cheek and her shoulder. He shook his head at both of their loose grips on sanity.

"Don't be impetuous, sweetheart," he said. "It doesn't suit you. Just keep an eye on a guy named Keagan for now. At some point, I might knock his block off myself. All in due time."

Weiss then asked Minka to get the pipe and opium. She leaned over the bed, the bare curve of her behind showing from beneath the sheets. She set up a hit and allowed him to light it. When the smoke drifted from their lungs to the ceiling, they again found silence, if not peace. She put her head on his chest as they surrendered to fatigue and drug-induced dreams.

13

Mid-April Storm

A light rain sprinkled down as Aiden McCarthy drove the Packard toward the Lanski home off Damen. It was about two hours after he had dined with his parents, not offering them any lies regarding his whereabouts. He told them he was helping Dean O'Banion with some business after Friday classes at Holy Name. He only omitted a few facts. For one, the work had nothing to do with flowers. Also, George Moran would be riding in the passenger seat with a shoulder-holstered Colt revolver.

As they drove north, they didn't notice the Cadillac following from a leisurely distance. They parked in front of the Lanski house thinking about little else but the family inside. It had been nearly a week since Bruno's kidnapping.

Bruno answered the door with his Ruger revolver in his left hand, ready for any unfriendly faces. Behind him, Jozef Kaminski stood, favoring the place he'd been nicked in the shoulder, having come to the Lanski household to help out how he could. He also helped partake in food that North Side Gang allies had brought for the past several days.

The man of the house relaxed his grip on the pistol and beckoned Aiden and Moran to join Jozef and his daughter inside. After peering north and south along the street, he shut the door to protect the warm refuge against the world.

In the kitchen, Aiden took out two loaves of bread and some baked ham while his superior revealed a fifth of Canadian Club. Bruno accepted the help, offered a rare, grateful smile, and ushered them to take a seat at his table.

Anna lay in a bed on the other side of the room. Although O'Banion had paid for doctors, soreness festered in her gut. Her father ordered her to rest in bed as he took over the household duties and cared for her. He and Jozef had prepared a soup from donated potatoes, onions, celery, and garlic.

Bruno invited the men to sip a small dram of the whiskey. He offered to make a ham sandwich for Aiden and Moran, but both declined with grim grins and shakes of their heads Aiden helped Jozef prepare sandwiches for the members of the household.

"So tell me how we're gonna deliver justice on those dagos and their friends?" Bruno asked. "The Genna boys oughta have their fingernails plucked out for striking my daughter, but I'll settle for an explosion at one of their rotgut factories."

Aiden couldn't blame Bruno, but he knew they had to quash vengeance to North Side Gang needs. He clenched his jaw as he yielded the floor to Moran. The lieutenant had to play diplomat in light of gangland agreements, even if Bruno got the shorter end of a deal.

"O'Banion cannot aid fighting that goes against our arrangements with the Italians," Moran said. "The boss feels for you, but the reason you are alive and still able to earn dough for your family is because of a deal he brokered last week through Torrio."

"You tell me that if those guineas pull any more bull, I have to talk to O'Banion, and he'll get on the telephone with that bastard Torrio?" Bruno asked, enraged. He stood at his dining table, thumbing his paring knife.

"Mr. Lanski, we North Siders gotta follow agreements," Moran said. "You'll make three times the money of any immigrant working at the stockyards, but you gotta keep in line. I've no love for Torrio, nor the Gennas, but a war would be worse."

Bruno threw his hat on the ground.

"*Gowno!* I'll be a good boy for now. But if those degenerates pull any more gypsy crap, Torrio can go to devil or whack the horse."

Blood flushed Moran's cheeks before he winked at Aiden.

"I think the boss can agree on self-defense," Aiden said. "It's why my pa has only gained a limp instead of lost a life. What do you say, gentlemen?"

Bruno and Moran both gave a nod to Aiden before they toasted and drank their small drams of whiskey. The two took their leave as the Lanskis and Jozef prepared to dine. Bruno and the lad brought nourishment to Anna. They sat around her and all began to say grace in Polish before being interrupted by a cacophony outside.

- - - - -

Several minutes after Aiden and Moran left the Lanski household, a screech of tires ripped through the dark, damp evening air. A Cadillac barreled south toward them on Damen before a shotgun blast interrupted a fleeting glimpse of familiar faces. They hit the ground and rolled to avoid the spray of pellets.

As they crouched in Lanski's yard, Moran drew his Colt pistol and fired at the driver's side door. The Cadillac abruptly swerved, hit a curb, and jack-knifed from over fifty feed away.

Bruno burst out the front door just before the crack of collision. He pointed his Ruger at the wreckage and fired a few rounds. He just missed the escaping driver, who ran east along Shakespeare until out of range and out of sight.

The passenger, being stupid, arrogant, or an unhealthy combination of both, lurched from the wreckage and began to stagger toward the Lanski home, shotgun raised. Aiden recognized him and scowled.

"You dirty mick, you better back away from my sister or I'll finished what my father started," Vincent Golino said, pointing the gun toward where Aiden crouched.

Aiden grabbed his stiletto, realizing at once that it would be useless. He shouted to Vincent, pleading with him.

"Put your gun down before one of these fellas shoot you. What about your sister? We won't be doing her any favors if we're both dead."

The lunatic continued his advance.

"*Figlio di puttana!*" Vincent swore before a crack punctured the air and cut him off.

As Bruno tucked the Ruger behind his back, Aiden ran to Sophia's brother and dropped to Vincent's side. He looked over the wound, took a flask from his jacket, and poured the contents on a bloody gash.

Moran ran up to them and knelt down for a moment. He then grabbed Aiden's arms, pulling at him and trying to lead him away. He had to use his full body weight to get his young associate to move.

"We'll be less useful than dead meat if we don't get out of here," Moran said through gritted teeth.

Moran brought Aiden to the passenger side of the Packard, and shoved him inside. He then hurried to Bruno and told him to stay inside with his daughter and Jozef. They were to act like innocent, concerned neighbors when the friendly Officer O'Neill showed up.

After returning to the Packard, Moran drove a slow, indirect route to Aiden's home.

"I don't blame Bruno a bit," Aiden said in a soft voice during the drive. "Matters are out of control. Who are the coppers gonna pin the noise on?"

"Aiden, you didn't shoot Vincent," Moran said. "That's what you gotta keep on your conscience. Officer O'Neill is a good copper. He won't point it at us."

Once the two had arrived at the McCarthy home, off of Chicago Avenue, Aiden nodded to Moran before he stepped out of the Packard.

"Thanks," he said. "I'm still not used to gunshots and don't plan on returning them. Not sure I've got the nerve."

241

"You'd be surprised at what a man will do should he be put in a certain position," Moran said. "A man who thinks before shooting is the kind of man you want to be. Get some rest; even if it takes a hit of laudanum. Get yourself ready for the next day."

Aiden nodded again before he made as quiet an entrance as he could into the Chicago Avenue house in which his parents slept. The peacefulness inside welcomed him to a sense of home in spite of the stirrings in his head.

- - - - -

News of the shooting near the Lanski's struck John Torrio like a right hook from Jack Dempsey. He grunted in exasperation when the name Vincent Golino came up. His oak table at the Four Deuces club and a late night brandy called to him as he stewed, miffed that an underling had played loose with the rules

Politicians and police were as loathe as Torrio to draw attention to more gangland blood rivalry, and he instantly regretted giving more confidence than what was due to Silvio's son. After slamming the brandy, Torrio reminded himself it wasn't time to dither. He called Capone to his table.

"We gotta be sure we come out on top, regardless of any pain to the Golino family," he muttered to Capone "How the hell did that little degenerate get a hold of one of our Cadillacs and the firepower to carry out his own little vendetta? He had to have had a driver."

Capone called a call girl over to fill his boss's drink.

"Mr. Torrio, I'm thinking any driver had something to do with our muscle. One of our recent hires was Irish and didn't have a taste for hookers. It was only one of the traits about him that rubbed me the wrong way. You don't have to worry about anything, I'm gonna take care of it."

"You see," Torrio said to one of his top-earning prostitutes as she attempted a blush not as genuine as her red hair or the hue of her silk robe, "I knew all along to put my faith in a New York Italian rather than that little Golino grease ball. Like father, like son. Ambition without brains—"

"I've got some of the skinny as well as fun in the sack" the prostitute said. "I seen that Irish doorman pallin' around with a some gal outside the club. I think they might be bunking west of here."

Torrio gave a respectful nod to Capone and asked the redhead to fill him in with what she knew. Alphonse Capone spoke with other doormen and dames-for-hire on word on where he might find the Irish tough guy.

- - - - -

Minka Summer got another round of Canadian-made "bourbon" for several men before checking back in with Torrio. She pecked the Outfit boss on the cheek and was rebuffed from further service. She headed back to the third floor of the Four Deuces.

In her room, she was happy to see Earl Weiss in her bed. After a round of whoopee, she told him needn't worry about any fella named Keagan. In a haze of opium, she assured that the turncoat's death would be an Outfit-organized job.

243

14

Next Day Fallout

Harriet Rosenstein woke with a startle when she heard pebbles ring against the wall her boarding house room. Curiosity and alarm won the war against her desire for comfort in the hours before dawn. She cursed herself before she got out of her bed on the second floor, put on a gray, ankle-length robe, and looked down to see what was the matter in the hours before dawn.

The sight of Keagan below on the street made her crack the window open several inches. She stooped down, picked up a pebble from the dirty floor, and threw it at him. She missed, but at least noise stopped.

After shutting the window, Harriet padded down the stairs in her bare feet to the front door. Having not seen Keagan in a week, she had too many unsavory questions to ignore. She soon met him with a bemused stare she had practiced on the steps. The door was opened only the width of her face.

"Long time, no see, fella," she said. "Looks like some sort of pickle brought you here. What's the skinny?"

Danny Keagan came closer, prompting Harriet to narrow the gap between the door and frame. His brow furrowed and his eyes focused. A bead of sweat streaked down hardened cheekbones from a clenched jaw.

"*Ma cherie*," he said in a low voice, "I'll have my gangster employers and their competitors after my head soon. Could I stay here until daybreak? We could leave on a train—"

"I ain't going anywhere with you, bub," Harriet said. "I overheard you talking about Johnny Torrio last week. If you don't give it to me straight, I'm afraid you're on your own with no place to stay."

She watched him with arms folded in front of her chest as Keagan shifted from foot to foot.

"I just came from driving a hit on North Side territory," he said. "It was a blood rivalry between two families, from what I could gather. The gunman got shot. I think the target got away. Torrio's not likely to be pleased."

"Remind me why I should care," Harriet said. Remembering Sophia's brother was a tool for the Outfit, she snatched a broom near the door and pointed the handle at Keagan's face. "Which families are you talking about? Who'd you help?"

Keagan gulped and attempted get a foot in the doorway to no avail.

"Someone named Vincent wanted to knock off a guy named Aiden I used to work with," he said. "The fella paid me twenty dollars just to drive. Seemed like easy enough job until a bystander pulled a gun on us—"

"How old was the schmuck who shot Vincent?" Harriet pressed. She hoped it wasn't Aiden, thinking for a second she had put too much faith in Sophia's sweetheart.

"He was well into his forties." Keagan replied with hesitation. "Vincent looked like a lost cause. I ran from the car and heard gunshots and police sirens. I kept running and then snuck onto a streetcar. I got off well before heading here. Didn't see a tail."

Stone showed on Harriet's frowning face. The specter of him attracting attention and the pull of fatigue lingered as she made a decision.

"I've little warmth for people who give up on a 'lost cause,'" she said. "There's a shed in the back where you can hide until morning to slink away and catch a train."

Keagan stepped toward the entrance, but had to dodge the end of a broom handle.

Harriet yawned before she shut the door, set the lock, and returned the broom to its place. After ascending the stairs, she tucked herself in bed for a few hours of shuteye.

Assertive knocks on the front door woke her at dawn. She tried to ignore it until hearing the crack of pine busting off hinges.

- - - - -

Alphonse Capone busted open the door to the boarding house. Gossip from Four Deuces doormen and a hooker had led him here in a bid to track down Keagan. A snub-nose driver and a bald ruffian soon joined him inside the foyer.

Capone figured coming here to find the putz was a stretch, but it was the only lead he had. He shot his Beretta pistol into the ceiling to hurry things along.

After a bang from his pistol, a few clumps of ceiling fell and two young women ran into view at the top of the stairs in their nightgowns. Capone beckoned for them to come to the ground floor with his pistol.

"You, head out the door and see if you find anything funny around this whorehouse," he yelled out to the driver. "Me and Baldy'll check in with these dames."

The driver nodded and did as told. When the women were down the stairs, Capone gave them a brief look-over before smacking his lips. He furrowed his brow as if to show concentration or disappointment.

"See these dames?" he asked his accomplice. "Neither of these would pass muster. The dumb Dora here is too homely. The others probably got too much moxie to please a john, don't ya, toots?"

Harriet responded with a swift smack between Baldy's legs, letting her hand linger as a threat. She gave a wink to Capone and smiled

"What do you say, palooka?" she asked. "Should I get him off or cripple him? You could shoot me after I do what you want, but that might complicate your day. Your choice...Just thought you and your pal would like to hear your options before wasting time with us good-for-nothin' gals."

Capone chuckled and gave a lop-sided grin. He liked the dame.

"You've made your point, toots," he said. "That's more hassle than I wanna deal with, *capisce*? I'm looking to keep it copacetic. What do ya say?"

"As long as you scram and leave me and my friend to our business," Harriet said with a shrug, keeping her hand steady, "I don't give a good damn what you do. Your move."

Capone tilted his fedora and walked just outside the doorway.

"I'll be seeing you around, baby," he said. "You coming, Baldy?"

Harriet kept her hand in place, but allowed Baldy room to limp outside. He and Capone were met with a slam with whatever was left of the door. Their driver was yelling for them.

- - - - -

The snub-nose driver sat behind the wheel of the Cadillac and beckoned with wild arms. Baldy limped toward the car before Capone grabbed his left arm and nearly threw him in the backseat. The car pealed away, heading north on Damen and right on Madison.

"What?!" Capone said.

In swift Italian, the driver said he investigated a shed to the rear of the boarding house. When he tried the door, Danny Keagan knocked him to the ground, grabbed his gun, and jumped an eastern fence. He ran back to the Cadillac so they could head the turncoat off.

Capone and his boys turned right on Ashland, scanning the street for Keagan. They were met with two shots to their tires from the south.

After the Cadillac swerved to a halt, Capone burst out the door with his Beretta. He shot at a streetcar headed south. The former Irish doorman was fortunate to have just boarded it.

Torrio's lieutenant consoled himself with fact that Keagan wouldn't show his face in Chicago again if he knew what was good for him. He could tell the boss whatever version of reality he wanted

"Good riddance," Capone muttered to himself as he headed back to the Cadillac. He helped his men change the tires, inviting them to drinks before driving back to the Four Deuces.

- - - - -

Later in the afternoon at Schofield's, gunfire from the previous evening weighed on Aiden's mind. How did Vincent not listen to reason? Could Bruno Lanski claim self-defense? How would Sophia take news of her brother? The lack of mention in the newspapers didn't cleanse his conscience. A cover-up by friendly police only picked at his still-ingrained Catholic guilt.

When the clock approached four o'clock, Aiden took off from arranging flowers to check on Sophia. He didn't even bother to check in with Crutchfield or any of the other workers before heading out the door.

On a streetcar south, Aiden kept his eyes to the floor, thoughts brooding. He walked the rest of the way west on Randolph to Peoria, hoping to be the first one, instead of a coroner, priest, or random gossiper, to tell her what happened.

After a soft knock on the Golinos' door, a middle-aged woman who looked like an older version of Sophia answered. She was likewise pretty, with gray shades gracing the hair by her temples. He figured that the woman was Sophia's mother, Celia, and adopted a tone he hoped was respectful, impersonal, and appropriate.

"Excuse me, ma'am," he said, trying to improvise with what he remembered from the ruse Harriet had used. "I am a deacon at Holy Name Cathedral. I was planning to meet with a Ms. Sophia Golino regarding her work with the Blessed Virgin Mother mission to serve misguided vagrants and recent immigrants."

Celia Golino wavered on her feet as she took in the young man before her. She then scrunched her face in a critical glare. Aiden figured she wasn't buying any of his baloney.

"If Sophia is doing charity work for the Church, then she was my second virgin birth," she said. "She's a good daughter, but as Catholic as Martin Luther. Some young boy's been sending her home with flowers. So give it to me straight, Irish. I'm not getting any younger."

Despite a crack to his nerves, Aiden had to grin at the woman's stones. She returned a sardonic smile, which somehow made delivering bad news more difficult.

"Yes ma'am," he said. "I sent the flowers. Sophia and I have been friends for weeks now. My apologies for not having asked your permission, but she said that her mother needn't be bothered. I understand it's been hard going."

Celia clucked her tongue and told him to enter the house. She told him to take off his cap before he could show her he had the good sense to do so.

"Mrs. Golino—"

"Call me Celia. Please."

"I came to deliver harsh news first to your daughter. It's best to come from a friend than anywhere else."

"Well, there's no need to dither around," she said after a graceless pause. "What's the matter?"

"I saw your son, Vincent, get shot last night after he

threatened me and some others with a shotgun. I warned him and came to his side, but was unable to help. The papers haven't reported about what I saw...and I'm not sure what to make of that."

Celia took a step back, nearly falling backward as she reached for a chair. Finding one, she collapsed into it as Aiden remained just inside the door. He stood attentive, waiting for any clue on what to do next. The ensuing silence was mercifully shorter than he expected.

"I figured my son had been messing with Torrio, even if I'd pretended otherwise, boy," she said. "I washed blood out of clothing, kept my mouth shut, and hoped he would get wise. But I figured rough stuff begets more of the same."

Celia got up and boiled water for tea, prepping a pot before she continued.

"I'm not sure that there was anything that would've stopped him from getting himself shot. Those damn gangsters will be the death of us all."

Aiden offered her a kerchief, which she refused. He accepted a cup of tea, letting her lead any talk. Themes of family and her hopes for her daughter mingled with the scents of spearmint and chamomile that calmed the air. Aiden limited talk about himself his parents, first seeing Sophia in Washington Square Park, school, and a job arranging flowers.

When Sophia came home within an hour, she dropped her coat at the sight of her mother and her steady talking. The two each took turns embracing her and catching her up with the events of the past day.

Sophia joined her mother with tears after Aiden told what he could about Vincent.

After talking and attempting to sooth each other for a while, Sophia and her mother were still sniffling when Aiden excused himself as the sun moved beyond the western horizon. He wanted to be polite, so just nodded with his hat in his hands to Celia.

Sophia embraced him at the door, and he wrapped his arms around her in response. After he stepped outside, he put his newsboy cap back on and walked over a mile north toward his own family. He pondered events as he took his time.

What mattered most to him is that there were tears of joy mixed with the sorrow between Sophia and Celia. The cooling air of the early spring evening made him hasten his pace as doubts raced through his head about courting Sophia. When he reached home on Chicago Avenue, the warmth inside gave him optimism.

15

A Sunday of Relative Rapprochement

The Rolls Royce Silver Ghost stopped at East Monroe Street off South Wabash Avenue, well within Torrio's territory, as evening descended on the Chicago skyline. At the Palmer House Hotel, Dean O'Banion received his guest, Mike Merlo, with a firm handshake, a wide grin, and guards armed with Police Special revolvers.

The added security was more for show. The two men had been friends well before Prohibition, but Merlo's recent ascent as head of the *Unione Siciliana* made him an even greater asset over competition.

O'Banion led the way into the opulent hotel, where the fresco ceilings of the lobby prompted Merlo to comment on childhood memories of the Sistine Chapel. They continued through black French doors to the gold column-decorated Empire Room.

Inside, O'Banion snapped his fingers for a server to show his friend a seat. Sam Genna, Torrio and his wife, Anne, and O'Banion's wife, Viola, stood in greeting before they all sat at a long mahogany dinner table.

Despite being in Outfit territory, O'Banion's ability to woo staff and treat them well showed in how workers treated his guests. The men received Cohibas and brandy at once as other attendants served Chianti to the wives. After the aperitif, servers delivered bowls of duck-broth and barley soup accompanied with a glass of pinot grigio.

"Mr. Merlo, thank you so much for meeting us here and partaking in our humble hospitality," O'Banion said after everyone had finished their soup. "Please accept these two bottles of Macallan Scotch, brought in from one of my distributors."

Genna and Torrio both flushed upon seeing attendants bring out the Scotch. O'Banion was beating them in hospitality to the Sicilian leader. Before his fellow Italians could offer their own gifts, Merlo struggled through any loss for words.

"Dean, you've outdone yourself," he said. "I'm your grateful friend, but there's more on your mind if you're calling us together like this. Let me know what I can do in my humble post as an emissary for Italian immigrants. We have shared friends in the business and public service communities."

Torrio and Sam Genna had no choice but to keep their mouths shut as O'Banion let the moment linger. The last thing they wanted to do was undercut Merlo, to show disrespect with territorial disputes. Their own associates brought bottles of champagne forth before Merlo nodded with the muted thanks required of him. All those seated at the table exchanged toothy smiles that varied in authenticity.

"Go on, Dean," he said. "Tell me what's troubling you."

"Mr. Merlo, despite a treaty between Mr. Torrio, Mr.

Genna, and myself, associates have betrayed the trust and goodwill between us," O'Banion said. "After we break bread, my hope is that we can come to an agreement on how to keep business copacetic with the community."

"*Signore* Merlo, all of our associates may have made ill-advised choices—" Sam interrupted, only to be hushed by the Sicilian leader.

"I don't know who started what," Merlo said, "but I'm sure than Dean is only looking for continued cooperation. I'm prepared to hear demands after this meal. If we aren't able to break bread and quench our appetites as polite men of means, then we'd be as uncivil as the Chinamen or the Negroes. *Buon appetito!*"

Palmer House servers soon brought *Bistecca Alla Siciliana*, cooked medium rare, and all parties partook of their steak and baked potatoes. Merlo was too busy with his steak to talk, but he made appreciative comments on O'Banion's hospitality and the beauty of the ladies present.

If the steak wasn't as well-prepared, Torrio and Genna would've been less comfortable being polite. They only took a break from their steaks to thank Merlo for his compliments on the women and return their own respects.

As the meal wound down with tiramisu and espresso, O'Banion secured Merlo's protection of his interests. He left the business of Vincent Golino unmentioned to avoid any disruption of potential, if coerced, goodwill.

"From here on out, I will verify that the actions my

bootleggers and warehouse staff abide by any territory agreements between myself, the Chicago Outfit, and our friends, the Genna brothers, in Little Italy," O'Banion declared. "With your blessing, I'm sure we can respect each others' businesses.

The leaders of the Outfit and Little Italy coughed in disbelief.

Undercut from his usual role of ultimate deal broker, at least with Merlo around, Torrio kept a respectful quiet that masked his temperament. His espresso tasted more bitter than usual. Sam Genna appreciated that past transgressions against the North Side Gang didn't gain attention, but twitching lines near his temples hinted at his unease.

"I tell you, Deanie," Merlo said, "if this is your idea of a negotiation between business interests, I'd be glad to mediate anytime. I respect your word and expect my countrymen to do so as well. Of course, if you, Sam, or John have any issues, please call my associates."

Neither Torrio nor Genna could challenge the bond between Merlo and O'Banion.

"I'm always glad to host a dear friend. *Cin cin!*" O'Banion said as he raised his glass of brandy and glanced in his competition's eyes. He clinked his glass with Merlo as everyone else nodded with neutered approval.

16

A Good Schooling

Aiden McCarthy got out of bed at 7:04 a.m Monday as Margaret finished preparing oatmeal in the kitchen of their home. After he showered and got ready for a day of classes, he joined his parents. Evan put down his *Daily Tribune* on their simple table and sipped his tea as breakfast was dished out. The normalcy was welcome.

"Mornin' Ma and Pa," he said.

"Mornin' lad," they both said before his father continued.

"Been hearing stories around the barbershop, lad," he said. "A few of my regulars talked about shots fired and speeding cars to the north on Damen. The papers didn't give it attention, but chatter makes you think that there's more to it."

"It's a good thing I lead a more prudent life," Aiden said, trying to change the subject. "Ma, it looks like a lovely day, I might need more of your wonderful tea if you have more to spare."

"I found blood on one of your shirts while doing the wash over the weekend, Aiden," Margaret said as she filled his cup. "There was a silver dollar-sized stain on your forearm; me and your pa are just worried. You said you were runnin' errands for O'Banion last Friday evening. Is that all?"

Aiden had become incapable of lying to his mother. Even if he tried, he wouldn't get away with it.

"Well, Ma. I don't go lookin' for trouble," he said. "It found me while delivering a meal and some company to Bruno Lanski. He's the North Side driver with the wounded daughter. An Italian lad threatened us and got shot. I don't know what happened afterward because one of O'Banion's fellas drove me home to safety. I don't want to make you worry, but I'm having a hard time keeping above the fray."

Margaret's face softened while Evan pushed the argument further.

"My boy," he said, "the lady you brought over for dinner Sunday several weeks ago was lovely, but I have to say she looked rather like a Golino. You shouldn't get yourself involved in gang disputes because of your attraction to a lass."

Evan realized that he had gone too far when both his son's and Margaret's faces went from one of diplomacy to defiance.

"You don't have to worry about her, Pa," Aiden said. "The only other woman I care about more than her is Ma. I'm willing to take risks for either, but I'm in no hurry make myself a martyr."

"You oughtn't get in over your head, lad," Evan said.

"I'm eighteen and I got a good head on my shoulders," Aiden said. "Mr. O'Banion saved your life and he'll look after someone who can be relied on."

Margaret poured herself more tea and sat down between her men, passing the pot from Aiden to Evan. She hummed to interrupt the silent tension.

After an exasperated sigh, Evan nodded to his son before pouring himself some tea. They finished breakfast in peace with the occasional ruffle of the newspaper. As Margaret cleared the dishes, Evan gave his son a clap on the shoulder and told him to be good.

Aiden replied with a respectful nod, kissed his mother, and went about his day, starting with classes at Holy Name. He vowed to himself that he wouldn't stray from his studies for the rest of the week to make his folks happy. His desire to be with Sophia and make good money would have to wait, tempered with visions of finishing school and getting a place of his own.

17

Midweek Mayhem

Crowds coalesced outside the Four Deuces a few hours after twilight while Jozef Kaminski and Bruno Lanski waited nearby, just a block north of 22nd Street. After lack of closure from the run-in last Friday, Bruno wasn't in the mood to adhere to agreements between rival rum runners, racketeers, and pimps. He didn't consider John Torrio more than a glorified thug.

The sight of laughing johns and hired women only stoked Bruno's fury. His daughter, Anna, was just well enough to return to studies. Jozef had recovered enough and was pleased to help hit back.

With nitroglycerin pumping through their veins as they watched the carnival of vice before them, the sight of one the North Side's own set off Jozef and Bruno. Earl Weiss, appeared to be a customer of the Outfit. Neither one could let this perceived slight stand.

"A traitor ought to get shot along with the heathens," Bruno said. "He'll get his soon enough. You wait here as I find out where the bastard's loyalties lie."

Jozef nodded, clutching the Winchester carbine.

Bruno followed Weiss and found a lady-for-hire

around his own age to use as cover within the Four Deuces. He headed to the third floor, following Weiss and a young redhead in an oriental, silk robe. He paid his own girl a dollar and told her to scram and keep her mouth shut. Outside the room where Bruno followed Weiss, he overheard the prostitute talking in a hushed voice.

"Well, sailor," the woman's voice said, "I thought that Golino boy would get bumped off. Alphonse Capone says Keagan is dead. So it looks like you've two traitors gone in a matter of days."

Bruno could see through a crack between the door and the frame. The desirable prostitute walked over to Weiss and kneaded his shoulders with the slender digits of her ivory hand.

"I suppose we oughta celebrate," Weiss said. "I can finally take a night off."

Bruno entered the room at once, leveling his Ruger at Minka Summer. She responded by dropping her robe and giving a scream.

"What in the devil is going on?" Bruno asked.

Weiss pulled his Colt on Bruno, starting a standoff as he took a smooth step back and aimed above the head. Neither seemed to notice the naked woman in the room.

"Now just listen, friend," Weiss said. "We may have a shared enemy here. You gotta listen to what I've got to say."

"I'm only with one fella, and it ain't Torrio," Minka interrupted, after retrieving her robe.

The three of them could hear footsteps racing up the

steps to investigate the scream. Weiss pointed his gun toward the door before two Four Deuces henchmen entered the room. They pointed their Remington shotguns at Bruno and Minka shooting him in the gut and her in the chest once faced with the pistols.

A split second after the shotgun blasts, Weiss returned fire and hit one of Torrio's tough guys between the eyes before the other took cover behind the door frame. As Bruno staggered out of the line of fire, Weiss shot Minka a tender glance. The last breath left her chest as he hurried to help his fellow gangster.

Bruno leaned against Weiss's left arm while they trained their pistols toward where the house guard was hiding. Weiss only let his aim waver when he dug his lighter from his left breast pocket. He dropped the lighter to his right foot and kicked it toward the door. The guard flinched to reveal a shoulder, which Weiss pierced with a slug from his Colt.

When he and Bruno made it to the hall, Weiss gave a kick to the goon with the shot shoulder before they continued toward the stairs. They stopped when they heard several men hustling up from the lobby. From the shouts in Italian below, they figured these other goons wouldn't be any more friendly than the first two.

The two North Siders regrouped. On the count of three, Bruno held himself against a wall as Weiss kicked through a door to a room facing the front of the cathouse. They ignored the interrupted liaison between a john and his hired company as Weiss shot out a window. Before the house hooligans came into the room, both North Siders leapt to freedom or death.

- - - - -

Jozef Kaminski watched the entire scene from a good fifty feet to the North, his mouth still gaping from the jump Weiss and Bruno made. An awning from the first floor interrupted the fall, helping their legs land with a jolt before they could limp toward him. Bruno seemed in worse shape with the gut wound. A fatal shot from the window above put him down for eternity.

"Dago *bastards!*" Jozef shouted before taking out his carbine and aiming toward the club.

He grinned when he hit Bruno's killer and knocked him out of the window. He continued shooting at the Four Deuces as Weiss limped away at the swiftest speed his legs could move. Police sirens could be heard somewhere nearby from the North.

Bullets stopped flying as two police cars came east on 22nd street. Any ruffians from the brothel stepped back inside to stash their guns.

Jozef doubted the police would do anything to help him. He had been shooting at the ones paying the bribes, after all. With the uneasy detente, he ran after Weiss. Adrenaline exploded in a punch when he caught up with Weiss near 19th and Clark.

Weiss fell and hit the pavement as hard as a stray barrel off a bootleg cart. He dodged the second punch, then a third by rolling to the side. His right hand found the Colt, but he tried to stay calm despite his instincts. He aimed the pistol at Jozef's neck, rested his index finger on the trigger, and tried to talk sense into the man in his sights.

"Bruno is dead," he said. "If you don't want the same

fate, you should skip town. There's nothing you can do but play stupid, innocent, or both when you're on the wrong end of a pistol. The only reason the dagos stopped shooting is that they are smart enough to know when the jig is up."

After releasing the carbine from his scarred hand, Jozef interrupted him.

"One of those thugs took out Mr. Lanski, leaving his daughter alone," he said. "I don't give a damn about myself as long as I get to—"

"Kill some dagos?" Weiss said. "Is that what you want to do? For what? The North Side Gang would disown you and the Outfit would pin you as another john gone haywire."

Jozef's shaking slowed, eventually coming to a stop. He wiped his brow as Weiss holstered his Colt. The young man spit on the ground before posing a question.

"So what now?"

"Get out of Chicago," Weiss said. "Go to Minnesota or Indiana for all I care. As for me, I'm going to get good and hammered."

Jozef rubbed his ragged-looking fist before helping his former coworker off the ground. He was about to give a cordial clap to Weiss's shoulder, but instead got a rapid punch to the temple to knock him out.

"Don't ever punch me unless you can finish the job," Weiss said to the unconscious form. "You oughta know that."

Weiss walked his limp off and thought about Minka. He remembered her ivory skin, the flame of her hair, and her laugh as he alternated between breathing the cool night air and inhaling fags from his pack of Lucky Strikes. After a streetcar ride north, he wandered to Carrie's Ax.

At the speakeasy, Weiss drained almost a fifth of cheap, diluted rum while shedding a rare tear into his bottle. He smoked the rest of his cigarettes before dropping a few coins in the dark-skinned musicians' jar. The Ax's owner showed him out in the wee hours of the morning, making him stagger home in hopes for a semblance of sleep.

Soon thereafter to the South, Jozef awoke and peeled himself off the ground. At dawn, he checked on Anna, delivered news of her father's death, and contemplated his next moves. He planned to stop by Dean O'Banion before making plans to get out of town. He didn't know if the visit would help him, but if nothing else, Earl Weiss might find himself in a pickle.

Anna Lanski urged him to come back for her.

- - - - -

Weiss meandered to Allen's Storage later that afternoon as rain drizzled atop his fedora during a shivery spring Chicago day. Rob Mullen's warm greeting at the door did little to improve his mood. The ache in his knee and his head only throbbed more when he saw his boss wave him over with a glare that would freeze the Dead Sea.

Dean O'Banion was sipping a non-bastardized dram of Canadian Club with one of the recent hires, a homosexual. The funny fella gave a smile that wasn't quite as fake as the jovial slap O'Banion gave to his lieutenant's shoulder. Weiss feigned a relaxed response despite the rattling in his skull.

"A Polish friend, Jozef, told me this mornin' about the run-in you and him had last night," O'Banion said. "I'm sorry to hear about your gal, even if she was one of Torrio's prostitutes."

The boss turned toward Weiss and looked him directly in the eye, continuing with dripping sarcasm.

"By the way, what are you doing looking for dames in that side of town? You know how I feel about tarnishing young gals for profit."

Weiss coughed and suppressed choking on his whiskey. He shifted from foot to foot and bowed his head. The gesture was meant to show humility, but hurt so much that the wince he gave made his boss grimace.

"I was rather fond of the girl," Weiss said. "I was not only necking with her, but trying to get an inside source in the Outfit. She had more hate than I do for Torrio. Believe me, I tipped her well and she was in on the ruse. I wasn't the one to tarnish her."

O'Banion's granite-hard eyes rolled. He then grabbed his lieutenant by the shoulder with an unfriendly squeeze. Red showed in the crevices of his otherwise charming face.

Weiss insisted he was telling the truth, rubbing his temple after having clenched his jaw. Mention of Jozef made him regret hitting the little cockerel, to a point. His curiosity persisted over pain.

"Speaking of Jozef," he said, "what's the word on him?"

"I think the lad will be alright. He's a soft spot for

Anna Lanski and I believe they'll both be heading out of town in due time. Mentioning me will give him a leg up wherever he lands."

Weiss had to smile, though his head and his ego still hurt.

"Why don't you get your house in order and come back tomorrow? You look and smell like horse manure. Come back ready to work once you get over the dame and get some of that oriental junk out of your system. You can make amends by helping out some of our new associates"

O'Banion nodded to the new hire and told him to go help other workers cut smuggled spirits with water, coloring, sugar, and spice. He relaxed his grip on Weiss's shoulder and gave a wink. He then ambled over to Mullen to crack wise and look over business.

Weiss took his cue and swallowed his pride. He welcomed another day off.

18

Salacity, Salvation, and the Sabbath

Saturday evening arrived at the Dil Pickle, and Harriet Rosenstein was in her element. During the week, she figured out that she had threatened a high-ranking Outfit lieutenant; the realization fueled her more than the tightly-packed crowd at her attention.

"I came across a kleagle today, my loves," she said to a rapt audience. "The unkind fellow called on Catholics, jigaboos, and other unclean sorts to leave America to the Americans, so I tempted him toward our garden of sin using my womanly wiles."

The several dozen men, a couple women, and a few of those in between whooped when Harriet shook her bosom, prompting a crash of cymbals among a quartet of a dark-skinned musicians. She waited until her audience settled before continuing.

"My friend, Silas, greeted us at the door. The kleagle couldn't believe he was fooled by a hebe whore and a darky. Mr. Robinson keeps out the riff raff, and the Puritan let it go. He may have learned that what you reap is what you sow."

At the drop of a pin, a drummer, two trumpeters, and

a clarinetist played a syncopated ragtime melody. Many in the Pickle hopped on the upbeat of the music, as those with more style danced a relaxed one-step. Harriet weaved her way through the masses toward the entryway. She kissed Silas on the cheek and thanked him for being game before.

"Mr. Robinson, I'm glad someone can make a gal safe from common brutes," she said. "Can a gal get you a drink?"

"Miss Rosenstein," he said, "it was my pleasure. I'm fine on spirits; however, I'll gladly join you when I'm not on the job. Some other time, when I'm not on the lookout for Klansmen or the Feds?"

"When we're not fighting the patriarchy," she added before they exchanged a wink, "it'll be my treat."

Harriet made her way back to the bar, where Sophia was lighting a palooka's cigarette and laughing at his jokes. From his cream-colored fedora, matching tie, and black and pink pin-striped suit, the sharp dresser exuded money and influence. He was too put-together for the average gin mill daddy and didn't seem to have a sense of humor when Sophia tried to tease her gams from his grasp.

"What's the matter, toots?" asked the grabby customer. "I don't believe for a second you're on your way to a convent."

"I told you, sugar," Sophia replied loudly enough to be heard over the din of the crowd. "That ain't my game. I'll gladly push you in the right direction."

"I don't pay for it."

Harriet didn't bother with coyness to keep things

copacetic. She laughed loudly, draping herself between her friend and the aggressive ape, grabbing his behind for effect.

"Jeepers creepers, my sheikh," she slurred, "I'm already zozzled, but a cuddly call girl'd keep you going all night."

The thug was about to get rough when a scarred fist connected with his temple, sending both him and Harriet to the floor. No one else seemed to notice, save for the Silas and Jeffery.

As club-goers danced or demanded more booze, the brothers escorted the lout out. The scarred hand was extended to help Harriet off the ground. The helpful gent was a blond haired fella, young enough to still go to school. Sophia and a shorter gal stood beside him.

"I appreciate the help, but I had the putz right where I wanted him," Harriet said. "Just the same, can I get you a drink on the house?"

The man turned his boyish face and whispered in the ear of the girl beside him. Harriet thought of her as a version of Lillian Gish, one decade younger. Her smallish lips were drawn into a pout until she gave a slight grin. She whispered back into her gentleman's ear, which made him smile from ear to ear.

"My lady wants a whiskey," he said with a Polish accent. "It's our last hurrah in this city for a while. I'll take a soda."

Harriet served them a double shot of undiluted Old Bushmills and the soda. She curtsied as if she were a well-to-do lady before receiving an overly formal response. The young mademoiselle bowed and the fella saluted, causing Harriet to blush. She felt more comfortable with the cross-dressers and nancies.

After she flashed a smile, Sophia led Harriet at once to dance and serve drinks to paying parties. An hour into the next morning, both ladies set queues to the saloon and took their leave. The young couple from earlier was nowhere to be seen. Harriet and Sophia said goodnight to Silas and Jeffery before they hoofed it to Randolph and Peoria.

- - - - -

At the Golino household, Sophia made them both tea and toast while being quiet enough to not wake her mama. She took a seat next to Harriet at the table, and a tear ran down her cheek as she poured water from a carafe. Her hands shook until Harriet grasped them with her own.

"Let me get that, honey," Harriet said, taking the carafe and pouring. "It's been a devil of a week, I imagine."

Several days ago, the friends had shared news about the week centered around Vincent's shooting. Harriet told about turning Keagan away. Sophia told her about Aiden's check-in and how he and Celia connected. That Harriet's version of events confirmed Aiden's version comforted Sophia.

The tea and toast rested on the table as Sophia spoke.

"I threatened my brother months ago with this same carafe," she said, looking with reddened eyes toward the glass vessel. "Vincent didn't always inspire that much anger."

Harriet got up from the table and crouched down near

Sophia's seat. She wasn't sure what to say, so she put an arm on her friend's shoulder while collecting her thoughts.

"I haven't many wise words as the only kind of sister I've had is you," Harriet said. "You've never given me reason to get angry with you, so I can't understand being mad at someone, yet caring enough to cry."

Sophia put her head on Harriet's shoulder, sniffled, and blinked back her sadness, holding onto her with both arms clasped.

"He could be a wretched rascal," Harriet continued. "But you kept hoping he'd come around."

Sophia sat up and put her hands on her lap after gesturing for her friend to take her seat. She wiped her eyes, took a bite of toast, and sipped her tea before Harriet did the same. A grin formed on her face before she spoke.

"You're a good friend, Harriet," she said. "Every once in a while, I remember teaching Vincent small tasks while growing up. I taught him how to tie his shoes, and Mama and I taught him how to read. The ebb and flow of life is bigger than my memories, and I'm unsure of how to deal with it."

"I'm not sure of the answer either, dove. I'm of the mind that we do the best we can, help the ones we hold dear, and try to enjoy ourselves."

"I'm keen on that."

Sophia and Harriet talked further into the early morning as they drained their tea. Just a few hours into Sunday, they crawled into bed and slept, lying together as sisters.

After waking up together later in the morning with smiles, Sophia and Harriet entered the kitchen. Both were pleased that Celia remembered her daughter's friend from Thanksgiving.

Celia gave kisses on the cheeks and told their guest to have a seat.

As Sophia boiled water for tea, she explained that Harriet was the friend who reached out under the pretext of helping the settlement house missions through Holy Name Cathedral. She spared her mother the details about her job at the Dil Pickle and any gangland drama. She wanted to keep events on an even keel. Her mama surprised her with a gust of sass.

"You have the slight look of a Jewish gal, so I commend you on getting my daughter to engage with the local nunnery," Celia dead-panned with a wry grin. "I've tried my whole life to get her more interested in the Church. To think that all she needed to do was find a non-Gentile friend."

"After spending my girlhood with a drunken wreck of a father, I realized Bohemians were my real family," Harriet said, her eyebrow raised. "I assure you I'm *not* one of the chosen people. If you have ham, I make a mean omelet."

Celia smiled before grabbing ham and some eggs she'd been saving in the icebox. Harriet went to work at once. In between sips of tea, Sophia joined her friend in the kitchen to saute some potatoes. All three were smiling as the room filled with aromatic rosemary, garlic, and fresh ground pepper

Between bites of their breakfast, the ladies exchanged

chuckles after railing against boorish men, politicians, and chauvinists of all stripes. They gave a sardonic laugh here and a knowing glance there while sharing in nourishment that fueled their stomachs and raised their spirits.

When Harriet went to Sophia's mother to say goodbye, Celia embraced her with both arms. Sophia kissed her best friend and her mother on the cheek before joining her mother to help clean their home. They then played cards before Sophia got ready for work.

It almost felt as if life was returning to some sense of normalcy.

19

End of the Week, Fresh Start

After an early evening spent arranging flowers at Schofield's on Sunday, Aiden McCarthy strolled north toward the Dil Pickle. Inside the club, he stole glances at Sophia; the tassels of her navy blue dress danced just above the knee of her sculpted legs, hypnotizing him and others.

Sophia charmed the crowd and got patrons to drink bootleg, dance, hire company for the evening, or all three. Aiden cut in from time to time to dance with her. Several glasses of Canadian Club helped him bide his time until the last song of the evening.

As drinkers, prostitutes, liquor-slingers, and revolutionaries filed out, Aiden asked Sophia if he could escort her toward her home. She agreed before taking off a white peony hair clip. They greeted Silas and Jeffery Robinson with a fist bumps at the door before heading off the second hour after midnight.

"I'm not in the mood to head back home just yet," Sophia muttered to him.

She took him by the hand and led him north on Dearborn Street from Tooker Alley. They walked the short distance to Bughouse Square. After sitting in an empty bench, she nuzzled into his shoulder to keep her warm. The silence between them seemed natural as vagrants, communists, and drunks wandered the periphery of the grounds. Despite the occasional shiver running from Sophia's shoulders to her toes, the two remained undisturbed.

"So where've you been all week?" she asked after putting her right hand on his knee. "Haven't seen you around since you met my mother and delivered ominous news about my brother."

Aiden furrowed his brow and put his left hand on her right.

"I've been trying to convince my parents I have my head on straight," he said with a slight chuckle. "I figured a week of only arranging flowers in my gangster boss's shop and keeping my nose in the books would help. Also, you and your mother could use some time, but I can't stay away from the woman whom I fancy too long, consequences be dammed."

Sophie smiled at him, her hazel eyes were happy despite large pupils, dilated with fatigue. Her tongue flicked between her lips for a quick, quiet moment.

"The space worked out. Celia is getting into the swing of things with a bit of fire." she said. "You left a good impression on her, so you've no need to be a stranger."

"I was just trying to—" Aiden was saying before being stopped by her lips. He responded in kind, putting his hand on her waist. He traced a line from her lips to her left cheek to the point of her neck below her right ear.

Sophia giggled as she noticed a few citizens of the

square gawking from a healthy distance. She moved her left hand to his chest and shrugged him off her neck. Blood rushed to dimples on either side of her slight grin.

"My dear, Aiden," she said. "Our necking is drawing attention. Would you take me to my house now?"

He helped her to a standing position and offered his arm to her. She took it before they continued the long stroll south along Dearborn. They meandered to the Golino home on Randolph and Peoria, taking turns to talk about bootleg, family and how their own passions could fit into the picture.

Birds started to sing outside the Golino household before dewy grass and warmer air could welcome a day more expected of spring. It was peaceful. She tickled his stomach as they lingered outside her door before dawn.

Aiden gave a lop-sided smile and caressed the small of her back with his left hand as he moved a stray ebony strand of hair off her cheek with his right. He glanced at the small cleft of flesh above her lower-than-proper neckline before he returned her gaze and gave a wink and a squeeze.

"I'm not about to anger the mother of my steady," he said. "I'll just have to try and get few hours of sleep when I get home, impure thoughts be damned."

After their lips met, she put a hand on his chest, giving a light push in what he took to be teasing. Devious thoughts reflected as they peered in each others' eyes.

"I'll see you around then, handsome," Sophia said. "Don't go necking with any other gal, though. I'll have to get rough with her."

He returned a smirk before she blew him a kiss and entered her house.

During Aiden's near mile-walk home, his cheeks flushed with color and his step lingered longer than usual. He promised himself he'd never let his gal down.

20

The New Deal

After his classes at Holy Name, memories of Sophia's early morning kisses flooded Aiden's brain as rain through an afternoon drizzle to work at Schofield's Flower Shop. He entered via State Street with a damp trousers, hung his coat and newsboy cap by the door, and returned Dean O'Banion's nod. The boss's reddened cheeks had a ruddy hue as if he was firing himself up, hitting the giggle water, or both.

Aiden waited to be addressed, only exchanging nods with Crutchfield and other workers. There was nothing to be gained by being cocky, at least not yet.

"I've been wondering if you'd take a gift from me, McCarthy," O'Banion said. "Business has been as unsavory as pimped rotgut. There's the gunshots outside the Lanskis' and inside the Four Deuces. We lost Bruno. It'll help if you carry one of these."

The boss handed his young associate a Colt pistol before Aiden coughed a laugh and shook his head.

"I'm not interested in a gun," Aiden said. "Dead bodies are not the best thing for profit. I'm no killer and would prefer not to be put in situations where it's either myself or some other unlucky bastard. What are you up to, boss?"

"I consider calamity counterproductive to cash too, lad," O'Banion said. "One of my better friends is a Sicilian gent who can hold off dirty dagos for now. Still, you oughta protect yourself. It's your decision whether to use it."

"I can't deny getting a thrill out of stealing, or to put it as a gentleman, 'to take advantage of business opportunities.' My folks and my steady gal don't want me to die and I'm not too fond of dying either. I'll go ahead and carry it, but I've little intention of shooting it."

"It can be good for show as well, lad. Now join me for a dram of the good stuff before getting to those carnations and chrysanthemums."

Aiden unloaded the Colt, pocketed the bullets, and hung the pistol and simple holster in his coat by the door. After taking a seat at a table, his boss poured them each a dram of Canadian Club.

Aiden felt a warm chill with the shot of booze and the bullets lingering in his front pants pocket. As he arranged flowers, his boss tried to assure him he'd have safe work with bootleg in Allen's Storage, under Rob Mullen's guard. On more secure bootleg routes from Canada through Detroit, Aiden agreed to help as a driver.

"Now lad, could you hand me some of those mums for this bouquet for Mr. Merlo's mistress? I owe her a bit of thanks for letting the head of the *Unione Siciliana* come and tell the local dagos to play nice and shoot less at us.

Making nice is one of my favorite parts of the job."

Aiden and O'Banion stayed for another hour, sipping more undiluted Canadian Club whiskey and chatting about rival bootleggers and moonshiners. They got Schofield's ready for another week of orders from churches, lovers, funerals, and weddings. With Crutchfield organizing arrangements in the back and replenishing flowers, ribbons, baby's breath, and other supplies, the time went quickly.

After Aiden returned home off of Chicago Avenue, Evan and Margaret listened as he talked about arranging flowers with O'Banion. Though the blush in his face remained, he left out the part about the gun, whiskey, and bootlegging.

Evan's face remained taut as if he sensed his son was hiding something. He shook his head and figured trying to press wouldn't do any good. Margaret made ham sandwiches, boiled potatoes, and announced that she was opening a bottle of red wine she had bought before Prohibition's start.

Aiden smiled after his mother justified to Evan that since she had bought it in accordance with the law, she could "damned well drink it." Evan had little choice but to agree as his wife filled their glasses.

21

Outfit Stirrings

Capone straightened his navy blue and light gray pin-striped suit in the morning light of a typical Thursday. He lit a Lucky Strike and and wandered into the saloon at the Four Deuces Club. His surroundings reassured him that the Outfit was becoming a force in the local economy.

Fellas lined up before noon for moonshine in plain sight. Gals of all ages and nationalities were exchanging favors for dough while roulette wheels spun and cash changed hands at the tables upstairs. Similar endeavors flourished around Chicago and to the West.

After ordering a double espresso, Capone sat at Torrio's oak table and waited for his boss to appear. His otherwise relaxed face grew taut when one of the pretty, pale-skinned prostitutes told him he had a call. It was his bookkeeper associate, Jake Guzik.

"Capone, we got a situation," Guzik said. "You gotta get over here 'cause there's a fella causing a ruckus at Jacob's Ladder. Some big grease ball called me a hebe and even slapped a few servers across the mouth."

Capone said he'd be right over and gulped his

espresso in one swallow, not surprised an out-of-control wino was disrupting his morning. More and more, he was finding himself having to clean up messes with his pistol.

Jacob's Ladder was a rather small speakeasy, but the owner was one of Torrio's most trusted clients. Capone jogged over a half block south, all the while grumbling to himself that Guzik's 280 pound girth, while making Jacob's Ladder's best customer, kept the man from putting up any fight.

"That blowfish oughta throw his weight around in a more useful way," he said to himself. "At least my fat friend won't blab about anything."

The sounds of breaking glass could be heard well outside the plain brick walls of Jacob's Ladder, but Capone was pleased that nothing had yet smashed the front window off of the South Wabash dive. He barely got the door handle turned before erupting through the entrance. Everyone, including seven other customers, the barkeep, and two prostitutes, went silent when he fired his Beretta into the unsealed oak floor under his feet and told everyone to freeze. The troublemaker was holding up one part of a smashed bottle after having knocked Guzik down.

"Say, *diablo*," Capone said, "Why you gotta rough up my pal, Guzik, and any of the rest of our clientele. Can't you just sleep it off or beat up some hobos.

The havoc-wreaking wino was over six-foot, but the halting gait and slouched spine made him seem smaller. He gave a lopsided grin meant to be cocky.

Capone winked and waited.

"You oughta know better than to deal with Jews," the man slurred. "Ah rats, you're a dumb, degenerate, dago pimp—."

During his speech, the fella had dropped the remains of the bottle and was trying to snatch a pistol in his pants pocket. Before he could finish, however, a bullet from Capone's pistol pierced him between the eyes.

After the shot, Capone was quick to leave out the door he had just entered. He walked with a relaxed step back to the Four Deuces, content that any official fallout from the speakeasy's brawl wouldn't touch him. Anyone who could give police a reliable tip knew better than to rat on their benefactor.

Capone's man, Guzik, told police that an unknown assailant had killed a customer with a shot to the head and fled on Wabash before he could get a precise description. From the information Guzik gave, police were looking for a tall, skinny, dark-skinned man that looked like he was on "illegal substances."

When Alphonse Capone returned to the Four Deuces, a brunette server clothed only in a cream-colored kimono greeted and escorted him to Torrio's oak table. After taking a seat, she served him a glass of Macallan Scotch and a Cohiba. He was too surprised and charmed to argue.

Within a few minutes, John Torrio joined him, telling Capone to stay seated as he sat down. A man in a gray vest and red bow tie served them steaks that were so rare they were sitting in warm blood. A dark-haired gal from Italy soon served them Manhattans made from Canadian Club and vermouth smuggled from Turin.

The dash of bitters came from Door County, Wisconsin to the North.

Capone's face was flushed and clammy, but he swallowed and toasted his boss. He realized the wonderful drinks and food were available from Outfit connections. The largess rendered him speechless for the first time since relocating from the East Coast.

John Torrio wiped up a pool of blood from his steak with bits of potato and bread before dabbing the corners of his mouth with a serviette. His lieutenant had been quiet during the meal, only commending Torrio on the steak and the Manhattan between bites. He figured Capone was nervous, noticing the tension in his jaw despite the tenderness of the beef.

"Well, I would tell you did a good job at Jacob's Ladder," he said, "But you look too shook up to take compliments."

Capone sipped his Manhattan and shivered despite the warmth that flushed his cheeks.

Torrio tasted his Macallan, nodding at the beautiful brunette who had brought it to him.

"Alphonse," he said. "I've got a Stiletto switchblade here and need to test your mettle. Give me your hand for a minute."

Capone laid his right hand, fingers spread, in front of Torrio before any hired muscle was needed to compel him. Torrio only returned a smile before sticking the blade between digits at a relaxed pace. Before pretending to aim for a finger, he pulled away the blade and released a loud laugh.

Torrio ordered another Macallan to be served to his white-faced lieutenant. He closed his blade and looked Capone in the eyes.

"I want you to inherit my place in the Outfit, *mio figlio*," he said. "One day, the Outfit will be yours to govern with all the problems and benefits it brings. You offered your hand when asked. I need you to remember that lesson and take care of one thing before you are my *numero due*."

Torrio explained to Capone that he'd have to extend Outfit condolences to the remaining Golino family members. It had been a week and a half since Torrio'd received word of Vincent's shooting, and he hadn't gotten around to cutting off any possible blame from his mother, Celia. Since O'Banion's associate was sweet on Sophia, appearing innocent was all the more important. Torrio told his lieutenant to think about his task.

"I've got faith in you," Torrio said. "You remember, it takes more than being a meathead to keep things copacetic Why not take a day, take the wife out, and gather your wits?"

22

Friday Night Fun

Aiden McCarthy rushed along Randolph Street to meet his gal and her mother for dinner as the sun graced the western sky with an orange glow. After classes at Holy Name, he had stopped at home to inform Margaret about dinner with the two. Her surprising, eager approval showed in his swift steps.

He shifted a bunch of chrysanthemums, courtesy of Dean O'Banion, in his left hand as he noticed the weight of his holstered Colt pistol. His pulse quickened to keep pace with his steps as he saw the Cadillac outside Sophia's house on Peoria. It was similar to the one he'd last seen outside Bruno Lanski's house. He willed himself to not worry as he readied himself to use the Colt.

Aiden's spirits didn't improve when he saw a man he recognized as Alphonse Capone being repelled from the Golino household. He had to admit being intrigued that the aggressor was Sophia. She held a Browning shotgun, backing the Outfit lieutenant down the walkway at the point of a double barrel. Along with the intimidating firearm, Sophia's above the knee, crimson skirt caught his eye.

"Hey, baby!" Aiden said with a voice loud enough to command attention. "Would you mind telling me where you're taking John Torrio's lieutenant? His boss is liable to rain down unholy hell on you and your ma should your trigger finger itch."

Sophia's arms showed no slack, in spite of a nod to her sweetheart. She continued to advance toward Capone as he held his hands up.

"This bastard said the Outfit apologizes for Vincent's death," she said. "Had my brother never gotten involved with them—"

Before Aiden could try to calm the situation, Sophia stumbled, almost falling to the ground. Capone had an opening and pulled a Beretta pistol, bringing it up to aim it at the gal.

With smooth, swift moves, Aiden retrieved his Colt with his right hand and pointed the barrel at Capone. Sophia had dropped the Browning, but still stood as Celia screamed from within the doorway of the house. A stand off began.

The nerves on the nape of Aiden's neck tingled when he saw Sophia on the bad end of a gun. He hoped Capone would be more interested in surviving than *maschilismo*. He told himself so to calm his worries. Keeping his arms steady was another matter.

"What do you say, Mr. Capone?" Aiden said. "My finger is shivering against a trigger that could end your life. I'm awfully fond of that gal there, so I'd be happy to make a deal."

Alphonse Capone smiled in spite of his position. He

made his own demands to save face and forestall any shooting.

"I suppose you've got a good point," he said. "My biggest asset is my alliance with Torrio, and that ain't much if I'm dead."

Capone cursed in Italian before he continued.

"What do you say, tough guy?"

Aiden kept his gun trained as he closed the short distance between them. He directed Capone's gun to aim at himself before he asked Sophia to take the Browning and her mother into their house. After he said *please,* she rolled her eyes and did as asked.

"As long as you aim your pistol at me, I'll be aiming at you," Aiden said when the women were out of harm's way. He held out his left hand to Capone to show it was empty. "I'll be waiting for you to get in the Cadillac and scram."

Capone paced to the Cadillac while he kept his pistol trained on Aiden. The two only dropped their aims as Capone started the car and headed east.

Aiden steadied himself with deep breaths, only putting his Colt away a while after Capone had left. He joined Sophia and Celia Golino in their house, leaving his pistol at the door next to the Browning.

Celia gestured for him and Sophia to sit at the table. They all said grace in Latin, Aiden's right hand still shook until Sophia grasped his shoulder. She pecked him on the cheek and he gave a grin and a hand squeeze in response.

Celia got a flask of moonshine she had gotten from a friend at St. Therese. She smiled as she poured them all a heavy dram of semi-poisonous spirits. After two more drams and a small meal of bread and butter, their faces flushed and chuckles pierced the air as they felt warmer.

Numbness climbed over Aiden until a few hours later.

- - - - -

A quarter hour after Alphonse Capone had left Aiden, he arrived at the Four Deuces. A guard led him to Torrio's usual spot at the oak table in to the saloon, where the boss gestured for him to sit. A brunette gal clad in a blue silk robe soon poured them each several ounces of whiskey.

"I'm glad to see you in good health," Torrio said. "Took you longer than I thought it would. How's tricks with the surviving members of the Golino family?"

Still paler than usual, Capone filled the Outfit boss on the stand-off between him, the Golino women, and the mick he recognized as Aiden McCarthy. He said he would have liked to bump everyone off, Sophia in particular, but her sweetheart made some good points.

"I don't like being put in that sort of position," Capone said. "But it beats death and, as you requested, *signore*, I restrained myself. At your command, I'd be more than happy to shoot the hellion and his broads."

Torrio finished his whiskey with a grimace and looked Capone in the eyes.

"You ain't gonna take out these Golino *puttane* unless they pose a threat to Outfit business interests. The same thing goes for Aiden. I wouldn't waste the bullets for now. O'Banion's his boss and we wanna stay on the mick's good side. Him and Mike Merlo are tight."

"You call the shots, boss," Capone said. "If you will it, I'll do it. If you'll allow me the honor of being your *numero due*, I accept."

"You make me proud, Al," Torrio said. "Do you mind if I call you Al? Al Capone's got a ring to it, don't you think? I think you and I will make history in due time."

Al Capone drank the rest of his whiskey. He and Torrio conversed about the future of the Outfit over several more drams of brown plaid. Capone said he'd appreciate it if Torrio could pay to relocate his mother, Theresa, and brother, Frank, to Chicago to help further their empire.

"You may not believe me, Mr. Torrio, but Frank's almost more refined than I am. My mother, God bless her, is a saint."

"We're not all on the level here, Al. So no need to oversell it. I'm sure your family's swell," Torrio said before waving the brunette for more drinks.

Later in the evening, Capone called a Cadillac and took his mentor home about five miles south. Anne Torrio was less than content, if not surprised by her husband's drunkenness. The lieutenant gave her a chaste kiss on the cheek before bidding her goodnight and returning to the car to drive to the Four Deuces.

At the club, Capone sauntered toward the brunette who had served him and his boss earlier. He handed her a sawbuck, told her to join him on the third floor, and swatted her behind before they ascended the steps.

In her room, he stripped into his undergarments and told her to light a few hits of dope. She did as told before shrugging the silk robe off her slender shoulders and joining him in bed. He wanted whoopee later. For now, he'd get stoned and rest against a warm body. A content smile crept on Capone's face as him and his company drifted off to rainbow-hued dreams.

23

Beautiful Headaches

Aiden edged toward consciousness well before dawn Saturday due to the faint sound of a police whistle in the background. He was lying to the right of Sophia in her bed, clothed in his undershirt and slacks. His shoes and button-down shirt lay crumpled on the floor next to a skirt at the foot of an armoire.

The events of the evening bounced around in his head when he noticed faint light from an outside street lamp hit the Colt pistol lying on the bedside table. Sophia's warm, even breaths on his left shoulder put him at ease. The sight of the smooth, bare leg stemming from her nightshirt and edging over the quilt reminded him he shouldn't be here.

He didn't want to be anywhere else in the world, but lingering Catholic guilt and so-called common sense overtook him. He would've called his parents last evening if they had a telephone. Instead he had fallen asleep in the arms of his sweetheart. He attempted to nudge awake the reclining beauty beside him with a kiss to the forehead.

Sophia's immediate response was to embrace him

with her arm and lovely leg. Aiden pecked her on hooded eyelids before they revealed a lovely shade of hazel.

"Wha, what?" she whispered while grappling with the waking world. "Aiden, I've never had a man in my bed before. You staying for the night? It's awfully late and I can smell rain on its way."

Aiden smiled at the hint of tease in her voice.

"Love, I'd fancy that," he said. "But I ought to be on my way to keep things proper while we're still living in the house in which we grew up."

Sophia groaned and gave him a mock pout after pulling her leg under the quilt.

Aiden pecked her on the neck just below the ear. With grudging urgency, he got out of her bed, put on his shirt and shoes, and returned his pistol to its holster. She followed, clothed only in her nightshirt and undergarments. She grasped his left hand with her right and walked him out of her bedroom and to the door of the house.

The pitter-patter of early morning rain made him grimace as she looked up into his eyes. Sophia pressed his body to the door with her own, kissing with lips open to his. He returned the embrace, patting her behind with his right palm.

"I'll be seein' you later," Aiden said in her ear. "We'll meet after Mass and before we get to work."

"Looking forward to it," she said while he put his cap on. She returned a smack on the behind as he left and she returned to a still warm bed.

He didn't look forward to the trip a mile or so north

toward home.

- - - - -

Aiden jogged north in the rain, hoping to reach his parents' house on Chicago Avenue within fifteen minutes. He was tired beyond belief after a lovely, if mostly proper, interlude with Sophia. Worries stemming from his not-so-lovely run-in with Capone percolated in his mind as his holstered Colt weighted on his hip with every step toward home. With swift, shivering breaths, he eventually unlocked the front door and breathed in warmer, drier air.

Creaks from the floor interrupted any attempted sense of peace as Aiden made his way toward his room. The audible yawn from Evan and the dim light of a candle made the scene even more uncomfortable. Evan's eyes were sleepy slits when he addressed his son as if waking from a shallow dream.

"Shh," Evan said, "keep it down so you don't wake your mother. She told me you were at Sophia's house for dinner and not to worry. If you know what's good for you, lad, you won't make a peep that might wake Margaret. Keep your trap shut and sit down at the kitchen table."

Aiden did as told as his father placed two coffee cups in front of them, filled with a brown liquid that had the mild oak and caramel hints of whiskey, and sat. The younger McCarthy's cheeks warmed as the hairs on his neck stood to attention. His father made two gulps from the cup and motioned for his son to do the same.

"I say, this stuff is still smooth even though it's illegal," Evan continued. "Should I commend you, son? Or does

301

O'Banion deserve credit for selling the less poisonous stuff? I asked him to sell me a bottle while picking up chrysanthemums for your ma. Go ahead and drink up, seeing how you aren't a lad anymore."

Aiden gulped his cup the same way his father had done. The rush of blood to his cheeks had as much to do with the whiskey as a healthy serving of humble pie.

"Pa, I'm helping Mr. O'Banion deliver a better product." Aiden said. "I'm not in the business of delivering anything that people don't ask for. I told you and ma, I don't look for trouble if I can avoid it."

"If you want to make money and provide for yourself and those you love, you'll have to answer to the consequences, son," Evan said. "You'll be done with school soon and you'll be free to work with whoever you want."

Aiden sat somewhat dumbstruck as his father finished his whiskey, propped himself up, and refilled his cup with water. He gulped down the water and re-filled the cup from the tap before giving a final word.

"You gotta know when to stop and pace yourself. You'll sop up the mess you've made from the rain before headin' to bed, won't you, son? I'd hate to have your mother continue to clean up after you. If you want to be man of the house, you gotta keep things spiffed up."

Aiden watched his father and limp to the water closet before heading to bed with Margaret. He sipped the rest of his whiskey and dwelt on his father's wisdom before grabbing a cup of water for himself.

Afterward, he put a towel down on any wet spots he had brought in from the rain. He cleaned the floor and cabinets before he put the bootleg in a high shelf. He stored any cleaned dishes away before calling it a morning. He headed to his room, shed his clothes, put the colt in his sock drawer, and climbed into bed. The dispute with Capone faded from his head as a sense of peace stole his body and soul.

Aiden got about four hours of rest before being woken by a smiling Margaret. She had prepared tea, eggs and ham that filled their small house with the scents of smoked meat, fried butter, and bergamot. He followed the scents after donning clean pants and a shirt.

"I appreciate how wonderful it was that some cultured lad would clean up the kitchen and help the lady of the house," Margaret said to her grinning son. "Or should I thank some mischievous monster who fancies a clean house?"

"It was my pleasure, Ma," he said. "I hope I can give you and Pa evidence every once in while about raising me right."

Aiden noticed his father's approving wink despite reddish eyes before he returned to reading the *Daily Tribune*. Brief worry hit him that Evan would spot evidence in the paper about last night's skirmish outside the Golino home. Then he realized both journalists and his father wouldn't worry about a stragglers like him shouting on Randolph and Peoria.

Aiden set their table as his mother finished cooking. He helped his mother serve breakfast, kissing her on the cheek before they ate together. Neither parent bothered him about his plans when he got ready to leave in an hour. He retrieved his coat, his cap, blew kisses to them both, and was on his way.

24

Checking In

Aiden had to see Sophia before heading to help O'Banion set sunflowers for Schofield's spring bouquets. He ran north on State to grab a dram of whiskey with her at the Dil Pickle just as her own shift began. He greeted the Robinson brothers with a smile and gave the doorman in drag a firm handshake before he entered like the regular he'd become.

He smiled when he saw the lass who tickled his fancy.

Near the stage, Sophia's shoulders shook with the snap of a snare drum, her hips swayed to a clarinet, and the swing of muted trumpets kept everyone else hip. She played a celibate seductress to prurient patrons looking for paid pleasure. The role suited her well, and her so-called virtue wasn't just for show.

He gave her a nod in tempo with the music, enjoying her spirit before getting his watered-down whiskey. His patience paid off when she shook her hips while she strutted over to join him. She pecked him on the cheek. The peony clipped in her hair set off the shine of her hazel eyes.

"You could use your assets to get a dime out of

dimwit," he said. "Yet, I'm the lucky one in the crowd. Can I get you some firewater?"

"You're not the brightest candle in the monastery," Sophia said with a wrinkle of her nose, "but you'll do. Also, I've a soft spot for a gentleman with guts. You can chat up a gal and play the tough guy, all while respecting your ma. By the way, would you get me a Bee's Knees?"

Aiden rolled his eyes before she poked him in the tummy. He gave her a wink before ordering.

The two sipped their drinks and eyed the dancers, drunks, revolutionaries, poets, and other entertainers before them. After joining the rest in a rare slower jazz number, he grasped her hip and told her she was beautiful. They kissed with open lips before Sophia whispered in his left ear:

"You still got that Colt on you or are you just excited to see me?"

Aiden looked her in the eyes and shrugged before giving her a lop-sided grin and responding:

"I'll show you how to shoot sometime."

Sophia answered with a roll of her eyes.

Aiden whisked an ebony tendril off of her face before pecking her ear. She gave him a healthy smack to his backside before finishing her drink, curtsying, and joining cross-dressed men and women to dance.

He left an hour before the western horizon eclipsed the sun. During the stroll south to Schofield's, he took his sweet time as his thoughts wandered to Sophia lathering up a lascivious crowd. His slight jealousy interested him more than it upset him. He figured it was a good sign.

- - - - -

Aiden stepped into the front door across the street from Holy Name Cathedral. He hung his newsboy cap on a hook before he saw Dean O'Banion hunched over ledger books. The ding of a bell made the boss look up.

Despite the fixed glare of baggy eyes, O'Banion, gave a smile from his flushed cheeks. He paused his pouring over the ledgers to do so with a fifth of Canadian Club in a lowball glass set before him. He offered a separate dram for Aiden and motioned for his young associate to sit. His eyes returned to the ledger books.

"You seem frazzled, boss," Aiden said after sitting. "Something I can help you with?"

"Torrio's been poking beehives, talking about a North Side lad who threatened to shoot Capone while the goombah was paying respects to a family. It all happened on Randolph on the near West Side last night," O'Banion said. "Say, doesn't that Sophia Golino gal, *your sweetheart*, live around there?"

Aiden shrugged, forcing a grim grin on his face.

"I'm not in a mood to celebrate my virtues," he said. "Do you want to clarify what you're implying...sir?"

O'Banion laughed before standing up.

Sudden apprehension gripped Aiden as he lowered his head and waited, unsure if he would be harassed or hailed. O'Banion placing a black, felt fedora on his head was the least expected. He lifted his chin and gaze to meet his boss, smiling in silence.

"Lad, you've pissed off the lieutenant of the most powerful gangster in town besides me," O'Banion said.

"Even if you wanted to stay a simple flower boy and delivery driver, it'd be impossible. With the blessing of my Sicilian pal, Mike Merlo, I can protect you as long as you're helping me out. Torrio's in no hurry to start a gang war but won't find too much a problem bumpin' you off if you want to go it alone."

That last part gave Aiden pause, and his smile wavered before he spoke.

"If that dago calls another shot on my family or my gal," he said, "I won't give a good damn about any gangland treaty."

The smile crossing O'Banion's cheeks also slackened. His temples creased before his head tilted to one side.

"I see what you're getting at," he replied. "You still oughta remember that goin' off half-cocked is no way to earn a profit or help your family. But as I've said before, I'm no expert on morality."

"Like it or not, boss, I guess you, me, and the rest of the North Side Gang are in this together. If the Gennas and the Outfit lads play along, we'll all be ducky. I think I made that clear to Capone last evening."

"Naturally," O'Banion said with a wink, "Now hand me some of those sunflowers and take your hat off indoors. I don't care how important the guy who gave you the hat is, a real man knows some bloody etiquette."

Aiden gave a huff and took the fedora off of his head before getting to work. He joined the leader of the North Side Gang and a later arriving George Moran and William Crutchfield to start flower orders for the week. Talk of the Black Sox scandal, Mayor "Big Bill" Thompson's love of Outfit speaks, and City Hall's protection of South Loop brothels dominated any banter.

O'Banion only brought up the potential for gangland friction with Aiden as they closed up for the night.

"Lad, you shouldn't worry yourself too much about keeping in line threats," he said. That's mostly a task for our good friend Rob Mullen. You'll be helping us mostly with information. If someone you love, an innocent, or both gets threatened, you might have to fight dirty. There's no shame in that."

"I'll keep that in mind, sir," Aiden said. "Let's hope other hooch slingers know to keep things on the level."

"You're a smarter lad than I was," O'Banion said. "Now go home to your mother. You oughtn't let her worry."

Aiden simpered and gave half a chuckle before returning a full and firm handshake to his boss and a wave to Moran and Crutchfield. He left, thinking of when to honor advice, play with the rules, and make his own way. The answers were part of fine-tuning his talents to thrive in a tantalizing, if tarnished world.

25

The Graduate

The day before, Aiden accepted his diploma from Holy Name School for Boys. The height of ceremony was when he shook the headmaster's hand and beamed with politeness that hid his sense of freedom. Evan and Margaret were proud, if not more relieved than any other parent present.

Margaret was currently roasting a turkey and potatoes for Sunday dinner, despite the warmth of early June air. Neither of her men complained as the scents of rosemary, melted butter, and garlic flowed out the open windows. Having rolled up his sleeves, Aiden cleaned with a dusting cloth before he set a polished table with extra chairs for expected guests.

Aiden washed himself afterward in the water closet while his parents played cards at the table, waiting for the guests and the turkey. A knock at the door jolted his nerve as he finished shaving without nicking himself. He considered the impression he'd make greeting his guests with blood on his neck. The thought made him chuckle as he heard the chipper lilt of his mother's voice flow from the kitchen.

"I appreciate you joining us for dinner. Come in, come in," Margaret said to Sophia and Celia at the door. "I'll take the cabbage and the carrots you dears prepared. Don't you dare trouble yourselves with anything else. Evan, offer our guests a beverage, if you please."

Evan did as told, receiving requests as Margaret set the food. He poured tea for Sophia and retrieved whiskey in a higher cupboard for Celia. Aiden appeared in the kitchen, washed and groomed with hair parted to his left. He made formal introductions between his parents and Sophia's mother before they all took to the table to enjoy the feast.

Evan got himself and Margaret drams of whiskey, denying Aiden's request for one, instead serving tap water. Their son gave a sardonic smile, but kept his mouth shut. Margaret led them all in grace and Evan stood to carve the turkey. Aiden was told to pass the potatoes to their guests before he had a chance to serve himself.

Aiden swallowed any snark with his water after passing food to Sophia. He was too uncomfortable to make conversation and knew better than to talk about bootleg or thoughts about his work with it. To his relief, Margaret was better at polite chit chat.

Between chewing, sips of refreshment, and passing more food, Margaret asked Celia about Mass at St. Therese. She had heard of the mission to the Orientals and wondered what their guest thought of it. When Celia replied with an Italian curse word, Sophia giggled and everyone else followed suit.

Margaret shifted the discussion, bringing up Aiden's

looser relationship with the catechism with her fellow Catholic mother. In turn, Celia complained about her daughter's lack of interest. Cordial commiseration over their kids allowed the two to carry on as Sophia and Aiden rolled their eyes, nudged each other under the table, and didn't argue. Evan just enjoyed the meal, nodding his head from time to time.

When supper drew to close and plates were empty, Celia and Margaret were pals. They invited Sophia to help them clear the table as Evan motioned to Aiden that they should take a walk. He pecked Margaret on the cheek before he mentioned they'd be back in about an hour or so.

"I must beg pardon of our guests," Evan said to the Golinos. "I'd like to have a few sage words with my son. He has a diploma, but he still has a lot to learn."

"You mind yer pa, now, Aiden." Margaret said with spirit that wasn't entirely serious. "Don't ever think you're too big for your britches."

Aiden clicked his tongue, gave a grin and donned his fedora.

"Yes, Ma," he said before following Evan outside.

- - - - -

The two McCarthy men meandered east. Evan limped and Aiden stepped with silence between them as they approached a space of green-grassed land about a half acre in size. The lot was just short of Market Street, and the only shade of green further east was in the lights that adorned speakeasies and gambling dens.

Evan stopped them with a wave of his right hand. He first brought out a silver flask and then a tarnished, silver-colored revolver from his jacket pocket.

"Son, this is a Schofield Model 3 Smith and Wesson that I got from your grandfather," he said. "Grandpa John was in the U.S. Calvary after the Civil War. He didn't talk much of it, and I gathered it was a hard time for him. This was the first gun he taught me to shoot."

He handed the gun to Aiden, who accepted it with a nodding head in reverence. Evan put a protective hand on his son's shoulder.

"This gun kept me safe in my past life when I was cracking safes with your ma's uncle," he said. "If you want to go around with the same type of fellas, it'll do me good to give you lesson in how to shoot. I need to know that you can use a pistol."

"What did you have in mind, pa? You want me to shoot that tree over there?"

Evan gave his son a firm, but friendly pat on the cheek with his left hand.

"It's best not to shoot at anything living unless you have to," he said. "If you hit this flask, then we'll have a drink and you can keep the gun. I'll keep the flask."

Evan directed his son to place the flask at the edge of the park, about fifty yards from where they were standing. The flask was placed in front of a wall to block any potential misfires. Once Aiden returned to his side, he showed the Schofield's sights, how to align them, and proper shooting stance.

Aiden inched his feet apart around shoulder length, gripped the pistol with two hands and aimed deliberately before a loud bang from the .44 caliber gun pierced his concentration.

The flask didn't move. The bullet took a chunk out of the wall in the background.

A small laugh from Evan broke the background buzz of the city.

"Why don't you try aiming about seven or so inches to the left of your target? I'll give you another shot. Also remember it helps to pull the trigger after you exhale."

Aiden aimed to the left and exhaled with his arms more relaxed. A warm bead of sweat was the only thing moving on his face before he pulled the trigger.

The flask flew onto the nearby sidewalk before Evan laughed again, with more heart than before.

"Well, my pa played the same trick with me, and I'm still here to talk about it. The gun's sights aren't perfectly set," he said. "This may come in handy if anyone else takes your gun."

Evan then took the gun, took a few seconds to aim, and then shot to nudge the flask another yard or so. Aiden deferred in awe to his father as they walked to take their target from the sidewalk where it lay. The elder McCarthy unscrewed the top and took a slug.

"Your grandfather's moonshine," Evan said. "This is the last of it made before he passed away in 1912. We oughta enjoy the last few drams of it to celebrate your worldly education. From one son to another. I hope it'll be from one father to another some day."

Aiden took a slug of it before coughing as if he had consumption. After the theatrics, he took a slower sip, able to work his lower jaw to sooth the burning. His father swilled it through his throat as if it were water.

"I get the feeling that you can't back away from the

shenanigans of these gangsters, even if you wanted to," Evan said. "But I've seen that you can shoot and that you can at least pretend to drink like you've got some experience."

"Alright then, Pa," Aiden replied. "I'm always more cautious than cock-sure. I'm not callous toward those I care about."

"At least we raised you with a whisper of wisdom."

The two finished the remaining ounces of John McCarthy's moonshine and took their time walking back to the house. Once there, they watched a card game between the ladies before everyone called it a night. Evan shook hands with Sophia and Celia, and Margaret gave each a cordial hug before Aiden left to walk his lady and her mother south to Randolph and Peoria.

Outside the Golino household, Celia hugged Aiden goodnight before heading through the door. Sophia remained standing in front of him. Her head, accented by whatever starlight still remained in the Chicago night sky, soon rested on his shoulder. He kissed the space between her temple and the top of her ear, relishing the calm.

The couple knew peace wouldn't persist. Neither of them, nor anyone else in the Windy City pretended otherwise.

Afterword

Aiden McCarthy's story is fictional; however, characters such as Dean O'Banion, Earl "Hymie" Weiss, George Moran, Alphonse Capone, John Torrio, the Genna Brothers (Sam, Mike, Vincenzo, Angelo), Mike Merlo, Jake Guzik, James Colosimo, and Victoria Moresco are actual figures in Chicago's mob history. Also, many of the politicians mentioned actually existed during the time.

I've used the books below to research *North Side Hellion* in my attempt at authenticity, not necessarily at accuracy. Please don't hesitate to check out these nonfiction sources at your favorite library or bookstore if you wish to explore more of the actual history of Prohibition, and Chicago's role in particular.

Beck, Frank O., *Hobohemia: Emma Goldman, Lucy Parsons, Ben Reitman & Other Agitators & Outsiders in 1920s/30s Chicago.*

Bergreen, Laurence, *Capone: The Man and the Era.*

Keefe, Rose, *Guns and Roses: The Untold Story of Dean O'Banion.*

McCutcheon, Marc, *The Writer's Guide to Everyday Life from Prohibition through World War II.*

Okrent, Daniel, *Last Call: The Rise and Fall of Prohibition.*

Acknowledgments

North Side Hellion would not have been possible with the help and enthusiasm of family, dear friends, and my readers.

My good friend, Mark Marohl, has helped me through many stages of this novel, acting as a sounding board and editing eye. I always appreciate the feedback.

Thank you to Louise Schwaegler, a family friend who helped me with Italian translations. If anything is incorrect with them, I take responsibility.

Editor extraordinaire, Maria D'Marco, gave wonderful advice to work through plot holes, develop characters, and language. I thank her for doing more than an editorial assessment and I would appreciate any chance to collaborate in the future.

Thanks to Nuria Marquez for the book cover design.

I must extend my thanks to all library and bookstore workers for helping to provide information and making many viewpoints available and accessible. In particular, many thanks to Chicago Public Library staff.

My wife, Caroline, and my parents, Marcia and Dale, join a large extended family to be my best supporters. Thank you.

To all: stay well-read!

About the Author

Ben Broeren is a native of Wisconsin and has a couple of degrees from the University of Wisconsin-Madison. He has worked as a freelance writer for newspapers and alternative weeklies in Chicago and Madison, Wisconsin. His journalism has been published in *Isthmus*, *The Capital Times*, and *New City*.

In addition to journalism and academia, he has experience as a dishwasher, a kitchen assistant, a cook, a warehouse tractor driver, a mail clerk, a hotel clerk, a personal service assistant for disabled adults, a bookseller, a volunteer for a presidential campaign, a volunteer legal clerk for a civil rights firm, and a volunteer for WORT community radio.

He currently lives with his wife, his son, and his dog in the Bridgeport neighborhood of Chicago. When not writing and editing, he likes to cook various types of cuisine, read, ride his recumbent trike, and keep up with what's going on through the news and conversing with neighbors.